M000230216

THE COLLECTION GIRLS

Emily Slate Mystery Thriller Book 2

ALEX SIGMORE

Dark Woods Press

THE COLLECTION GIRLS: EMILY SLATE MYSTERY THRILLER
BOOK 2

1st Edition

ebook ISBN 978-1-957536-08-8

Print ISBN 978-1-957536-09-5

Prologue

"WHAT'S GOT YOU SO ON EDGE LATELY?" MARGARET ASKS, sitting across from her best friend.

Hannah Stewart barely looks up from her drink. The music in the bar is loud, but not loud enough that she can't hear her friend. Her thoughts are so erratic the only thing keeping her from breaking into a thousand pieces is the cosmopolitan in front of her. But she's doing everything she can to keep it from showing.

"Hannah? Did you hear me?" Margaret asks.

She shakes her head and offers up what she hopes comes across as a genuine smile. "Sorry, I was just thinking about work. We got a brand-new shipment in today and we've got to catalog it before we can begin testing."

Margaret sits back in the booth, her face pinched. "Uh-huh. Is that why you've barely touched that?" She nods at the drink.

Hannah puts the rim of the glass to her lips and takes a sip. She can't afford to get tipsy, not right now. It's funny, she never would have thought getting drunk with a friend would be something she'd no longer be able to do, but here she is. This is her life now.

She glances around the room, nervous. But as far as she can tell, everything seems normal.

"God, you are so *wired*. What the hell is going on?" Margaret isn't someone she can bullshit forever. They've been friends ever since college, moving to the same city together after graduation. Even living together for a short time before Hannah moved out on her own after her promotion came through. She knows Hannah, and she won't let this go. Hannah's only hope is to resolve this situation before it gets any worse. Before people begin to find out.

"I don't know," she replies, trying to sound tired. "I think I'm just under a lot of stress." It wasn't a lie...technically.

"That much is obvious," Margaret says. She reaches across the cracked veneer of the old wooden table. This place isn't the classiest in Bethesda, but it is where most of the young professionals hang out. Thus, it receives a lot of wear and tear. Margaret places her hand on Hannah's exposed arm. "Whatever it is, I want to help."

Hannah wants to tell her; she really does. But doing so would put Margaret in danger, and she's already made enough bad decisions regarding this whole fiasco. She isn't about to bring her friend into this mess just because she's feeling skittish. Alonzo said six days. It's only been four. There's no need to freak out yet. Come Monday...that'll be a different story.

Hannah shakes her head and takes a long sip from the cosmo, perhaps more than she should, but she needs something for her nerves. She plasters the best smile she can on her face and levels her gaze at her friend. "How's the new project going? Are you making any headway?"

She sees the sadness in Margaret's eyes as her friend pulls her hand back. It's obvious she's hurting the person she trusts more than anyone. She just wishes she could tell her it's for her own good. If Margaret finds out what Hannah has gotten herself into, not only will she be appalled, but she'll probably disown her. And right now, Hannah can't afford to lose any friends. She has to find a way out of this; she needs more time.

"Okay, I guess," Margaret says, playing along. "We got a couple new interns in. They're…competent."

"Like we were at that age?" Hannah asks, trying to keep the mood light.

Margaret smiles. "Yeah. Something like that."

Hannah manages to hold on to the conversation for the next hour. Draining the cosmo and then another. Finally, by the time eleven comes around, she's feeling better about the whole situation. Maybe it won't be as bad as she thinks. Alonzo is a reasonable person, and if she doesn't have everything he needs by Monday, she'll still be able to get it. It'll just take a couple more days. And who knows, maybe her luck will change after all.

Hannah looks down at her empty glass, her vision doubling before focusing again. Definitely shouldn't have had that second one, but she needed a pressure valve. These last few weeks have been nothing if not brutal. "I guess I should probably get back," she says.

Margaret nods. "Big night with Tyler?"

Hannah barks a laugh, perhaps too loud. She looks around, unable to stop herself from giggling at her outburst. Though no one seemed to notice. "He wishes."

"Things aren't good between you two?" Margaret asks.

Hannah shrugs. She wasn't going to mention Tyler tonight, but considering everything else she's been keeping from Margaret, she owes her this one. "Things are…okay. They're not terrible, it's just…"

"Not knocking your socks off?"

"I guess you could put it like that," Hannah says, pulling out her phone. She needs to call for a ride-share. Normally she'd walk since her apartment is only six blocks away. But given everything that's happened over the past few weeks, it's better to take precautions. She opens the app on her phone, setting up the destination.

"You deserve to have someone who wows you," Margaret says. "If he's not doing that, then you're just wasting your time."

"Someone who wows me," Hannah repeats. "I don't think I've ever found anyone like that. You know me, it's the work that really gets me off." She barks another laugh, though when she thinks on it, she's not even sure it was funny. But who cares?

"You good to make it home?" Margaret asks.

Hannah gets the confirmation on her phone of the pickup, quickly showing it to Margaret. Six minutes. "Yeah. I'm going home and right to bed. I've...got a lot going on tomorrow." She tries to flag down the server, but the place has only gotten busier as they've been sitting here. It's significantly more crowded than it was an hour ago.

Hannah stands and the room tips slightly. She holds on to the table to get her balance, then makes her way over to the bar where she has to almost yell to get the bartender's attention. She points out her table and tells him to put it all on her tab. Margaret deserves some free drinks considering what a shitty friend Hannah has been to her lately.

Once she closes out the tab she makes her way back to the table.

Margaret looks behind her, like Hannah might be hiding it behind her back. "Where's the bill?"

"It's all taken care of," Hannah says.

Margaret shakes her head. "You must be feeling *really* guilty. I can't remember the last time you paid."

Hannah can't help her emotions from rising to the surface and she turns away.

"Hey," Margaret says, putting a hand on her shoulder.

"I'm sorry. I didn't mean...c'mon, I'll ride with you back to your place."

Hannah shakes her head. "No, that's okay. I just...I need some time alone."

"Hannah," Margaret calls as she walks away. But right now Hannah can't even look her in the eyes. She's right, she's been a shitty friend and a shitty person. But come Monday, all of that is going to change. She's going to start making better decisions. She's going to get out from under this bridge she's found herself under. It's time to start living a life other people can be proud of her for. It's time to stop being so damn selfish.

Hannah heads out of the bar on to the side of the street to wait for the ride-share. She's going to make this up to Margaret. And everyone. She just needs to figure out how. There are a couple other groups of young people out here, most huddled in groups, smoking cigarettes, or vaping. Hannah checks her phone. Only two minutes until the car gets here. Based on the map, it's only about a block and a half away. She takes in the cool evening air and shivers, wishing she'd brought a jacket. She hadn't realized how chilly it was going to be tonight.

The world tips and moves, and she wishes she hadn't had that second cosmo. They always go to her head. She should have stuck with something tamer, like an IPA. She has to lean up against a signpost so she doesn't accidentally tip over or trip, which would make things ten times worse. All she needs to do is get in the car and get home. Then she can crawl under the covers and figure all of this out tomorrow.

But as she's standing there, she becomes aware of how quiet it's gotten. The groups of people have disappeared, either dispersing or heading back inside. And Hannah feels the hair on the back of her neck stand up. She glances behind her, trying to do her best to focus, but it's difficult with all the shadows along the street. Is there someone standing down there, at the end of the block, watching her?

She can't be sure. All she knows is that she's a target. Where the hell is that car? She reaches into her purse and wraps her fingers around the small can of mace she's been carrying for the past six months. Her heart is pumping. Should she go back inside? Or is she over-reacting? She blinks again and the shadow person seems to disappear. Were they even there to begin with?

Finally, a pair of lights comes rolling down the block. Hannah lets go of the mace and pulls out her phone again, checking the make and the model of the car, along with the license plate. All of them match up with what's shown on the app.

The car rolls to a crawl in front of her and the passenger side window rolls down. "Hannah?"

She smiles. "That's me." Finally. Some relief. She opens the rear door and slips into the back seat, slamming it shut behind her. Shutting out any possibility of that person grabbing her...or worse.

"Wedgewood apartments, right?" the driver asks.

"Yes, thanks," Hannah replies, sinking back into the seat and relaxing for what seems like the first time all evening. The world continues to spin when she closes her eyes, but it no longer matters. The car rumbles on beneath her and she takes a deep breath. Everything is going to be okay.

"Fun night?" the driver asks.

"I guess," she replies. "Do you mind if we don't talk? I'd just like to get home."

"No problem."

As the car makes its turns and begins heading down the main thoroughfare, Hannah can't quit thinking about that look on Margaret's face. She had hoped going out tonight would help relieve some of her stress, but now Margaret's pissed, and she feels like crap. She should have realized until she resolved this situation with Alonzo, she'd have to keep everyone at arm's length. But after Monday it's going to be a different story. After Monday she's going to come clean…even go to the cops if she has to. She's tired of being intimidated.

The back of this car is stuffy. She opens her eyes and tries to roll down the window, but when she pushes the button it doesn't respond.

"Excuse me," she says. "Can you unlock the windows? It's a little stuffy back here."

The driver doesn't respond.

Hannah sits up a little straighter. Now that she thinks about it, how long has she been in this car? She looks at the app on her phone and realizes they are way off-course. Her apartment is in the opposite direction.

"Hey," she says. "What the hell? You can't just go wherever you want. They're tracking you."

She's about to dial 911 when the driver speaks again. "I wouldn't do that, Hannah. You don't want word to get out, do you?"

A chill runs down her spine. She leans forward, trying to see the driver's face, but he's put some kind of mask on, she can't see him anymore. What did he look like before, when he picked her up? "Alonzo said I had until Monday! You have to give me the time, I'll have everything as we agreed!"

The driver brings the car to a stop. Hannah tries the doors, but they're locked and she doesn't see any way to unlock them. As she's working the handle, just wanting to get out of this situation, there's a pinch on her exposed thigh. She turns back to see the driver removing an empty needle from her leg.

"What the hell is this?" she yells. She fumbles for her phone again, but before she can dial, it's knocked from her hands. She tries searching for it, but her vision is going hazy and she's having trouble concentrating. Her eyes are heavy, though she knows she can't fall asleep. She has to get away from here. She tries for the door again, but she doesn't even have the strength to pull the handle anymore.

Hannah flops back onto the seat, her head feeling like it's going numb. The last thing she hears before her world goes dark is, "Sorry, Hannah. But you're not going to make that appointment after all."

Chapter One

You just need to stay calm. Stay calm, and think your way through this.

I take a deep breath and open my eyes. I'm sitting, cross-legged on the floor. My apartment surrounds me, with too-few decorations and too-many case files brought home from work. My Pit-bull, Timber, lays about three feet away, basking in the afternoon sun streaming through the French doors that lead to my small patio. Soft jazz plays through my Bluetooth speaker and there's a glass of amber liquid sitting on the table beside me.

I have full control of my environment, everything is in order, just the way I like it. My mind is clear, so why am I having such a hard time concentrating?

Nope, no negative thoughts, remember? Just openness, and a willingness to accept things as they are. But doing that means accepting someone didn't just straight-up murder my husband four months ago and make it look like he died of natural causes. Accepting things as they are would mean letting go the fact that the exact same thing happened to a suspect in one of my most recent cases. The man who had killed his wife in cold blood, sewed her eyes shut, then buried her in a box in the middle of the woods. I'd had him, he was in custody, and he was going to pay for his crimes.

And then he was dead. Not from the two bullets I put into him, but from a heart attack. Just like Matt. And just like Matt there's no evidence of foul play. Which is all a load of bullshit.

"This *whole thing* is bullshit," I say, standing back up. Timber stirs and looks up at me, gauging whether I'm going into the kitchen or not. When I plop down on the couch and reach for my glass, he puts his head back down and resumes sunning.

I don't know why I ever thought meditation would work. Maybe because I've tried everything else and yet I'm still no closer to figuring this out. "Great detective work, Emily," I say. "Really great. You're a real sleuth. Can't even figure out the identity of one person." I hold up my glass as a salute to my ineptitude and drain the entire glass in one swig. It doesn't burn as much as it would had it been straight, but that was because I cut it with some Amaretto. But even my favorite cocktail isn't bringing me any relief.

All I'm concerned with is finding the name of the woman who walked out of Stillwater General Hospital almost a month ago and disappeared into the ether. But first I need to find actual evidence she was there so everyone else will stop thinking I'm crazy. No one has come out and said it yet, but I can see what they're thinking. That the stress of losing Matt has finally gotten to me, despite the fact I managed to catch a serial killer in a case that everyone thought was dead in the water. Despite the fact I've proven myself in the eyes of the FBI and have been fully reinstated, assisting on dozens of other cases. But I see them talking behind my back.

Everyone except Zara, of course.

There's a term we use in the FBI for people like me: *Roasted*. Agents who have, for one reason or another, succumbed to the stress of the job. That might have been true three months ago when I was attempting to finish a delicate operation days after my husband had died. That had been a bad call, on everyone's part, despite the fact we interrupted a national kidnapping ring and reunited forty-two kids with their families. It wasn't enough to keep me from being suspended and placed on unpaid leave. When I came back I was assigned to desk duty for three weeks until the case in Stillwater came up.

A case no one thought anything about.

But with some help, we managed to bring a killer into custody to face justice. Had it not been for the woman I passed in the hospital, I'm dead sure Gerald Wright would still be alive today and preparing to face trial for the deaths of two women and the attempted murder of his own children.

I think what upsets me the most is that no one will even consider the possibility. Wright was older, he had risk factors that are normally associated with heart attacks. So it was no surprise when it happened. Except for the fact they'd given him a clean bill of health hours before. I think the hospital and the local Stillwater P.D. is just covering its ass, considering they had an officer posted outside his door. Except when he wasn't, which was when I saw that woman leaving the hospital.

The way she smiled at me…like she knew me…it was, unnerving.

Ever since coming back to D.C. I've spent the majority of my free time searching for her, trying to find any clue that might lead to her identity, but so far I still can't even get a picture. None of the angles at the Stillwater hospital picked her up, and apparently no one else noticed her but me.

But I know she did it. She knew who I was, even if I couldn't return the favor. And if I ever find her again, I'm going to make sure I get the information I need.

My cell rings and I grab it from the counter without even looking at the number. "Slate," I say.

"It's Simmons."

I double-check the clock on the microwave. "It's four-fifteen on a Sunday afternoon."

"Just got notice," my boss says. "Daughter of a federal judge here in D.C. has gone missing."

I smirk. "Missing, or run off with her friends for a week in Cabo?"

"Parents say she's missing. They've filed an official report." My boss, SAC Janice Simmons, is all business, no-nonsense. She talks like she's reading the newspaper.

"When was the last time they heard from her?"

"Last night. Apparently she never made it home."

I take a deep breath. The alcohol is already in my bloodstream, but it's not enough to affect my performance. Still, I hadn't planned on going into the office today. I've been going over the details of Matt and Gerald Wright's deaths ever since I got off on Friday. I had hoped *this* would be the weekend when I made a breakthrough, but honestly, my mind feels like mush. Maybe getting out and working a case would do me some good.

"Who's the lead?" I ask.

"You are."

I'm taken aback for a moment. Sure, I did a passable job in Stillwater when we found Wright, but not being able to bring him to justice was a blow. At least I was able to get the corrupt police chief out of there before he did any more damage. Even though they welcomed me back into my division with open arms, I haven't been given my own cases yet. I've just been assisting other agents, providing support where I can. I figure it's the last part of my penance for going off the rails a few months ago.

Still, to have my own cases again…it's what I've wanted ever since.

"Wow, thank you, Janice," I say. "I won't let you down."

"I know you won't," she replies. "It should go without saying how much I trust you to be doing this so early."

"It does," I reply.

"You are one of my best, as long as you can keep your head on straight," she adds. Even though it's probably deserved, it feels like a backhanded compliment. Proof that I haven't completely redeemed myself yet. I look down at my leg, even though I can't see the raw scar under my jeans. My little reminder that I need to be more careful in the future. I almost died.

"Can I bring on another agent to assist?" I ask. Even though I know I can handle it, it never hurts to have a little backup.

"Foley?" Janice asks, exasperation in her voice.

"She's been cleared for field work."

My boss pauses on the other end of the phone. "Might as well. You two work well together anyway. Who better for her to get her feet wet with?"

"My thoughts as well." Zara Foley is the closest thing I've ever had to a sister. She was a big help on the Stillwater case and had expressed the desire to get out of analysis and into field work with the Special Agents. She's as smart as they come.

"I'm emailing you all the case files now. Get on this one now, Emily. The judge isn't a patient man, and this is his only child. If we don't find her quick I'm gonna have the AG breathing down my neck to get this case done."

"We're on a clock, got it," I say, shuffling around my apartment, grabbing what I'll need for a late night out. I take a glance at Timber, who still has barely stirred. I'll need to leave him dinner before I go.

"Let me know what you need and keep me in the loop," she adds. "We're going to have a lot of eyes on this one."

"Got it. Talk to you soon." I hang up and search through my phone for the email, which pops up a second later. There's not much in the way of case files yet, just the missing person's report and the parents' address.

I grab one of Timber's cans and begin opening it as I dial Zara's number. Within seconds he's right beside me, looking up at me with those big, brown eyes.

"I gotta work late tonight, buddy. I'll take you for a walk when I get home."

He licks his lips as I begin spooning food into his bowl, balancing the phone between my ear and shoulder.

"Helloooo," Zara says, playfully drawing out the word.

"Good news," I say. "You've got a case."

"What?" she replies.

"Well, more accurately, *we've* got a case. Judge's missing daughter. You ready?"

"Now?" she asks. "I just sat down to play Call of Duty."

"This is how field work goes," I reply, smiling. She's a beast at that game. She convinced me to play a few times, but she trounces me every time.

I set Timber's food bowl down and he goes to town. "Okay, yeah I'll be ready in five," she replies. "Meet you there?"

"I'll pick you up on the way," I reply. For the first time since I came back from Stillwater, I'm feeling excited again. As long as it's something other than frustration and regret, I'll take it. "See you in six."

Chapter Two

I TURN OFF THE CAR AND STEP OUT. FOR MID-APRIL IN D.C., it's still unseasonably cold. I was hoping this chill would break by now, but with the wind I'd say it's still in the low forties, especially now that the sun has gone down.

I look over to my new protégé, stepping out of the passenger side. A month ago she would have been unmistakable with her electric blue hair, but since Zara has been granted field duty, she had to dye it to something that doesn't stand out as much. She's gone with a platinum blonde which seems to skirt the limits of department policy, but Janice lets her get away with it. The problem with blue, red, purple, or green hair is that it makes you stand out in a crowd, which is exactly what we don't want to do. It also makes us easier targets.

I have to say, Zara took the change in stride.

"I hope you gave my boyfriend extra love before you left," she says, making her way around the car.

"He got plenty of dinner," I reply. "Plus sometimes I hide treats around the house so he can have a little scavenger hunt."

"Oh, no wonder he was always looking around the floor,"

she replies. Zara took care of Timber while I was in Stillwater. Maybe I shouldn't have kept him after what happened with Matt. I pull long hours, and because I don't have family commitments anymore, it's easy for me to take on additional shifts. Keeping Timber around was supposed to help normalize some of that, and to give me someone to look after, someone who counted on me. I rescued him after he was rehabilitated from a local dog fighting ring just outside of D.C. Matt fell in love with him immediately. But sometimes I feel like I leave him alone too much. It's too bad pit bulls aren't eligible for K9 duty.

We've pulled in behind the black and white that's already here. The judge has an impressive house, I'll give him that. The driveway is a semi-circle, connecting to the street in two places, and the front of the house is a mirror image of that semi-circle, with a portico held up by four two-story columns. The entire house is white with black shutters, windows, and the main double doors of the front entrance, which are glass-paned.

Through the glass I spot a plain-clothes detective speaking with a man dressed in what looks to be workout gear, though his hair is almost all gray. I assume this is our judge.

"How do you want to approach this?" Zara asks.

"Let's just hear what they have to say first. If this really turns out to be nothing more than an impromptu trip with some friends then we don't have anything to worry about."

"You really think that's the case?" she asks as we approach the front door.

I shake my head. "I'm trying not to make any assumptions." Old Emily would have done that. She would have made a judgement call before even getting all the facts of the case. New Emily is trying to be better, to show them that I really am worthy to hold my own caseload again.

I ring the doorbell which catches the attention of both the detective and the man standing in the foyer. The detective approaches the door and opens it for us, and I'm hit with the scent of lilacs and peonies. The foyer is large, with a checkerboard marble inlay floor and in the center of the foyer is a large table with an ornate bouquet of fresh flowers, which I assume is where the smell is coming from.

"Detective Dunn," he says. "This is Judge William Stewart."

"Bill," the man says, stepping forward and taking our hands.

"I'm Agent Slate, this is Agent Foley," I say.

"Thank God you're here," he says, turning to Dunn. "No offense, but we just feel better now that the FBI is on the case."

Dunn does a good job of hiding his displeasure, but I still catch a couple of micro expressions. "Of course."

"Please," Judge Stewart says, leading us into a sitting room right off the main foyer. Inside sits a woman, also in activewear. Even though she's sitting, I can tell she's tall due to the length of her legs, which are tucked halfway under her on the couch. Another detective is standing next to her, looking flummoxed.

"Honey," Judge Stewart says, "the FBI are here."

The woman practically jumps up and approaches us. "Have you found anything yet?" she asks.

Now that she's closer, I see that her looks belie her actual age. She could probably pass for someone ten or even twenty years younger than she actually is. It's clear the Stewarts take care of themselves. But given the size of this house, I assume they have the money to do so.

"Not yet, Mrs. Stewart," I say. "We were only just made aware of the report this afternoon."

"This afternoon?" she says. "But I made the call last night!"

"It took a little while to get through the system, Mrs. Stewart," Dunn says. "Being the weekend and all."

She throws up her hands dramatically. "I can't believe in this day and age it takes almost twenty-four hours before the proper authorities are notified when there's an emergency. My daughter is *missing*. Do you have any idea how important the first forty-eight hours are to solving a case?"

I slip a glance at Zara and she has to turn away, hiding a grin. This happens more often than not. People who think they're experts on the criminal justice system after watching a few hours of true crime TV or documentaries. The officer who tried to explain has also turned away from her, but I feel like his reasons are more anger-based.

"Honey," the Judge says, taking her arm. "Come, let's let them do their jobs." He turns to me. "What do you need from us?"

"I know you've already given your initial report, but we'd like to hear it firsthand. Can you tell us how do you *know* she's missing?" I ask.

"Oh my God, this is pure incompetence. Ask *them*," Mrs. Stewart says, pointing to Dunn and his partner. "Why can't you people get your information straight? You are wasting valuable time!"

"Amanda!" Judge Stewart yells. His wife stares back at his face before returning to the couch where she picks up a bottled water and chugs it.

"I'm sorry," he says to us. "We know because she always texts us when she gets home each night. No text last night, and she's not answering her phone today. I went over to her apartment after we called it in just to make sure, but she wasn't there."

"Anything out of the ordinary?" I ask.

He looks perplexed by the question. "Not as far as I could tell. I don't go over there very much…why?"

"We'll need to go over and take a look for ourselves," Zara says. "Assuming that was where she was last seen."

"Of course," he replies. "We're just so worried. She's never done this before."

How many times have I heard that from unsuspecting parents? Usually, a statement like that means they've never been caught before. I'm not willing to send out the dogs yet. "When was the last time you heard from her?"

"Friday night," Mrs. Stewart says. "She texted, like she always does. Every single night since she moved out on her own. She's never missed a night."

"Is it possible her phone just died, and she hasn't had a chance to charge it, wherever she is?" I ask.

"And where would she be, other than at home? She has to work tomorrow."

"Where does she work?" Zara asks.

"CurePharm," Judge Stewart says. "She's been with them ever since she graduated. Just got a promotion not too long ago, which is when she started living by herself."

"I told her," Mrs. Stewart says. "I said she should stick with a roommate until she had a serious boyfriend. This is a dangerous city, and people are just *looking* for opportunities to hurt young, attractive women."

"Have you received any kind of demands, anything that makes you think this is a kidnapping and not..." I trail off.

"What?" Mrs. Stewart says. "Go ahead. Say it."

"A night out on the town," I say, trying to remain diplomatic. Mrs. Stewart is a complete powder keg. If I'm not careful, she'll shut down.

"You mean was she out whoring herself out to random guys?"

"*Amanda!*" Judge Stewart says again. "Why don't you take a minute? Go cool off."

Mrs. Stewart huffs and leaves the room through the other doorway, which I assume connects to some other opulent part of this house.

"I'm very sorry, Agents. This isn't like her. She's been on

edge ever since last night. Hannah is our only daughter and we're both…well, we're protective of her."

"That's okay," I reply. "I'm an only child myself, so I know how parents can be. Your wife's anger is misplaced frustration and fear."

"For both of us," he says. "But no. We haven't received any kind of ransom demands. No communication whatsoever."

I turn to Zara. "Can you get someone down in surveillance to put a trace on Hannah's phone? I want to know if it's still on or not."

"Sure," Zara says, pulling out her phone. "Do you have her number?"

"I've got it," Dunn says and huddles up with Zara as I turn back to Judge Stewart. "Has Hannah ever disappeared before? Ever gone off with friends or a boyfriend without telling you?"

He shakes his head. "Not to my knowledge. If she has, she's hidden it from us."

"Is there anyone you know of who might be a threat to your daughter? An old boyfriend, anyone?"

His eyes glance over to the doorway his wife left through. "Not directly. But as you know I'm an appeals judge. And sometimes defendants aren't very happy when their appeals are denied or their decisions aren't overturned."

"You're thinking this could be blowback from one of your cases?"

"I didn't say that," he says, though he's quick to recover. "I'm just saying that's the only kind of danger Hannah has ever had in her life. Not that we've ever had to deal with anything like that before, thank God."

I feel like he's hiding something, especially the way he keeps looking back at where his wife went. I'm not sure what's going on here, but I can only press him so much. If I'm going to get the answers I need, I'll have to redirect. "No history of any mental illness or trauma, I assume?"

He shakes his head. "Nothing."

"Do you know who would have seen her last?" I ask.

He shifts on his feet. "Probably either her boyfriend or Margaret."

"Margaret?" I ask.

"Friend from college. They were roomies and have been together ever since. They actually shared an apartment until recently, where, like I said, she moved out."

"Was there trouble between them?" I ask.

"Not as far as I know. But Hannah wanted her own place. And with her promotion she could finally afford it. Though we're still working on getting her place furnished."

I look around this opulent house and have a hard time believing Hannah wants for anything. But maybe I'm wrong. She might be one of those kids who wants to make it on their own, just to prove to their already-successful parents that they can. That they don't necessarily need their help. "What does Hannah do at ChemPharm, do you know?"

"It has something to do with medial research," he replies. "But it's all very hush-hush. Non-disclosure agreements and such. She can't really talk about what she's working on."

Zara rejoins us. "I got Lukas to put a trace on her phone," she says. "It hasn't been on since eleven last night. He's pulling the call records for us now."

"Good," I say. "When you were over at her place, was her car still there?" I ask.

Judge Stewart nods. "It was, which was why I actually felt silly that we'd already called in a missing person's report. But when I searched her place there was no sign of her. Purse and phone were both gone."

"No signs of a struggle?" I ask.

He shakes his head. I want to check it out myself to make sure. But a federal judge can probably tell when someone has been fighting for their life not to be abducted. Still, we need to check it out. But it sounds like Hannah never made it home last night.

"Okay, I say. Thank you for all your help. We'll get started right away."

"Tonight?" he asks, stepping forward as he wrings his hands together. "It's just...my wife is right. Time is of the essence."

"Yes, sir," I reply. "We're starting right now."

He only looks mildly relieved. "Thank you. And if it does come down to it, if they want money, we're willing to pay anything. No negotiation. We just want her back."

"May we use your key to her apartment?" I ask.

He retreats into the hall and comes back a moment later, pulling the key off his ring. "It's Wedgewood Apartments, off Old Georgetown Road. Number Six-oh-one."

I give him a final nod and we excuse ourselves from them and the detectives, heading back out to the car.

"So? What do you think?" Zara asks.

I sigh as I slip in behind the wheel. "I think it's going to be a long night."

Chapter Three

When I pull up to Wedgewood Apartments, there's already a local Bethesda P.D. unit sitting outside. Zara and I step out of the car and approach the officer on the scene.

"How long have you been here?" I ask.

"About an hour," he replies. "My partner is up on six, keeping an eye on the door."

"Anyone in or out?" I ask. He shakes his head. I indicate to Zara that we should head in.

"You're so much more serious on the job," she says once we're inside the lobby. Wedgewood is not some crappy apartment complex on the edge of town. The entire lobby area has been designed by someone with good taste. Everything looks modern, sleek. Despite the building being older. They must have renovated which no doubt has kicked the rent up.

"What do you mean?" I push the button for the elevator. It seems like a quiet Sunday evening and since it's chilly out, it doesn't look like any of the residents want to brave the weather.

"You just…you're like laser-focused," Zara says, a small grin playing on her lips.

"I'm always like that."

"You *think* you're always like that. But in reality you can be pretty chill when you want to be."

I roll my eyes at her as we step into the elevator. I'm the last person anyone should consider chill. Relaxing just isn't something I do. The building is only eight stories tall, so it looks like Hannah should have a good view from six.

The other officer stands in the hallway from the unit downstairs. We show him our badges and he nods. "Has anyone been through here?" I ask.

"A couple of residents. One lady asked me what I was doing. That's it."

I nod and pull Judge Stewart's key from my pocket. "Gloves," I say, pulling a pair out of my jacket pocket and slipping them on before slipping the key in the deadbolt. "Keep a sharp eye."

"Only if I get to drive back," Zara teases.

The deadbolt clicks and the door opens on a dark foyer. The entryway leads into an open kitchen and living room. It's not a ton of space, but more than enough for one person. There's a small bathroom off to the side. The living room faces out on Bethesda, and in the distance I can see the top of the Capitol building and the Monument. Not a bad view for someone only a few years out of college. Off the living room is a spacious bedroom with its own private bathroom. Everything in the apartment is clean and tidy, tidier than my place.

"See anything out of the ordinary?" I ask.

"Just that her taste in books leaves something to be desired," Zara replies, looking through the few books on her shelf. "I bet she hasn't read half of these."

"Not everyone loves ghost sex."

"Hey," she says. "It's called paranormal romance and I'll thank you to stay out of it."

I look around for any sign of a struggle, or indications Hannah knew she was leaving and not coming back for a while. But nothing seems out of place. Her clothes are neatly arranged in her closet and there's a suitcase inside, which means if she did leave of her own accord, it was unplanned.

I check her bathroom, finding all her makeup and hair products. Stuff she probably wouldn't have left behind if she could help it. Her cabinet is full of medications, which I start examining one by one.

"Zara?" I call.

She comes into the bathroom. "Hey, nice countertops. Is that travertine?"

"I don't know what that is," I reply. "Look at this." I hold out the bottle for her.

"Lorazepam? Isn't that for anxiety?"

I suppose that's not uncommon. There's another, unmarked bottle near the back. I shake it a few times, and the rattling inside indicates it is very full.

"Whoa," Zara says opening the bottle. Tiny clear pills fill the bottle to the brim. "Ex?"

"I'm not sure. We'll need to get them tested. But she's got at least two grand worth here if it is."

"You think she's dealing?"

I can't say for sure yet. There aren't any other unmarked bottles in her cabinet, and most dealers I know aren't foolish enough to leave their merchandise on display like this. But I'm starting to lend more credence to the kidnapping theory. If she was in trouble with someone over drugs, they might have decided to take their payments out of her rather than wait for her to pay them back.

"Could this mean her parents were right? Someone took her?" Zara asks.

I pinch my features together. "It's nothing more than a theory at this point. We don't *know* anything yet. But unmarked drugs don't help things. I've seen stuff like this before, where the kidnappers don't even want a ransom. They might just want to teach her a lesson. Or use her as an example, which could make our job infinitely more difficult." I hand Zara the bottle. "Let's get this back to the lab so they can figure out what we're dealing with here."

She places the bottle in an evidence bag. "You'd think if they were upset about drugs, they would have come looking for them."

She's right. If this was drug related, why take the girl, and not come back for the merchandise? This place should be a wreck. "I suppose that's what we need to find out."

"C'mon, on a scale of A to D, how did I do?" Zara asks as we pull up to the FBI's underground parking lot entrance. Gus stands watch at the gate and checks both of our IDs before opening it, even though he's known us both for years. The man in the booth does his normal scan, making sure the car doesn't have any kind of explosive devices or other potential dangers strapped on it. You can never be too careful these days.

After they drop the pylons and wave us through, Zara shakes my arm. "You're killing me here!"

"Why is your scale only A to D? What happened to F?"

"Oh, I don't get F's," she replies, smug.

"Never? Not even in something insanely hard like Organic Chemistry?"

Zara shakes her head. "Nope. I don't get D's either, but I figured asking on an A to C scale would have been too cocky. Now come on! Tell me what you thought!"

I smile. Making her squirm is something I have to admit I enjoy. "I dunno. Passable, I guess. Maybe a B minus."

"*B minus?*" she practically screams. "Are you *kidding?*"

"Whoa there," I say, pulling into an open spot. "No need to blow the windows out."

Zara punches me on the shoulder. "You're screwing with

me, I know it. That was a solid A performance back there. With the Judge. And then at the apartment. I was smooth."

I shoot her a side glance. "A minus at best. And that's because I'm feeling generous."

"Whatever." She steps out of the car at the same time I do. "I was made for field work. I can feel it."

As we make our way through the underground entrance and the first level of security, I go over what we know so far in my head. We need to get Hannah's phone records first, just so we can figure out the last people she spoke with before her phone went down. If we're lucky, the call will lead to the person who sold or gave her the drugs. At least it will give us a starting point.

"What are your first impressions?" I ask as we retrieve our bags from security.

"Girl from a nice family gets involved in the drug trade and screws over someone she has no business dealing with," Zara says. "They come back for retribution."

"Maybe, it's a good theory, at least. I'd expect something like this if Hannah was a bit younger, maybe still in her early twenties. But she's been out of college a few years now. She has a stable job, responsibilities. Why get involved with something like this?"

"Maybe she has a secret addiction, or is looking for some excitement," Zara says, swiping us through to our office block. Once inside we take the elevator up to level four. "But if she was taken, how in the hell are we going to find who's responsible? It isn't like they label these bottles with their gang signs." She shakes the bottle in the evidence bag for emphasis.

"That's what we need to find out," I reply, heading for my desk. "Get those phone records and start going through her socials. I'm going to run the basic background stuff. See if I can't figure out who this girl is and what might have motivated something like this."

"What about the boyfriend?" Zara takes a seat at her

station, focusing hard on her computer while she talks. Having come from Intelligence Analysis, she's a whiz on anything computer related. In fact, before she was approved for field work, she used to work through the nights, electing to sleep during the day because she said it made her more productive.

I check my watch. "It's already past ten p.m. He's not going to be much good to us tonight. We'll hit him first thing in the morning." I'm already antsy about talking to the boyfriend. After how my last case went, with Victoria's husband, Gerald, being such a good liar that I couldn't see through his deception, I'm more than a little gun shy. Part of me feels like I've lost my edge, my ability to intuit a person's motives just by how they speak, and stand. All the tiny little things that a person does unconsciously, that telegraphs their true intentions. I missed those with Gerald, and it nearly cost two children their lives. I can't afford to be that sloppy again.

"Well, well, aren't you two burning the midnight oil." I look up to see Agent Nick Hogan standing a couple of stations away, a white mug in his hands.

"Evening, Nick," I say.

"Big case?" he asks. Nick and I have always been something of rivals, though I don't even really know how it started. I think we both just have those kinds of personalities, where we have to keep proving ourselves the best over and over again, otherwise we feel a little worthless. Nick was with me on our last big sting, the one that got me suspended. Because of my inaction, he ended up shot, but thankfully recovered well. He says he doesn't blame me for it, though with him I can definitely tell that's not the whole truth. There's something else going on there that he doesn't want me to know.

"Not sure yet," I reply. "Judge's daughter is missing. We're trying to determine how serious this one might be."

Nick takes a sip from his mug. "Sounds thrilling."

"Yeah, and what are you doing here so late?" Zara asks as

she types furiously on her keyboard, not looking up. "Trolling the criminal database for your next date?"

"Funny," he replies, though he doesn't grin. "No, I have my own cases, thank you. And they're not exciting. Just time-consuming."

"The best ones," I say, running Hannah's name through a general background and credit check. I want to get a look at her financials too. See if she really is living on her own or if she's still taking handouts from her parents. Did she need money? Or were the drugs more for a thrill?

"Yeah? You want to trade?" he asks.

"I'm sure you're more than capable," I say.

He lingers for a moment longer. I can't tell if he's really bored or if he's looking for something else. And honestly, I really don't care. I don't have time to deal with Nick Hogan right now.

Eventually, he leaves, allowing me a moment's respite as I can finally look away from my monitor for a moment. I glance back at Zara, who shrugs. She dives back into her work. "Oh! The phone records just came in from Lukas."

I'm behind her chair in half a breath. "Looks like it's mostly outgoing calls. Only two incoming."

"Last incoming was from a Tyler Lozano. And all her last outgoing was to a Margaret Webb."

"Let's get a workup on both. Tyler, that's the boyfriend. And the other one is the friend from college Judge Stewart mentioned. We'll need to interview them tomorrow."

"You got it." Zara gets to work.

I feel bad for initially thinking this might have been nothing more than Hannah wanting some time to herself. And now I find myself in the unenviable position of trying to find *two* women who someone doesn't want found.

Chapter Four

"You look like hell," Zara says as I pull up.

"Thanks." She gets in, gasping as she looks in the cupholder.

"Is that a Cocoa Frappe Single Serve with a dollop of whipped creme and cinnamon top?"

I grin. "Maybe."

She grabs it and takes a long sip, relishing the dessert in a cup. "Oh, that's better than sex." She reaches down to my cup. "What did you get?" When she opens the top her face turns sour. "Black? Really? Not even creamer?"

"What can I say? I'm a simple kind of woman."

Zara turns, looking in the backseat. "I see my boyfriend has been here. You've got hair everywhere."

"I dropped him off at doggie daycare this morning," I say. "I got tired of feeling guilty for leaving him alone."

"They were okay with that?" she asks. "Given his history?"

I shrug. "Ever since he was re-trained he hasn't so much as growled at anyone, including other dogs. But they said they'd have to take it slow, keep him with people first and watch him carefully. If nothing else, he'll get a lot of human interaction."

"I'm glad you did that; he's such a sweet pup," she says, taking another sip.

"Get any sleep?" I ask, pulling away from the curb. First on our list of stops this morning is Hannah's boyfriend's place. After what happened last time, I'm not taking any chances. And if it looks like for even a microsecond like this guy had something to do with her disappearance, we're taking him in. No questions asked.

"I'm still adjusting," she says, yawning. "Usually I'm going to bed around now. Not getting started."

"Pitfalls of the job, I'm afraid."

"Anything come back on the pills?" she asks.

"Nothing yet, the lab still has them. In the meantime we've got some questions to ask."

It takes another thirty minutes to get over to Tyler Lozano's apartment. It's on the east side of town, not close to Bethesda at all. Which is strange, I would have assumed he and Hannah would have lived closer.

The apartment building is decidedly less fancy than Hannah's. There's no lobby, like her mid-rise. Only a two-story siding-clad set of buildings all clustered around a central area with a pool that's been covered up for the winter. I check his address in my notes and we head for eighteen fifty-six, in building four.

I knock on the door a few times, hoping it's still early enough he hasn't left for work yet. The door opens a crack and I see a bloodshot eye covered by a mop of brown hair staring back at me.

"Yeah?"

"Tyler Lozano?"

"Hang on a minute." He shuts the door and calls out. "Tyler! Cops are here."

"Wow, is it that obvious?" Zara asks. "I mean, I know the pantsuits don't exactly scream carefree, but couldn't we be Jehovah's Witnesses or something?"

"I don't think Jehovah's Witnesses dye their hair platinum blonde," I say. "Plus the butt of your weapon is sticking out of your coat."

Zara looks down and pulls the front of her jacket in front of the weapon, only for it to flop back again. "Well, shit," she says, pulling it in front again. Like a bad cowlick, it flops back. "Whatever. Let 'em see it."

The door opens again, and this time we're greeted by the fresh face of a man who looks like he's trying to be everything his roommate is not. He's clean-shaven, with a button-up shirt and tie on, though his shoes are untied. It looks like we caught him in the middle of his morning routine.

"Yes?" he asks.

I lean closer to him. "Are you Tyler Lozano?" He nods. "Do you know Hannah Stewart?"

"She's my girlfriend. Why?"

"When was the last time you spoke with her?" Zara asks.

"What is this? What's going on? And who are you?"

I show him my badge, and Zara does the same. "I'm Agent Slate. This is Agent Foley." When he sees our badges he takes a step back. I'm afraid he's going to close the door on us, but he leaves it open. I can't help but wonder if that was involuntary, or if he's worried we might suspect him in Hannah's disappearance.

"Has something happened to her?" he asks, his voice trembling slightly.

"We're just trying to collect some information," I say. "Can you tell us the last time you heard from her?"

"Um…Saturday, I think. I thought we were going to go out, maybe get something to eat. It's what we normally do on Saturdays. But she said she was meeting Margaret, that she couldn't."

"And you haven't spoken with her since?" Zara asks.

"I tried calling a few times yesterday. And I left her a few texts, but she never called back. I figured she was pissed at me for something."

"Why would she be pissed at you?" I ask.

He shrugs. "Sometimes she just…is. She gets really upset sometimes; I don't know why. And she doesn't like to talk about it. So yeah, it's not strange for a few days to go by without me hearing from her." He looks at us both in turn. "Is she dead?" His voice trembles.

"What makes you think that?"

"Two FBI agents show up at my door, what else am I supposed to expect?" He's agitated, and scared, that much is clear. I just can't tell if it's fear from potentially losing Hannah or the fact that we might be on to him.

"Do you mind if we take a look around?" I ask, peering into the apartment. From what I can tell, it's not nearly as clean as Hannah's was.

"Please," he asks, and his eyes begin to shimmer. "Just tell me. I can take it."

I let out a long breath. "She's missing. That's all we know right now."

"Missing? Since when?"

"Saturday night, we think," Zara says.

He furrows his brow, like he's trying to figure out if that's why she hasn't called him back. "Mr. Lozano?" I ask again.

He looks up, then seems to realize the request and steps back. We enter, though Zara stays close to Lozano in case he decides to try and make a run for it.

The apartment is typical for what I'd expect from a couple of twenty-something guys. Beer cans litter the table in front of the worn couch, where the roommate sits, a headset on and a game controller in his hands. On the TV is a racing game. I step in front of the TV to examine the rest of the apartment, but he barely notices, just ducks and looks around me.

The kitchen is an absolute mess. Stains everywhere, half-eaten containers of fast food on almost every surface, and a pile of dishes in the sink. Again, more beer cans. Actually, considering how they're all arranged, there's no way there's been a struggle in this place. Cans sit precariously on surfaces that with even the slightest bump would send them crashing to the ground. Tyler wouldn't have taken Hannah from here.

I head into the back, checking the bedrooms. One is little more than a mattress and sheets on the floor, but the other has an actual bedframe and proper furniture. It's not hard to guess which one belongs to Tyler. His laptop sits on the desk in the room, open, but off. I tap one of the keys, but it only brings me to a login screen. The rest of the room looks standard to me, I don't see anything out of the ordinary.

I return back to the "living room" where the roommate continues to play his game, oblivious to the rest of us.

"Where were you on Saturday night?" I ask.

"Here," he replies.

"On a Saturday night?" I ask. "Seems like a low key night for someone not too far out of college."

"Yeah," he replies. "And saddled with a ton of debt. It's a lot cheaper to drink at home, trust me."

"Anyone here with you?" I ask. Tyler points to the guy on the couch, who is completely engrossed. I reach over and grab the headphones off his head. A split second later he's paused the game, staring up at me.

"What the hell, man?"

"Where were you Saturday night?" I ask.

"Here," he says, like he's offended to be anywhere else.

"Anyone here with you?" I ask.

He points to Tyler. "Got your ass kicked on GT six, didn'cha Tyler?" he teases.

"Jerm, Hannah's missing."

"What?" he asks, then looks at Zara, and then me. "Oh, is that what they're here for?" Tyler nods. "Damn, man. I'm sorry about that. I liked her."

"It doesn't mean she's dead, Jerm!" Then he looks at us,

his eyes pleading. "Right? You haven't found anything yet, so she could still be alive, right?" The sheer terror in his voice has me convinced he didn't know anything about this until we walked up to his door this morning. Though he does seem fixated on her death. If he'd already known, he wouldn't have acted so surprised. Not to mention there's nothing here that would make me think Hannah even stepped foot in this place recently. I can imagine for a neat freak like her, a place like this would be intolerable.

"We don't have any evidence to suggest that, no," I say, trying to remain level-headed. I don't want to give Tyler false hope, but at the same time I don't want him shutting down completely. "Do you happen to know anyone who might have wanted to do her harm? Anyone she was in trouble with?"

He shakes his head. "No, but she doesn't tell me everything. And lately, I've seen her typing on her phone a lot more than she used to. I try not to think that she's talking to another guy, but it's hard not to think that, you know?"

I glance at Zara, who seems as perplexed by this information as I do. We didn't see a significant spike in text messages in her call data. Which means she must be using an app for messaging, rather than just the phone's texting feature. And that means we'll be digging through data for days.

"Has she exhibited any mood changes in the past few weeks? Anything that would make it seem like she's more...on edge?"

"Yeah," Tyler says. "She has been more short with me lately. I just figured it was because I was doing something to upset her. Like the way I chew."

"The way you chew?" I ask.

"She says it's annoying and I need to cut it out."

"That's cause she's a grade-A stuck-up bi——." The word dies on "Jerm's" tongue when he looks at us. "Uh...princess. She's always complaining about something he's doing wrong. I told him he needs to find someone who appreciates him."

"And you're the expert on women?" Zara asks, incredulous.

"Sure," he says, giving her a wink. "I'm sure you and I would go great together."

Zara stifles a laugh. "Em, if you're good, I think I'll wait outside."

"Sure," I nod, turning back to Tyler. I hand him my card. "If you hear from her, or think of anything else, anyone shady she might be involved with, you call me immediately. Doesn't matter what time."

He takes the card and nods, though I can see in his eyes he's already lost hope. But honestly, if Jerm is right and this is the way Hannah treats him, maybe it's the best thing for him. Some people might say her needling would be enough for a motive, but I'm not getting any vibes off Tyler that tells me he has anything to do with this.

Still, I've been wrong about that in the past. Which is why I want a second opinion.

I join Zara back outside at the car. "So?" I ask. "What do you think?"

"That Tyler needs to stand up for himself," she replies. "And he probably doesn't have anything to do with this. He seemed genuinely surprised at the news. And scared he might never see her again, even if she isn't very good for him."

"Thank God, I was afraid there for a second I was completely misreading him. Ever since Wright…" I trail off, shaking my head. "It's messing with my confidence."

"You'll get it back," she says, giving me a wink. "You just need to get back in your groove. Who's next? The friend?"

"Yep," I say. "And it looks like we're going to have to deal with some beltway traffic. She'll be at work or on her way by now."

"Then we better get a move on," Zara says.

"You sure? Don't wanna go back in there and get *Jerm's* number?" I give her a wide grin.

"Not in a million years. And if you don't leave right now I'll go back in there and give him *your* number."

I smile to myself as we pull away from the complex. I have to admit, bringing Zara on was the best thing I could have done for myself.

Chapter Five

WE'RE STANDING AT THE FRONT DESK OF BIOLABS, INC, WHICH happens to be a subsidiary of one of the largest drug manu-facturers in the country. If this was anywhere else I would have pushed my way past security by now and gone to find Margaret Webb myself. But unfortunately, she works in a clean room, which means no one can go in that hasn't gone through a rigorous safety check and donned the appropriate equip-ment. Basically, a full static-free suit along with face covering and gloves. It also means that it takes someone in that environ-ment a while to transition back out.

"How much longer?" I ask the desk clerk, a stern-looking man with a blue ballcap that matches the rest of his uniform.

"Shouldn't be much longer, ma'am," he replies. "Ms. Webb was in the middle of handling some very volatile mate-rials. She can't just drop everything, not unless you want this place to suffer a biohazard."

"What kind of stuff are you guys processing back there?" Zara asks.

"Sorry, I can't talk about it," he replies. "I'm sure someone in the FBI can understand our need for secrecy."

This guy has a very punchable face, like it's begging my fist to slam into it. But I obviously can't do that, as good as it would feel. Still, the urge is strong.

Zara nods at something behind me and I turn. A young woman in a lab coat is walking toward us, her face pinched with worry. Her hair is short and curly, light in color and her features are soft. She doesn't wear much makeup, if any at all, but I can tell her cheeks are already flushed.

"Ms. Webb?" I ask.

"Yes?" she says, taking my outstretched hand.

"I'm Agent Slate. This is Agent Foley. May we go somewhere to speak privately?" The lobby of BioLabs, Inc isn't exactly bustling, but there are people coming and going, not to mention the guard at the front desk.

"Of course," she says, "Please come with me." We pass the guard, and she leads us into a small conference room off the main hallway. "I have to tell you now, if this is about some of our proprietary products there's only so much I can say. Even to the FBI. You'll have to get a full warrant with some very specific language if you're looking—"

I hold up my hand. "That's not what this is about."

"Oh," she says, and visibly relaxes. It makes me wonder just what they're doing here and if it's something we *should* be investigating. "Then what can I help you with?"

"When was the last time you spoke with Hannah Stewart?" Zara asks.

"Hannah? Well, I saw her on Saturday night," she says. "But I haven't spoken to her since. Why, what's going on?"

"You haven't received any calls, or texts?" I ask. She shakes her head, slowly. "Unfortunately it looks like Hannah is missing."

"Missing? As in…she ran away?"

I try to keep my face neutral. "Actually, it's looking more like she was taken."

"Abducted?" she asks, her voice a pitch higher. "Why? What would anyone want with her?"

"That's what we're trying to figure out," I reply. "It seems you might have been one of the last people to see her. Can you tell us what happened on Saturday?"

Margaret shifts in her seat, cutting her eyes away. "We met up for a few drinks. Ever since she moved out we haven't been getting together as much. It was supposed to be like a commiseration. You know, try to get things back to the way they used to be."

"Were you two not on good terms?" Zara asks.

"It wasn't really that," she says. "It's just…the past few weeks Hannah has been acting kind of…odd. Not like herself. She used to be so outgoing and carefree and lately she's been very closed off, not returning phone calls, missing dates we'd set. It used to be that you couldn't pay Hannah enough to miss a chance to let loose at the bar for a couple of hours. But I practically had to threaten her to get her to show up on Saturday."

"Threaten?" I ask.

"Not literally," she says. "But you know how it is when you know someone is ducking you. I told her if she didn't have time for me in her life anymore, to just tell me to my face. Stop with all this passive aggressive bullshit."

"How did she take that?" Zara asks.

"She was overly apologetic. Saying she was sorry for leaving me hanging so many times. She promised she'd be there on Saturday, and she was."

"How did everything go? Okay?"

"Yeah, I mean, as well as could be expected," she replies. Though I notice her shift in her seat some more. She also starts cracking her knuckles one at a time.

"Is there something wrong, Margaret?" I ask.

"No, why?"

"You just seem…nervous."

"I'm sitting across from two FBI agents, just now learning my best friend is missing, possibly kidnapped," she says. "How am I supposed to seem?" There's a fire in her eyes for a brief moment before it's gone again, and she takes a deep breath. "I'm sorry. I'm not usually so wired. I've been working with some very…volatile products lately and it's frayed my nerves."

"That's all right," I say. "Did you happen to see anyone on Saturday that might have been stalking Hannah? Anyone watching her?"

She shakes her head. "Not that I recall. But she did seem a little jumpy. And a little out of it, like her mind was somewhere else. She kept scanning the room, like she was looking for someone. I thought she was just being cagy about her and Tyler."

"What about them?" I ask.

She hesitates, like she's betraying a secret, but decides to speak anyway. "They're not really a great fit, and she knows it. I think she's had it on her mind a while that she's going to break up with him, she just hasn't come out and said it."

Zara leans forward. "Have they been together long?"

"Only about a year," she replies. "When it got to the point where he was hinting about moving in, especially after she got her own place, I think she realized she didn't feel the same way about him that she did when they started dating. It happens. Sometimes people grow apart."

Somewhere deep inside me, I can't help but think about Matt. About how we never grew apart, only closer together. We thought we had decades left.

"So do you think her odd behavior was because she was nervous about breaking up with Tyler?" Zara asks, taking the lead, for which I'm grateful. I had promised Janice I wouldn't let Matt's death affect me on the job anymore, and here I am, falling back into an old pattern again. I have to focus.

"No, this was something else. She was worried about something…serious. Tyler, forgive me, isn't serious. Not to her."

"Do you know where she would have gone after?" I ask,

refocusing. "Could she have headed out to another bar? Or gone to meet someone else?"

Margaret shakes her head. "She went home. She said she had a lot going on the next day. I offered to come stay over with her, but she declined."

"Do you have any idea what she meant by that?"

"No clue."

I sit back, crossing my arms. "Where did you guys meet up?"

"Arnie's, down off Arlington," she says.

"That's only a few blocks from her apartment," I say, pulling out my phone so I can double-check the route she may have taken. "So we're looking at roughly a six-block area where she could have been abducted."

"No, she called an Uber," Margaret says.

I glance at Zara. "You're sure?"

"Yes," she says. "She showed me the driver was on his way before she left."

"You didn't leave together?" Zara asks.

Margaret's face flushes. "The night didn't end well. She said she wanted to be alone, so...I didn't follow her. Now I wish I had. But I was hurt too. It's been...tough."

"I'm sorry to hear that," I say. "But this is helpful. We can just contact Uber and they can at least let us know if they picked her up. If we can figure out where she was taken, it will really help us find her." I nod to Zara, who stands back up and makes the call.

I lean closer to Margaret. Compared to Tyler, this woman is a damn Hannah encyclopedia, which shouldn't surprise me. People are often more open with their best friends than the people they have sex with. "Do you know if Hannah was having any issues with drugs?"

"Drugs?" Margaret asks. "Like pot?"

"Like ecstasy, or something similar," I say.

She shakes her head. "No way. Hannah isn't into that stuff. She's never gone for it before."

"Maybe not using, but would she ever sell it for someone? For some extra cash?"

Margaret twists her face into something resembling revulsion. "Why would she do that? Her parents are crazy rich. And she makes good money at ChemPharm."

"We found a stash of pills at her apartment," I say. "We're analyzing them now. But they're not normal prescription pills. They look to me like recreational drugs."

"I don't understand," Margaret says. "Hannah wouldn't even know where to get something like that—much less sell it to someone else. Not unless she's been lying to me for a lot longer than I suspected."

I lean back again. "Maybe she was too embarrassed to mention it."

"Trust me, Hannah would never deal drugs. It's just not in her nature." I have to physically restrain myself from reacting. People have no idea what they're capable of until they're under the gun. If Hannah found herself in some trouble, a quick drug flip might have seemed like an easy way out. Except something went wrong.

Margaret glances toward the door; she's ready to be done. Which means we won't get much more from her, at least not voluntarily. I hand over my card. "If you think of anything else, please call."

Margaret takes the card, then reaches out and places her hand on my arm. "If you find her, please tell her I'm sorry."

I hope she'll be able to deliver the message herself. But in my experience, it's unlikely.

Chapter Six

"NOTHING FROM UBER," ZARA SAYS AS WE MAKE OUR WAY down to Arnie's. It's not far and since all the morning traffic is already over, it makes for a pleasant drive. I'm actually appreciating how green everything is today. Spring was always Matt's favorite season; I wasn't sure how I was going to manage it this year without him. "They don't have Hannah Stewart in their system."

"Margaret must have been mistaken," I say. "Try Lyft. We need to make sure no one else picked her up."

Zara nods and gets on the phone again, calling into the ride-share.

I go back over the meeting with Margaret. I let my emotions regarding Matt override my better judgement again. And for the second time while on the job, I got distracted thinking about him. Thankfully, this time it wasn't in the middle of a high-stakes negotiation ending in a firefight. But still, I can't be letting my guard down like that. It's been four months. I need to be able to maintain my focus or this homecoming is going to be short-lived.

Instead, I think about Hannah. It's obvious she was afraid of someone. And I have to assume whoever she was on the lookout for has something to do with those pills we found. But finding whoever sold or gave them to her is going to be near-impossible, if Margaret is to be believed. Hannah isn't the kind of person who has a lot of contacts in that world... though there may be a few rich kids who've dipped their toes in. And if the drugs are spreading from friend to friend, maybe we need to look at her other acquaintances.

Still...it's strange. I'd expect this behavior from a high schooler or someone in college, not a professional in the work-force. Which brings me back to my original hypothesis: the drugs have something to do with money. Money that Hannah needs for whatever reason. And I have a feeling once we find whoever sold or gave them to her, we'll find who took her.

"Still nothing," Zara says, hanging up. "Maybe Margaret only thought she saw Hannah schedule them."

"Maybe," I say. "But aren't there a few local ride-share companies? We need to check those too, just to make sure. People these days aren't loyal to one company over the other; they're going to use whoever can get them home the quickest and cheapest."

"Right," Zara says, checking her phone. "There's one local called *Ryde 4 Lyfe*. That's Ryde, with a 'y' and the number four. In case you were wondering."

"Sounds like a winner," I say as we pull up to Arnie's. There's no parking on the street so I have to pull around the building and park in the back. There's only one other car here, which doesn't surprise me, given it's Monday morning. They probably aren't even open yet. But that suits us better. It would be a lot harder to get what we need with a crowded lunch or dinner rush.

"You want me to..." Zara holds up her phone as we get out of the car.

"Once we're done here," I say. "Let's see what they can tell us."

The front door is locked, so we have to go around to the

side again. I end up banging on the door for a solid minute before I hear a deadbolt shoot on the other side and the door swings open, almost smacking into me.

"What?" A large man with a square jaw says. His eyes are bloodshot, but his face looks like it's been chiseled from stone. He's got a five-o'clock shadow that's gotten out of control and is glaring at the two of us like we've just kicked his dog.

I badge him. "Agent Slate with the FBI. This is Agent Foley. May we have a minute?"

He lets out a long breath like he's considering slamming the door in our faces. But eventually he steps aside to let us in.

We come back through the kitchen which looks clean, for the most part, through a swinging door into the main bar area. The whole room is dark, and the chairs are all up on the tables.

"Wanna tell me what this is all about?" the man asks, following us in. He goes to a tap behind the bar and pours himself a water which he downs in one gulp.

"Rough night?" I ask.

"It's basketball season," he says. "Seems like every night is a rough night." He pours himself another water.

"Are you the owner?" I ask.

"General manager," he replies. "Ed." He holds out a hand.

I take his hand. "Got a last name, Ed?"

His eyes flick from me to Zara and back again. "Bauer." Zara stifles a laugh while I have to bite my lip. "Yeah, yeah, go ahead," he says. "I've heard it all before."

I shake my head. "No, that's fine Mr….Bauer." I shoot Zara a glance, but she turns away, chuckling to herself as she pretends to inspect something behind her. "Were you here on Saturday night?"

Ed's eyes stay on Zara for a minute before returning to me. "I'm here every night. Robbins won't give me a night off. It's bad enough I have to open every morning too."

"Robbins?" I ask.

"Jerry Robbins, the guy who owns the place. Though you'd never know it by coming in here. About the only thing he does around here is count the money."

"Sounds like you need a new job," I say.

He shrugs, taking another sip of water. "Things will be better once the season is over. Another week and I can start sleeping again." He walks over and flips on some of the lights, bathing the main room in fluorescents.

I pull out my phone and bring up Hannah's picture, showing it to him. "Did you see this woman on Saturday night?"

He studies the picture for a moment, then shakes his head. "Maybe. I'm not sure. We were slammed. Tons of people in and out all night. She could have been here, but she doesn't stand out to me."

I put the picture away. "Em," Zara says, pointing to small black orbs nestled in the ceiling and in the corners of the room.

"Fancy cameras," I say. "Those look like the kind they use in casinos."

Ed nods. "Yeah, Robbins is paranoid someone is going to steal off him. He's got more cameras than he has employees."

"Do you still have the footage from Saturday night?" I ask.

Ed shoots a glance back in the direction of the restrooms. "Yeah, it stays on the server for a month, but…"

I look at him, then look at the empty room. "You need to get things started here."

"I'd show you if I had time, but the other employees won't be in for another hour and I need to start setting up. If I don't, we won't be ready when the lunch rush comes in."

"I understand," I say. "I used to wait tables in college. Once some of your other employees come in would you have time to show us?"

He nods. "Probably."

"Great, we'll wait out in our car." I motion to Zara that we should head out.

Ed rubs at one eye. "That's not necessary." He pulls a couple of chairs down from one of the tables. "It's not like you're going to disrupt me in here. What do feds like to drink anyway?"

"Blood," Zara replies. "The fresher, the better."

"Coffee will be fine, thank you," I say, shooting her a look. She smirks at me as we take a seat. Ed grins at us and retreats into the back. "You can call that ride-share now," I say.

"And miss the sexual tension between you and Mr. Eddie Bauer?" she laughs. "No way."

"Will you shut up?" I say, hushing her. "And I don't know what you're talking about."

"Sure," she says. "You don't see the way he's looking at you? I mean jeez, Em. Look at those muscles under that shirt that fits him just right. If you're not going after Coll, you should at least give this guy a chance." She reaches over and takes my hand. "It'll be good for you."

I withdraw my hand. "I'm just not ready yet." She gives me a knowing look as Ed brings over two cups of steaming coffee. "Thank you."

"No problem. I'll let you know as soon as we can start looking at those videos." He heads back and disappears behind the swinging door to the kitchen.

Zara nudges me. "Feel it yet?"

"Don't you have a phone call to make?" I ask.

"Yeah, okay," she replies, stepping away from the table to make the call. I take a sip of the coffee as I watch the swinging door swing back and forth until it stops. I don't know what she's talking about; I didn't feel any tension. Am I just oblivious, or is she making it up? Then again, I really don't know how to flirt or recognize when someone is making a move on me. I've never been good at it. My friends in college used to tease me that I was completely blind to anyone who showed an interest in me, going so far to say that people needed to spell it out before I'd get it. Which is ironic, considering what I do for a living. You'd think with all my skills as an investigator and a profiler I'd be able to tell when someone is interested in me, but I'm just not wired that way. When it comes to anyone else, I can see as if I had 20/10 vision. But when it comes to me, it's like I'm walking around with my eyes closed. Back then I would always just explain it away, that I only had eyes for Matt, even during those brief times we weren't together. It was less embarrassing than telling them I couldn't tell someone was hitting on me.

"Got it," Zara says, sitting back down. "Well, maybe."

"What do you mean?" I ask.

"Hannah is a registered user with them, but they're not willing to release their ride records," she says.

"What? You told them who you worked for, didn't you?"

"I told him. The guy on the phone was a complete ass. Told me I better serve him with a warrant if I want a look at his records and then hung up on me."

"Oh, we are definitely going to visit him next," I reply. "Once we see what's on these tapes."

"These what?" Zara asks, winking at me.

"Ha. Ha. Yes, I realize no one uses tapes anymore. I can't help it; I grew up with people saying that all the time. I even made a mixed tape or two back in the day, before I had a CD burner."

"Oh, now you're really dating yourself." She laughs.

"You're like, one year younger than me," I say. "You've got no room to talk."

"Tell me about Napster, grandma. Did you really wait three hours to download a file just to find out it was a foreign language version?"

I take a sip from my cup. "Keep it up and you're gonna find this coffee all over that new blouse of yours."

We banter back and forth for a while as more employees

of Arnie's begin to show up. A few of them shoot us looks, but most ignore us as they go about their morning opening duties, one making his way around us to finish taking down all the chairs and get the tables ready for customers. After about forty-five minutes Ed reappears. "Ready?" he asks.

"Thanks again for the coffee," I say, raising my empty mug to him. "It was good."

"Local brew from here in town," he says, leading us to the restrooms. Beyond the doors is a third door marked "employees only" which also requires a key.

Inside is a standard office with a desk, a couple of filing cabinets and a shelving unit overflowing with purchase orders, and inventory lists. There's a second room off the first, which houses little more than a desk, a computer and four monitors. The room is significantly cooler than the first office, and it's a tight squeeze getting all three of us in there. Eddie takes a seat and taps the space key, bringing up live feeds of every angle of the place. I see now what he was talking about; this Robbins guy has some high-quality cameras for a bar. Which is good news for us.

"Saturday night?" Eddie asks. "What time?"

I check my notes. "She was here between eight-thirty and almost eleven."

He taps a couple of keys and the images on the monitor change, showing a busting bar, full of people. "This is eight-thirty," he says, looking back at me. "Just use the arrow keys to skip forward or rewind. Space will take you back to the bank of cameras, just click on whichever one you want." He gets back up and has to squeeze past me to get out. I can't help but feel a slight tingle as his body brushes up against mine.

"If you need anything else, just come and find me. I'll probably be around the bar."

"Thanks, Mr. Bauer." Zara snickers.

I shoot her a look. "Thank you, this is really helpful."

"Good luck," he says, giving me one last look before leaving us to it.

Zara giggles as she sits down in the chair, giving me a knowing look. "I know you had to have felt *that.*"

Chapter Seven

IT TAKES US NEARLY AN HOUR, BUT GIVEN THAT THE BAR HAS
nine different cameras, and all the footage is in black and
white, it took some time to pick out Hannah on the various
feeds. The good news is we have a clear view of her for almost
the entire evening. The bad news is it's almost impossible to
tell if someone was watching her or not. With so many people
in the bar, it's possible someone could have come in, clocked
her, then waited outside for her to leave. Unfortunately,
Arnie's only has two cameras outside. One is on the side door
which we came through and the other is on the front door.

"Okay," Zara says, peering at the screen as she makes the
image larger. "Here's Hannah at the end of the night, with
Margaret. There, see?"

The two figures on the screen are unmistakable. It looks as
though they're having an argument. Margaret was right,
Hannah looked nervous the entire evening. "That must have
been when Margaret offered to come back with her."

"And there, she's not even looking at her phone as she
leaves," Zara points out. "But here," She switches to another
view, this one using the camera outside the building at the

same time code, "*Now* she's looking at it, like she's checking the status of her ride."

"So she definitely called someone," I say. "Maybe we have this wrong. She could have called another friend to pick her up."

"Possible," Zara says. We watch as Hannah makes her way around a small crowd of people to wait by the street. Eventually the crowd dissipates and she's out there alone. I can tell by the way she's holding herself she doesn't feel safe. Why doesn't she just go back inside to wait? Is she too afraid of running into Margaret again? Finally a car pulls up, but it's so far away from the camera I can't tell the make or model.

"What is that?" I ask.

"Some kind of sedan. Light in color. Could be gray, or a light blue."

"Definitely a ride-share," I say. "She's checking with the driver first before getting in the back." Once she's in the car pulls away slowly. If we had a better angle we might be able to at least see the taillights, which would give us a better indication of the model. "Rewind it to the car and screen shot it. I want to send that over to analysis. They might be able to get something on the vehicle."

Zara taps a few buttons and I hear the printer in the other room starting up. We run back through the whole sequence again, starting at eight-thirty-three when she walks into the bar. Other than Margaret, she went up to the bar twice and ordered something before returning. Each time it looks like a different guy tries to pick her up, but she refuses both of them.

"What do you think?" Zara asks as we watch the encounters over and over again. "One of these guys might have followed the ride-share?"

"Maybe," I say. "Looks to me like they ignore her the moment she rejects them, moving on to other targets."

"Any luck?" Ed calls from the other room. I look behind

me to see he has two wrapped packages in his hands. "You guys missed lunch. Thought you might be hungry."

"Yes, please," Zara says, taking one of the packages and unwrapping it. It's a turkey club.

"You didn't have to do this," I say, taking the other one. "Thank you."

"It's no problem," he says. "I figure you guys probably work through more meals than you'd like."

The smell wafting off the club makes my stomach rumble. I didn't realize just how hungry I really was. "Hey, before you go," I say to him as he's turning to leave. "Do you recognize either of these guys?"

Zara pulls up the footage of the two men who hit on Hannah. The angle isn't the best, but in one of them, Eddie is visible in the background, making drinks. He leans close to the screen, and I can't help but smell the aftershave on him this time. He shakes his head. "Sorry. They don't look familiar to me. We have a few regulars, but I don't recognize those guys." He stares at the image for a moment longer. "That's her, isn't it?"

I nod. "Hannah Stewart. In the flesh."

"I do sort of remember her now. She seemed really on edge, like she needed those drinks. Kept ordering cosmos. What do you guys want with her?"

"She's missing," I say, prompting a look from Zara. I wouldn't have normally revealed that to him, but I've just had a thought. It's possible this place could be the stakeout spot for the kidnapper. "Have you had any other reports of missing women from here?"

He shakes his head. "I don't think so. Not that I've heard about, anyway."

It was worth a shot. "Zara, go ahead and print out the pictures of these guys too. We need to identify them."

"Got it," she says, a mouth full of turkey club. The printer in the other room whirrs again. I pull out my card for Eddie.

"If you happen to see either of these men in here again, or Hannah, please give us a call."

"Sure thing." He pockets the card. "Is this your personal number?"

"Yep. Don't be afraid to call if you see something. I'm always available." He gives me something of a sideways grin and I realize what I've just said. I stand there, awkwardly, staring at him until he finally excuses himself and returns to the bar.

Zara bursts out laughing as soon as he's gone. "I'm always available!"

"Yeah, yeah," I reply. "Let's get the hell out of here. We have a weasel to visit."

She packs the rest of her sandwich back up and grabs the papers off the printer. "That was absolute gold. I'm gonna tell Janice I need to always be by your side, just so I can't miss these little nuggets."

"I suppose I deserve that," I say. "C'mon."

As we're leaving, I give Ed one last wave, mouthing him another "thank you". I can't help but appreciate the fact he has a nice smile.

"Where are you going?" I ask Zara as she makes her way to the passenger's side.

"What?" she asks.

"You're driving while I'm eating this delicious sandwich." I toss her the key fob over the roof of the car. She catches it in one hand.

"Fine. But only because I feel sorry for you." She chuckles again, shaking her head. "Always available."

———

Twenty minutes and one scrumptious turkey club later, we're parked in front of the corporate offices of *Ryde 4 Lyfe*, a local ride-share service officially based in Maryland but that covers the entire D.C. metro area. Given what a pain the tube is, I imagine they have to do pretty good business. But you'd never know it to look at the place. The primary office is nestled into a strip mall in between a vacant property and a barber. There isn't even a sign on the building above the door. Instead, there's a few pieces of paper taped to the inside of the plate glass window identifying this place as the Ryde 4 Lyfe corporate offices.

"What do you think? Cockroaches?" Zara asks.

"Definitely. Maybe even a rat." The building is located just outside Capitol Heights, and it fits right in. The parking lot is cracked and broken all over the place and the building could use a refresh, though considering the bars covering most of the windows I doubt that's the biggest of their worries here. "Let's see what we're dealing with."

We both step out of the car and I'm immediately aware of my surroundings. A couple of units down a man is sitting on a rusty metal chair outside, smoking. He watches us all the way to Ryde 4 Lyfe's door. When I give it a tug, it doesn't budge. "Locked."

Zara puts her hands up to the window, attempting to look in. She taps on the glass. "I don't see anyone."

"I wonder if your call spooked them," I say. "Which only makes them look more suspicious."

"How can they just not be here? Aren't they running a business?" she asks.

I pull out my phone and look up Ryde 4 Lyfe's customer service number. I give it a quick call.

"Hello, thank you for calling Ryde 4 Lyfe, where our priority is your destination. You've reached Dana, how can I help you?"

"Dana, this is Agent Slate with the FBI, could you tell us if your corporate offices are open today?"

The woman on the other end of the phone hesitates for just a second longer than she should. "Yes, of course. We're open today from eight a.m. until four p.m. However if you're having a problem with one of your rides I'd be happy to help you."

"I'm looking to speak with the owner of your company," I say.

"Oh, well," she stutters, and I can hear the rustling of papers in the background. I look over to Zara who shakes her head. "I believe he is out for the day. But if you like I can have him call you——"

"Listen, Dana," I say. "You sound like you're just trying to do your job. But I'm standing in front of your corporate offices right now and my partner just spoke to your boss not more than an hour ago. If he's not here I need you to tell me where he is. Otherwise, you could be obstructing a federal investigation."

"He's right here," she blurts out. I suppress a smile. "He just showed me a text telling me to tell anyone he wasn't in today."

"Then please, come open the door for us."

She hesitates again. "I'll be right there." A few seconds later the lights in the unit come on and a pretty, young redhead comes to the door, unlocking it. I glare at her as she holds the door open for us, though she just looks at the ground.

"Dana!" a man calls from the back. "You're fired!" He comes storming around an open doorway and stops as soon as he sees us. "You! You're not supposed to be here without a warrant! I know my rights. Out! Get out!" His face is red and flushed but he's younger than I suspected. He can't be a hundred and twenty pounds soaking wet, but he's acting like the biggest man in the room.

"Mr...." I begin.

"...Aruz," Zara says. "Robert Aruz."

"Mr. Aruz, we just need to ask you a few questions."

"No!" he calls out. "No questions, no cops. Get a warrant.

Until then, we are closed!" He approaches us to usher us out the door.

"I can assure you, Mr. Aruz, you do not want to touch us." He stops cold, his face frozen somewhere between outrage and terror. While he's within his rights to refuse to speak with us, he's not doing a lot for his case here. I can understand a certain kind of reluctance, but this is outright combativeness. What is Aruz hiding?

"I'm calling my lawyer," he says.

"I have to say, you seem awfully afraid of something," I say, looking around the small space. "What are you hiding here?"

"Nothing! I'm hiding nothing! I just don't like people poking into my business. How many times I gotta say it? Out!"

I have an inclination to stand here and argue with him, force him down, but I think it might be better to come back when he's less agitated. Though part of me is afraid he might try and flee. And I need to get a look at his records. We need to make sure Hannah was dropped off at her apartment before we can proceed any further. Once we can establish *where* she was abducted from, we might be able to gather some clue about who took her.

My phone vibrates in my pocket, and I pull it out, looking at the number. I quickly put it back away.

"Very well, Mr. Aruz," I say. "Expect another visit from us again soon." As we reach the door I turn back to him. "And don't take it out on your employee here, she was only doing what an officer of the law asked of her."

His face contorts again. Maybe Dana would be better off with a different job anyway.

We head back out to the car. "Did I miss something, or did we cave pretty quickly in there?" Zara asks.

"He's not going to give us anything in that state," I say. "But he's way too defensive for someone in his position. I want to go back and run some checks on him. See what Robert Aruz is really doing in there."

She nods, then indicates my phone. "Who buzzed you?"

"Dry cleaning is ready," I reply, getting back in the car. "I also want to start looking at those men from Arnie's. Maybe we can get a hit on these two guys in the facial rec system."

"You okay?" Zara asks. It's like she can sense something is off.

"Fine," I reply, starting the car. "C'mon. We've got a lot of work to do."

Chapter Eight

I PULL INTO THE MOSTLY EMPTY PARKING LOT SURROUNDING J.R.'s diner, which is close to Michigan Park. I dropped Zara off back at the office, telling her to get started on the men from Arnie's and to see if she could find anything we could use to persuade Mr. Robert Aruz to allow us access to his records without needing the warrant, which will take more time than we have. I feel bad about lying to her, but right now, she wouldn't understand. No one would. And this is something I need to keep quiet. It's better for her career and her overall wellbeing that she doesn't know.

Since it's well past noon, the diner looks to be in a slump, which is perfect. And hopefully we're far enough away from most of my usual travel routes that I don't see anyone else I know here. Even if I do, I could always explain it away as meeting a C.I. or having something to do with this Stewart case.

Speaking of which, I already have one voicemail on my phone from Judge Stewart looking for an update. But until we have something more concrete, I'm not about to call him back just to say we only have a few leads and no idea where his daughter is. I feel guilty enough as it is by taking time away from her case to deal with this, but it's important. And Zara is still on the job, so it's not like we've abandoned Hannah. Not at all.

I step into the diner, the smells of fried food and salt permeating the air. A waitress serving drinks to an occupied table looks over at me, but I wave her away. I spot the man I came here looking for in the far corner, reading a newspaper.

"Mr. Parrish," I say, taking the booth seat across from him.

He drops the paper lower so I can see the spectacles on his eyes. "Agent Slate." He folds the paper neatly, setting it to the side. In front of him is a mug of steaming coffee. The waitress comes over, her pen and pad ready.

"What can I get'cha, hon?"

"Just a water," I say.

Parrish arches his eye. He's probably in his late fifties, with a full, graying beard hiding a tight expression. He's still got most of his hair, though it's beginning to thin near the top. He's also a man who looks like he could hold his own in a fight, but who has also slowed down in the past few years. "Surprised you're not hungry," he says.

"I just ate. Working on a case." I nod to him. "Find anything?"

"You wouldn't be here if I didn't," he says. He begins to make a move under the table but pauses when the waitress returns with my water. She doesn't even give us any further consideration, instead heads back to the kitchen in a hurry. It looks like she's the only one working the entire diner. Thankfully, it's slow.

Parrish produces a manilla folder, sliding it over to me across the table. "It's like you said. There isn't much there. I spent two weeks going over that place, inch by inch, and still, this was all I was able to come up with."

Intrigued, I open the folder and remove a series of 8x10 blown-up photographs. They're all grainy to some degree, but they all show the same subject: a woman in a black coat, walking away from the camera.

My heart jumps, my adrenaline beginning to pump. "You found her," I say.

He chuckles, but it's mirthless. "If you call that finding someone, I'd hate to see what success looks like in the eyes of the FBI."

"No, you don't understand," I say, looking at the pictures. "Up until now, I've had nothing. No other witnesses. No photographic evidence. Nothing. But this is her, this is the woman I saw in the hospital." I look over the pictures again. I can just barely make out her long, blonde hair flowing over her coat as she walks away. "Where did you get these? I already checked all the hospital cameras."

He leans forward. "These two were from a dashcam in a Ford F-150 parked about a hundred feet away in the hospital lot," he says. "This one is from the bank that sits a block away from the hospital, which is why it's such bad quality, and this one is from a traffic camera at the intersection across from the hospital."

"Is there video to go along with this?" I say, my pulse racing. He nods to the envelope again and I reach back in, feeling a data drive inside.

"All show the same thing. The woman walking away from the front of the hospital, then she disappears off all the cameras a few minutes later. I can't find her after that, though I assume she got in a car and drove away. The nearest bus station is in the opposite direction of the way she's going."

I flip through the pictures again. To have actual photographic proof that I'm not crazy, that I did see someone at the hospital and that she most likely killed Gerald Wright—and probably my husband too—is such a weight off my shoulders. I can't even describe it. "I don't guess you found anyone else who saw her that day?"

He shakes his head. Not long after I got back to D.C., I

hired Parrish to go back to Stillwater and begin investigating this woman, since I couldn't do it myself. He's a retired cop who works as a private investigator now, and he's good. Expensive, but good. I can see now he's already been worth the money. But until I can actually put this woman in the same room with Gerald Wright, I'm still up a creek without a paddle. All this does is prove she exists. It doesn't give me any way to identify her or actually charge her with a crime. But I am dead sure that if I can get her in an interview room, I can get her to admit to both Wright and Matt. And then I can start getting some real answers.

It might not be much, but it's a step in the right direction.

"Do you want me to keep digging?" Parrish asks, breaking my train of thought.

"Is there anything else to find there?" I ask.

He shrugs. "I was thorough. I went through every resource I could think of. A few people working at the hospital thought they might have seen her, but none of them could be a hundred percent sure."

I sit back in the booth, already feeling the deflation setting back in. While it might be a step in the right direction, it feels more like a tiptoe.

"You look upset," he says.

I try to reset my face. "It's not because of you. You've made a huge difference for me. I just wish I had a little bit more."

He nods. "I understand. A grainy image of a woman in a black coat isn't exactly compelling evidence." He reaches down and hands over a second envelope.

"What's this?" I ask.

"Well," he grins. "I was planning on charging you extra for this one. But seeing as how important this is to you, it's on the house. Call it a professional courtesy."

I open the folder and this time instead of a grainy black and white image, this one is in color, and it's a front shot of the woman, full body. Enough to where I can see her face clearly.

"Holy shit!" I exclaim. Everyone in the diner looks up for a moment, then returns to their meals. Parrish chuckles again. "Where did you find this?" I whisper.

"This was captured by a surveyor almost a quarter mile away," he says, proudly. "They were doing some work for the city and taking full land surveys with a six-thousand pixel camera. It took his computer three minutes to resolve the entire image, and then we went in looking. There's no video here, but one of his images caught her as she was leaving the hospital. And it was high-res enough that it was relatively clear, even though he was thousands of feet away."

"Parrish," I say, "This is incredible! This is clear enough that I can run it through the FBI databases. I could get a hit!"

He pinches his features. "Are you sure that's a good idea, seeing as it isn't a real case?"

"It's a case all right," I say. "They just don't know it yet. Gerald Wright was murdered, and this woman was responsible. I just need to find a way to prove it."

"Didn't you say his toxicology report came back negative?" Parrish asks.

I nod. "So did my husband's. But Wright swore up and down that someone killed him. Then less than two days later he's dead himself? Tell me that's not suspicious."

"No, I have to give that to you," he replies. "Do you think this is enough to convince your bosses to reopen the case on Wright?"

I shake my head. "I don't know. But maybe if I can identify this woman first, then figure out what her agenda is, *then* I'll have enough. And I can finally put the questions about my husband to rest."

"Well, I wish you luck with it," he says. "I've seen cases with a lot more languish for decades. I hope that's not your experience too."

"Thank you," I say, gathering up all the photos and data drive again. "Really. This is a game-changer. I'll send the final payment via bank transfer."

"Works for me," he says, reaching across the table. "Good luck, Agent Slate. Let me know if you need anything else."

I take his hand and give it a firm squeeze. "I definitely will."

Chapter Nine

THE FIRST THING HANNAH REALIZES WHEN SHE WAKES UP IS she's cold. She looks down, realizing that wherever she is, she's been stripped down to her underwear. She sits up, her head pounding and making her dizzy before she can regain her bearings. Once the room stops spinning, she takes a moment to look around. There are some clothes on the chair next to the bed, but they aren't hers. Right now, she doesn't care. She pulls the fitted dress on and slips on the flats, finding they're the perfect size for her.

As best she can tell she's in someone else's bedroom. Her first thought is she's been drugged and raped, but she's not sore anywhere and she doesn't see any bruising. Still, her head is foggy and it's difficult to tell what's happened.

All she can remember is getting into that ride-share and realizing they weren't going back to her place. The driver had locked the doors, then before she could call someone, he'd stuck her with something…a needle. After that…she can't remember anything. But her mouth is dry and her muscles ache, like she's been out rock climbing or cross-country running. She looks around for something to soothe her throat, only to see a door placed opposite the bed. Opening it, she finds a small bathroom, complete with shower and toilet. The sink has a small glass with one toothbrush sticking out of it. Wherever she is, this person lives alone. She grabs the glass and fills it with water from the tap, drinking the whole thing in one go. Then she drinks another glass before finally replacing the toothbrush.

Where is she? And who brought her here? She returns to the bedroom to find there is another door, right beside the dresser. Though this one looks a little different. She tugs on the handle, trying to twist it, only to find it won't move. The entire door doesn't budge no matter how much of her weight she seems to put into it. She gets down on all fours, trying to see under the door itself, but it's sealed tight. No light escapes beneath it.

So she's a prisoner. Is that it? She looks around for the rest of her stuff, her phone, purse…anything she could use but it's all missing, just like her regular clothes. She goes to the far wall, expecting to find windows beyond the large curtain that covers the entire wall, but when she pulls it back, there is nothing but a blank slate.

"What the hell?" she says as her heartrate picks up. No windows? No doorway out? Someone has locked her in a box, no matter how much they try to fancy it up. Hannah grabs one of the lamps from the side table beside the bed, intending to use it to break off the handle of the door, only to find it bolted to the nightstand. When she tries to move the night-stand, she finds *it* is bolted to the floor. The room might look like a bedroom, but it is obvious someone has worked very hard to disguise its true purpose: a prison.

She places her hands against her head, trying to think about what happened. Had the ride-share guy abducted her as a crime of opportunity, or is this Alonzo's doing? He'd said she had until *Monday*, dammit. And it's still only…wait…she doesn't know what day it is. She doesn't even know what *time* it is. She could have been out for one hour, or fifty. But given how dehydrated she feels, she has to assume it's been at least a couple hours. Could Alonzo have really pulled this off? When she met him a few months ago, he hadn't seemed like someone who had these kinds of resources. But then again, she doesn't know much about the man. Maybe the person she'd met was just a persona—something to throw people off.

But the point is she hasn't gone back on her part of the deal. Not yet. Did it matter that she's considering going to the cops? Okay, maybe. But he had no way of knowing that. She'd only started thinking of it sitting there across from Margaret, knowing how disappointed she'd be if she knew what Hannah had gotten herself into. She doesn't want to be that person anymore.

Hannah returns to the bathroom, looking for anything she can use to break that door lock. The only things not nailed down are the cup and the toothbrush. Is the toothbrush for her? She'd assumed it was for whoever lived here, but it is slowly dawning on her now that this place has been set up for her. She is in a cell, and who knows for how long. Surely Alonzo won't keep her in here forever, right? He'll want to retrieve his goods. Even if he tears her apartment apart, he probably won't find them.

But what if he does? Then what use is she to him? Could he keep her here indefinitely? What would be the point? Unless he's hoping to squeeze her parents for money.

That has to be it. He's gone back on his word—what else did she expect from a criminal—and instead decided to kidnap her to get a bigger payday from her parents. But how had he even known? It wasn't like she went around announcing who she was. To him, she should have just been another customer, no one special. This was why she should have changed her last name once she was out of college.

This had been nothing but a disaster from the beginning. How did she think she could ever get away with selling drugs? She'd promised Alonzo she could sell the entire bottle in a week, then gone home and hid it, too afraid to approach her coworkers and friends. Too afraid of what they would say or think about her. And despite her promising Alonzo access to a brand-new market, one that had lots of disposable income, she hadn't even made one dollar yet. She suspected he had someone watching her, keeping tabs. He must have seen that she hadn't made any progress and gotten nervous. She should have just returned his goods to him, telling him she was out, that it was too dangerous.

But instead, she'd gone home every night, convinced she'd work up the courage the next day. And every morning she'd left for work without the pills, unable to bring herself to it. She just wasn't that kind of person; despite the fact she desperately needed the money. But if she'd known a prison was in her future, she never would have even gotten involved with it. She'd rather be in jail than in here. At least her family would know where she was. Because now she is pretty sure this was an underground bunker of some kind, and she isn't going to be getting out of here anytime soon, if at all.

Hannah walks over to the locked door and begins banging on it, though it's like hitting concrete. She isn't even sure the sound is making its way through. What is she supposed to eat in this place? Maybe he won't feed her, maybe she'll just waste away in this place, with no one knowing where she is.

Hannah hits the door until her hand is too sore to hit it any longer. Then she leans back against it, sliding down to the floor and wraps her arms around her knees. She just wants to go home. To explain what she is doing, even if it means going back to her parents. Right now even that seems preferable to this.

Hannah hears what sounds like a microwave beep and looks up. In the upper right corner of the room sits a small camera mounted to the ceiling, with a red light on. She blinks away her tears so she can see it more clearly. How had she missed that? So someone is watching her after all. Probably laughing as she nearly broke her hand on that door.

"What do you want, Alonso?" she yells. "If you ever hope to get those pills back, you'll have to let me out of here. You won't find them without me!"

There is no response. Of course not. Nothing she says in here will make a difference. She'll just have to wait and see what his play is. In the meantime, she'll have to try hard not to think about how small this room actually is. But when she looks up, there is an air vent, no larger than twelve inches by twenty inches on the ceiling. At least she won't suffocate. But even if she could move the furniture, there would be no way she could fit through there. Not without dislocating half her body.

"Not going to talk to me, huh?" she asks, taking a seat on the bed. "Fine."

"We can talk," a modulated voice says. It seems to be coming from the walls themselves. But she can't tell if it is male or female, the distortion is too great. Still. If she can communicate with him, maybe she can convince him to let her go. It's the only chance she has.

"First though," the voice says. "Who's Alonzo?"

Hannah freezes. Fuck.

Chapter Ten

LEAVING MY DOCUMENTS FROM PARRISH IN THE CAR, I HEAD
back to the office to meet up with Zara again. As soon as I get
a chance, I'm going to upload the woman's picture into the
facial recognition database to see if I get a hit. Parrish's words
keep echoing in my head that I'm going off-book for this one,
but I don't care. Once I determine who this woman is and
why she decided to murder our suspect, no one at the agency
will question it. This is one of those situations where it's better
to ask for forgiveness rather than permission.

It isn't lost on me that I'm now searching for two missing
women. But I'm not going to let this interfere with my search
for Hannah Stewart anymore. My business with Parrish is
done, which means I can handle everything from here on out
by myself and on my own time.

"Hey," I call out to Zara as I pass back through the double
doors that lead to our department. Now that Zara has been
assigned field duty and been given the new title of Special
Agent, she's been placed up here with the big guns, meaning
she has a new workstation. Back when she was an Intelligence
Analyst she'd do her work from anywhere, home, the office,
her car; wherever she could get a secure connection. Now,

because of the nature of the job, she doesn't have as much flexibility to work when and how she wants to. I think that's probably the only thing that bothers her about this job. Otherwise she seems to love it.

"Pick up your dry cleaning?" she asks.

I hesitate a second, asking myself if she suspects. But then I have to remember not telling her is for her own good. If for some reason this all does go bad, I don't want any of the backlash to land on her. "Yep, all taken care of," I say. "Have you made any progress with finding those two men?"

She shakes her head. "I'm still running them through NICS. But nothing so far. I decided instead to focus on our other friend."

"The ubiquitous Robert Aruz," I say, taking my own station. Part of me wants to go back to my car just to retrieve those pictures so I can feed them into the system right now. It's going to be hard to wait until I have a free minute, but I don't have a choice. I made a promise and I have to stick to it. "Found anything on him yet?"

"Not much, here." She sends over what few files she's pulled, and I go through the information. Aruz is only two years out of college, making him not even twenty-five yet. Not only did he build Ryde 4 Lyfe from the ground up, but he also runs most of it himself. It seems he has a small support staff, which may or may not still include Dana.

He graduated top of his class from MIT, then moved down to D.C. to be close to his family, most of which live just north of the city. It seems he managed to start Ryde 4 Lyfe with a few angel investors and venture capitalists, all, no doubt, people who he met up in Boston. But the company seems to be performing well.

"No arrests, no citations, not even a parking ticket," I say, going back through his record. "He's as clean as fresh snow."

"Has to make you wonder why he's so opposed to us being there," Zara says. She's not wrong. Somewhere along the line this guy has had a bad experience with the police. Otherwise he's just being an asshole, which, I suppose, is possible.

"Maybe it's not him," I say. "Could be a family member or someone else who had a run-in with the law."

"Ohhh, good point," Zara says and turns back to her computer, her fingers flying over the keys. "Here we go. He has an uncle in MCDC, and his father has been arrested twice."

"For what?" I ask.

"Looks like petty larceny and this other one...reckless driving?" She looks into the screen more intently, her face less than two inches from the surface. "But it was thrown out. The judge said it was abuse of police power. Looks like they might have been profiling."

I lean back in my chair, netting my hands behind my head. "That makes sense." No wonder he doesn't want us there. He thinks we're going to charge him with something he didn't do. He's probably grown up hearing horror stories about cops and how they can just bend the system to their own will. Which, I have to admit, is somewhat true. It's crazy what some officers get away with. But I have to believe there are more good cops out there than bad. And hopefully some of these systems are changing, though that didn't seem to be the case in a place like Stillwater, at least not until we got the current chief out. Places like D.C. are harder because they rely on a network of precincts that are run by the old guard: cops who have been around forever, or whose families have served since the early days. It makes it difficult to see systemic change when the people in charge won't give up their power and let younger generations take over.

Unfortunately, that extends to the FBI as well. Though I feel like things are getting better here. Twenty years ago I would have been fired for what happened four months ago. But because Janice is a senior agent, and the old boys club doesn't have the power it once did, I can count on a fairer outcome. I just hope we can keep things moving in the right direction.

"So what are you thinking? How do we get to him without trying to get a warrant?" she asks.

I really don't know. Without some kind of leverage we're up shit creek. It's unlikely we'd be able to get a judge to sign off on a warrant unless we can actually show Hannah used that app and at this point we don't even know if she was their customer. It's the classic chicken and the egg. We need one to prove the other.

"Did you check all the rest of the ride-shares in the city? Even the tiny ones?"

Zara nods. "She wasn't registered with any of them. It's this or nothing."

"That looked like a ride-share, on the video, right?" I ask. "I'm not imagining it."

"Yeah, unless she treats her friends like chauffeurs." Zara pulls out what remains of the sandwich from Arnie's, taking a bite into it. "So good," she says, her mouth full of turkey. "We should make that a regular stop."

"Uh-huh," I reply, not really paying attention. I'm trying to focus on how we can crack Robert Aruz. There has to be *something*. "There aren't any other cameras along the route to her apartment are there?"

Zara pinches her features together. "I'm not sure." She works on the computer a bit longer. "Looks like one. At a stoplight at Campbell. It's a cross street on the way."

"Can you pull the feeds from the city?"

"Gimmie a sec," she says. This is the good thing about Zara. She's been in these systems so long she knows most of them by heart. And even the ones she doesn't know, she knows who to talk to so she can get what she needs. It's impressive. "Requisition...rushed...approved, and...here we go."

I get up and look over her shoulder. "You are too good."

"Don't tell me, tell Janice. I want to make sure this isn't a temporary thing. Being out with you is too much fun."

"You realize that you'll probably be assigned your own cases, right? Most of us work alone."

She shrugs. "Yeah, I know. Still. It'll be fun while it lasts."

The database pops up for Saturday night. Zara begins running through the files during the proper time code. "So she left the bar around eleven-ish…"

"Eleven-oh-six, according to Arnie's footage."

"Right, so we'll start at eleven-oh-six and watch straight through. Shouldn't be more than ten minutes, tops." She brings the feed up and the timecode at the bottom of the camera shows the proper time. It looks out on to a desolate street, colored in all black and white. If we see the same style car, we can just get the license number and question the driver.

"Quiet street," I say after a few minutes have passed. Zara sped the feed up to 2X so we're not waiting around. "No cars yet."

"No nothing," she says. "No dog walkers, people heading home for the night, late-night pizza delivery. It's like the most boring street in the city."

A few seconds later headlights indicate a car is approaching under the light. It stops, then proceeds down the street. But instead of a car, it's a van. Definitely not the vehicle we saw.

We wait until eleven-sixteen. No other cars have come past. "Hold on a few minutes. Let's just make sure it's not a slow driver."

We wait until the counter shows eleven-thirty-one. The only other car that came through was a supped-up pickup. Definitely not a sedan. "That's not good," I say.

"So…what? The driver took her?" Zara asks. "How is that possible? The company would log if the driver deviated from his path...and that he didn't drop off Hannah like he was supposed to."

I shoot her a glance. "I think we just figured out the real reason why Mr. Aruz is so nervous."

"Is *this* enough for a warrant?" she asks.

I straighten up. "Screw the warrant. This is enough to nail the bastard. If he is knowingly covering up the fact one of his drivers may have acted improperly...not only is that a crime, he's aiding and abetting Hannah's kidnapping, whether he knows it or not. Trust me, we don't need the warrant."

"I like the sound of that," Zara says.

"C'mon," I say. "Let's go put the fear of God in him."

Chapter Eleven

I STEP OUT OF ZARA'S CAR AND FIND MYSELF STARING AT THE façade of Ryde 4 Lyfe for the second time in the same day. It's getting late in the afternoon, but the lights inside are still on and because of the illumination, I can see Dana still at her post. Which means there's a good chance Aruz is still in there too.

We make our way to the door, and I tug on it, thinking it's going to be locked again. But surprisingly, it opens. Dana looks up when it does, a surprised expression on her face. She wasn't expecting us back.

"Oh," she says. "Agents, I…um…did you already get the warrant?"

"We need to see Aruz. Right now," I say.

She heads into the back. Less than a second later I can already hear Aruz berating her. I give Zara a look and she nods. We both head to the back. The way he's carrying on it's like someone cut off his leg.

As soon as he sees us, he's out of his chair, which happens to be in the middle of a large bank of monitors and servers, all crammed in the room here in the back. "No! I told you. No warrant, no access. Now get—"

"Stop right there, Mr. Aruz," I say, pulling my jacket back to reveal my weapon. I unclip it from the holster but leave it in place.

He stops short, and his eyes flick from me to the weapon and back again. "You can't shoot me. I didn't do anything."

"Actually, you did," Zara says. "You've participated in a coverup. We have the authority to arrest you and drag you down to headquarters. Have you ever been inside the building? On a tour maybe? We've got some nice, comfy cells there."

"Coverup, what coverup?" he says, his face burning red. This man has zero respect for authority, which makes him even more unpredictable. "You're making this up. You're just manufacturing evidence so you can get access to my proprietary algorithm."

"I don't give two shits about your algorithm," I tell him, my patience wearing thin. "What I do care about is a young woman who seems to have been picked up by one of your drivers and then abducted."

"Impossible," he says, shaking his head. "We prioritize the safety of our customers above everything else. Every driver goes through an extensive background check and the program monitors every ride. Every client is delivered to their chosen destination. If someone deviated, I would know it in an instant. Do you realize what kind of liability risk this kind of business incurs? My insurance bills are insane."

"Did your program register any errors on Saturday night?" I ask. "We have a customer of yours who we think called your service, was picked up, and then just disappeared into thin air."

"You *think*? You barge in here to my place of business, threaten me with a weapon—"

I hold my hand out. "No one has threatened you, Mr. Aruz."

He turns to Dana. "You saw it, she put her hand on her

weapon." Before she can answer he turns back to me pointing. "I have a witness. Unless you plan on killing us both."

I keep both of my hands up to show him I'm not a threat. Aruz is more erratic than I gave him credit for; he's just looking for an excuse to blow all this up, and he wants to take us down in the process. If we keep up like this, we're never going to get anything out of him. He'll stonewall us until eternity. Especially since he's right. We don't *know* Hannah used his service. But we have a pretty good idea, having eliminated all the other services in the city. It's obvious from the video evidence she used a ride-share.

"Maybe you're right," I say. "Maybe she didn't use your service at all. We're just asking you to take a look at your ride records to be sure. Then we can cross your business off our list and never return."

"And I told you, that's not possible," he says in a huff. "I don't release my records to anyone, no matter what they want to accuse me of. You come in here with a legal warrant, signed by a judge and I will comply, but only within the limits of the warrant itself. You get nothing extra. And you get nothing for free!"

"This guy," Zara says under her breath.

"Listen to me, Mr. Aruz," I say, my voice as serious as I can make it. "We have evidence suggesting that one of your drivers picked up a woman but never dropped her off at her destination. And if you're covering for him, I can assure you this will not end well for you."

I can tell by his face he's not swayed in the slightest. It's like talking to a brick wall. "Ha! More threats. I know my rights. Do you have proof this woman used *my* service? Mine? Tell me now."

I exchange a glance with Zara.

"I thought not," he says, voice triumphant. "You are fishing. Which means you have nothing on me. Nothing. And I will not stand here and let you bully me into giving you what you want. You want the records, go through your 'justice' system. Don't come down here threatening me and my employees."

"Mr. Aruz, if we find you are obstructing this investigation by covering up a crime by one of your drivers, I can assure you, you'll face a punishment just as severe."

"And I've already told you, I would know if there was a problem in the system. I don't hire unreliable drivers."

"In fact, you don't hire them at all, isn't that right?" Zara asks. "They're 'independent contractors', aren't they?"

"It's for everyone's benefit," he says.

"Except for your employees, who don't get those benefits. They're responsible for their own health and dental insurance, while they take all the risk," I say.

He nods to Dana. "I provide plenty of benefits. And who the hell are you to tell me how to run my business? Like I have said all along, I have done nothing wrong. Now get out of here before I call my lawyer and have you censured for badgering."

"That's not actually a thing," I say.

"Oh?" he asks. "Then I'm sure the FBI wouldn't mind hearing that two of its agents are down here, harassing a small-business owner when they don't even have any evidence against him."

Aruz is really trying my patience. I pride myself on being the kind of person who can handle a lot of punishment, but Aruz is pushing it. I *know* Hannah used his service, but I just can't prove it yet. Not unless we can get hold of her cell phone and show that she actually made the reservation with his company. But given the kidnapper didn't leave anything behind, I highly doubt that will happen.

"You realize a young woman's life is on the line here, don't you?" I ask. "This doesn't have to be this difficult. Five minutes and we will be out of your hair."

"I don't care," Aruz says, and I really believe him. He doesn't care about anyone or anything, which only increases my suspicions about him. Even if he is covering for one of his drivers, I don't have enough yet to force him to cooperate. I had hoped coming down here with the fresh evidence that the car went missing would have been enough to compel him to cooperate, but it seems I underestimated just how hard-headed he would be.

I give him and Dana one last look. She looks as uncomfortable as a person could, her whole body is rigid. I'm sure she sees this kind of interaction every day with her boss. "Mr. Aruz, make sure you don't leave town," I say. "And expect another visit from us, very soon." We both head back out.

"That's right," he calls after us. "Go back to your big buildings of justice and your courtrooms and maybe do something productive for society for once. Stop picking on small businesses just trying to survive."

I grit my teeth and focus on planting one foot in front of the other just so I don't turn around and throw Aruz on his ass. The man is so skinny I feel like I could snap him in two if I really tried.

Once we're outside I suck in a deep breath. The late afternoon is slowly turning to evening and the temperature is beginning to drop. Behind me I hear the click of a lock. I turn to see Aruz standing behind his door, glaring at us.

"C'mon," I say, getting back in Zara's car. "I need to get out of here before I punch through that glass."

"I could just drive through it if you want," she suggests, getting behind the wheel. "It's an older car, the gear could always slip."

I smile. "I don't think that's going to help us get what we need."

"You never know, he might be so distracted you could run into the back and look up his records."

I hate that for a millisecond I consider it. "Nah," I say. "I'm sure he's got the entire system triple password and biometrically locked. Let's just get out of here. I still need to go pick up Timber. The kennel is going to close in half an hour."

Zara checks her watch. "Let's just go pick him up now. You'll never make it back to your car and all the way over there in time. Not with the afternoon rush."

My first instinct is to argue, because the pictures from Parrish are still in my backseat. And I know Zara will just insist on dropping me and Timber off at home rather than go all the way back to the office. But I can't think of an excuse that would sound plausible. Plus, it's not like I can do anything with them at home anyway, I had just hoped to study them further. I don't have much choice, not without making her suspicious. Zara is too sharp for me to pull one over on.

"Sure, thanks," I say. "That'll be a big help." I gesture to Aruz, still standing in the window. "If I have to see his face any more today, I think I'll lose it."

"You and me both," she says. "I don't understand why some people have to be so difficult. Do you have any idea of how you're gonna get that warrant?" She backs out of the space and heads for the main road off the strip mall.

"No clue," I say. "No judge will sign off on a gut feeling. We need some way to connect Ryde 4 Lyfe to the car itself, but we can't do that without the company's hiring list."

"It's too bad they don't have those bright lights the other companies use," she says. I shake my head. Even if they used them, the footage is from so far away it would be too difficult to make out on the car itself. And while we sit here, spinning our wheels, Hannah is God knows where, having God knows what done to her.

I hit the armrest, my frustration finally leaking out.

"Drink?" Zara asks.

"Definitely," I reply.

Chapter Twelve

A LIGHT BREEZE BLOWS ACROSS THE BAR'S OPEN-AIR PATIO, BUT it's not enough to make me get up. I've got my heavy coat on, and Zara has the same. Timber sits at my feet, lying on the cool ground with a bowl of water right beside his head. Apparently, he had a full day at day care and is all tired out. At least one of us was productive today.

"Here's to intimidation tactics gone wrong," Zara says, holding up her drink. It's a sex on the beach, which is completely inappropriate for the weather, but she's the kind of person who loves tropical drinks no matter what setting she drinks them in.

I have a tumbler half full of Knob Creek with a dash of ice. It's just enough to cut the sting of the bourbon, but still keep me warm as I sip on it. "I can't believe that little cretin has balls that big," I say, going back over our encounter with Aruz. Never in my professional career have I ever encountered someone so obstinate. Most people, even the contrarian ones, eventually relent. They see we're trying to do the right thing, and they eventually decide to help us.

But not Aruz. That man is firm and determined. Which sets off a series of bells in my head. Despite what he's been through in the past with his family, I feel like he's protecting something else. He's not just refusing us to look at his records because of his rights, he's got something to lose if we do. We just need to find out what that is.

Zara leans down, finding my gaze. "Whatcha thinkin'?"

I grin. "Who says I'm thinking anything?"

"Your face. You always look like that when you're concentrating really hard."

My thumb finds my temple and I rub it for a moment. "Aruz. He's hiding something."

"That much is clear," she says.

"No, I mean he's hiding something else. Something we haven't touched on yet. He's way too combative not to be. We need to find out what's going on in there."

"What's the angle?" she asks. "Dana?"

"I don't know. She seems more like someone who's gotten caught up in a tornado and is just looking for a way out without falling to her death. I'm not even sure we could get her to cooperate. And if we did, what kind of access does she have? It looks to me like he's got that place locked down pretty tight."

"Still," she says. "There has to be a way." Zara pauses for a moment, then looks back to me. "As long as we're sure Ryde 4 Lyfe is the culprit."

I hold my hands up on the table between us. "We checked all the rest, who else is left?"

"Private taxi?" she asks.

I shake my head. "Did that car look like a taxi to you? Nah, that was someone's personal vehicle. Someone smart enough to know where the cameras were."

"Either that or they're extraordinarily lucky," Zara says.

"I don't think so. I think they've been planning this for a while," I say. "It's someone who has been meticulous. A random kidnapping wouldn't have gone this smoothly. There would have been something left behind, some piece of evidence. But this screams like it was engineered from the start." I take a sip from my drink.

"So then Aruz is involved," she says.

"Has to be. Otherwise, how else would they schedule the driver to pick her up at that exact moment? We just need to find a way to squeeze him until he talks."

"You want me to drop you off and head back to the office? I didn't get very far this afternoon; I could keep looking."

I shake my head. "You need rest too. This isn't like when you're in front of a computer all day. Being on high alert like this, all the time, it will wear you down if you're not careful."

She sips on her pink straw. "If you say so. Maybe that's just what the old-timers want us to think."

"Who are you calling old-timer?" I ask.

She grins, her lips still on the straw. "No one."

I look down at Timber who's half asleep at my feet. But as soon as he sees me move, he glances up at me, that big smile on his face. "I think someone is insulting your mama."

He just stares at me with those inquisitive eyes of his. "I should probably get him back. He's exhausted."

"Okay," she says, slurping down her drink.

"Whoa, slow down there," I say. "You're not going to be able to walk, much less drive. I didn't mean you had to leave too. I'm getting a ride." I hold up my phone to show the newly-installed Ryde 4 Lyfe app.

A huge grin forms across Zara's face. "Do you think he knows yet?"

"I'm sure he does," I say. "I just registered with my full name. And look, they even have an option that allows pets."

"Whoa, that's a nice feature," she says.

"If we can't get into his records, I want to at least see what the experience is like. Maybe see what Hannah saw. I don't know if it will help or not, but I think it's worth a try. If for no other reason than to piss Aruz off."

"Go for it."

I scroll through the app and schedule my destination, then ask for a pickup that can handle a medium-sized dog. The app responds almost immediately with a driver who will be here to pick me up in six minutes.

"That was easy," I say, finishing off my drink.

"Let me know if you find out anything," Zara says. "And I'll be by first thing in the morning to pick you up."

I stand and Timber gets up as well, excited to be moving again. "You didn't have to do this. Thank you."

"What are friends for?" she asks, bending down and giving Timber a kiss on the top of the head. "Bye, bye, boyfriend," she says. "I'm gonna steal you one of these days."

For a brief moment I pause, considering whether or not to tell Zara about the photographs Parrish managed to find. Part of me wants to confide in her, but another part is telling me that all I'd be doing is resigning her to a doomed ship, destined to go down. I can't sabotage her like that. I've already done enough damage; this is my fight. As much as I'd love to tell her, I can't bring myself to pull her in like that.

"You okay?" she says when she notices me staring at her.

"Yeah, fine," I reply, flashing a smile. "Enjoy the rest of your drink. And try not to pick up too many guys here."

"You know me, can't stop banging dudes left and right." We share a laugh as I head over to the corner where my *ryde* is scheduled to pick me up, Timber trotting right behind on his leash.

"See you tomorrow." I wave and she waves back, going back to our table and her drink. I check the app again and see the car is right around the corner. When I turn back, I see Zara has decided to take her drink inside. Maybe she is after a hot date after all. But then again, for all the time I've known her, she has been very picky about anyone she brings home. She's not the kind of person who meets people at a bar. When Zara goes looking, she does a deep dive on someone before talking with them. Plus, I think she's still a little hung up on Coll. But he's been so busy going through the application process I haven't hardly heard a word from him. I had thought when I came back from Stillwater we'd find time to at least hang out, but it seems he's been too busy for that.

The car pulls up and rolls down the passenger side window. An older man wearing a cowboy hat leans forward. "Emily? With…Timber, right?" the driver asks.

"Right," I say.

"Hop in," he replies and unlocks the doors. I usher Timber in first, who crosses the seat and sits down on the far side, right behind the driver. I take the seat beside him. "There's a little latch hooked on the seat if you want to attach his collar."

"What?" I ask.

The driver turns. He's probably in his mid-forties, beard, with dark brown eyes. "It's like a dog seatbelt," he says. "Just in case I have to stop quickly."

I reach behind Timber and find the little hook at the end of a nylon band. I hook it on his collar. It still gives him freedom to move but isn't so constraining he can't lay down, which is what he does. "I need to get one of these for my car."

"They're great," the driver says. "Beautiful dog, by the way. How old is he?"

"We think about four," I say, using the royal "we" even though Matt isn't around anymore. "Is driving around people's pets difficult?"

"Not usually," he says, pulling away from the curb. "Most are well-behaved. Every now and again there's an accident, but I have a great detailer."

"How long have you been working for Ryde?" I ask.

"Only about six months. I actually work for the big two as well," he says, indicating a couple of different placard signs he has on the seat beside him. "You never know which service someone might be using."

"Is that common? For a driver to work for multiple companies?"

"Sure," he says. "I don't know anyone who *doesn't* do it. You're leaving money on the table if you do."

"Huh," I say, sitting back, the wheels in my mind turning. I'm wondering how likely it is that our mystery driver worked for the other companies as well. Though it's not like we'd know, considering none of them processed Hannah's request. But it might be a way in. I shoot off a text to Zara.

Cross check employees of the major ride-share companies. Let's see how many cross over.

A second later her reply comes through.

On it first thing tomorrow.

I stow my phone again. "Do you like driving for Ryde?"

He shrugs. "It's okay, I guess. It's a gig. Pays the bills."

"How are you assigned the people you pick up?"

"I'll get a notification on the app," he says. "Asking if I want to take a fare. But I have to be within a reasonably close distance. The company doesn't like you to be waiting around too long for a ride."

"And if there are multiple drivers within my range?"

He glances at me in the rearview. "It's whoever responds first. So if I'm quick enough, I can beat out another driver to get your fare."

"And thus get paid more often," I say, still thinking. "Would the app log if someone was idle for a long time? Say they didn't pick up fares all day, but were still quote/unquote *available*?"

"Why would someone do that?" he asks. "It'd be a waste of their time just to sit around all day."

"Humor me," I say, stroking Timber's back. He's almost fallen asleep to the soft rumble of the car.

"I mean, I guess," he says. "I'm sure the app tracks how long someone is using it. So yeah, if a driver sat around all day not taking fares, I'd think that would show up."

That's what I think as well. All of a sudden this is beginning to make more sense. Whoever was after Hannah may have been lying in wait, ready to pounce when the opportunity came. Which means whoever they are, they have a lot of free time on their hands. The question is, who are they working for?

The rest of the ride we spend in silence, Timber snoozing quietly beside me. As soon as we reach my apartment I wake him up and we both hop out. "Thanks for the ride," I say. "Five stars."

"Just make sure you rate that on there," he replies. "It affects our performance bonuses."

I hold up the phone in a half-wave. "Will do. Thanks again."

"Have a good night." He pulls away before I'm halfway to my building, Timber trotting along beside me. My mind is buzzing with the possibilities of a stalker lying in wait for Hannah. I hadn't thought it was possible they could reverse-engineer a ride-share before, but now I do. We're dealing with a professional here, which sends a chill down my spine.

We really need to see those records. The sooner the better.

Chapter Thirteen

"I APPRECIATE YOUR POSITION, AGENT SLATE, I DO. BUT without some connective tissue between this ride-share and Hannah Stewart, there's nothing we can do." Janice sits across her desk from me, that same stern look on her face.

Zara picked me up early this morning and after dropping Timber back off at doggy-daycare—which I think is going to be our new schedule, considering how well he did there—we were in the office early. And as soon as Janice came in, I scheduled some time with her to go over this apparent wall we've hit.

"But without the records, we can't prove she even used the ride-share," I say. "We need the records to prove we need the records."

"And therein lies the problem," she replies. "We can't just requisition them without cause. And a hunch isn't cause."

She isn't telling me anything I don't already know. But part of me, perhaps stupidly, had hoped she had a solution I hadn't thought of yet. Zara is already working on the information we received from the other ride-shares, comparing the lists to see common links. Again, it'll be nothing conclusive, but maybe it will help narrow down the list a little. Then again, there is no guarantee this driver was registered with anyone else. But my thought is he would want to be, just in case she used one of those apps instead of *Ryde 4 Lyfe*.

"Keep working it, Slate," Janice says. "You'll find another way in."

"Yeah," I say, getting up. This is one of those cases where time is of the essence. We can't waste it on dead ends, otherwise Hannah will pay the price, if she hasn't already.

As I'm leaving her office, my phone vibrates. "Slate," I say, pushing through the door back out into the bullpen.

"Agent Slate, this is Judge Stewart."

Shit. He's calling for an update and I've got absolutely nothing for him yet. "Morning, Judge. I promise I haven't forgotten you. We're still chasing down a number of leads, I didn't want to get back to you until we had something more concrete."

He holds the line a moment. "Agent, can we speak?"

"In person?" I ask.

"Yes. The sooner, the better."

There's an urgency in his voice I don't like the sound of. "Why, what's happened? Did you receive a ransom?"

"Nothing like that, but I don't want to talk about it over the phone. Can you come down to the courthouse? I have a break between nine-thirty and ten-fifteen." I check my watch. That's only twenty minutes from now.

"Sure, I can be there."

"Thank you," he says, then hangs up.

I head over to Zara's desk. She's deep in it, going through what looks like thousands of records. I knock on her desk, pulling her back out. She blinks a few times. "What's up?"

"Judge just called. Sounded kinda…weird."

"Weird how?" she asks.

"I'm not sure, but he wants a face-to-face. Right now."

Zara is out of her chair with her coat in her hand before I can say anything more. "Let's not keep him waiting."

"Off to bust another drug lord?" Nick calls from across the bullpen. He looks like he hasn't gotten any sleep and that mug is still in his hand.

"Nope, just your balls," I call back and he rolls his eyes, turning in the other direction. I don't know, but I'd like to think if he'd had a mental breakdown on the job and I'd been the one who had been shot, I'd probably be a little more understanding four months later, rather than continuing to needle him. But I guess that's the difference between us.

The Federal Court of Appeals sits on Madison Place, which is right off Lafayette Square in front of the White House. As it is, with all the tourist traffic and security precautions it's easier for us to walk than drive or take the tube. Plus, it's warmed up today and we manage to make it up to the building in only about fifteen minutes.

After a thorough security check and leaving our weapons behind, Zara and I make our way up to Judge Stewart's personal chambers. An officer of the court stands outside his door. I show him my badge as we approach.

"He's expecting you," the officer says, opening the door for us. We both walk into Judge Stewart's lavish chambers, and I attempt not to gawk. The whole room is done up in wood paneling, fitting for a judge. His walls are covered with shelves full of law books, and those walls that don't have shelves to fill are instead adorned with awards, commendations, accolades, philanthropic gift thanks and pictures with the rich and powerful. His degrees from Harvard are mounted directly behind him, between the two large picture windows that look out onto the square itself.

Judge Stewart sits behind an impressive desk, full of binders, books and papers, all scattered across the top. He rises when he sees us, holding out his hand. "Agents, thank you for coming so quickly. Please excuse my office, the past few days have been…stressful."

We take the seats across from him. "I don't doubt it. I'm surprised you didn't take some time off."

He shakes his head. "Can't do it. Not with Amanda stomping around the house. My presence only seems to enrage her further, so it's better if I'm here. Plus, this isn't something we could talk about in her company anyway."

I furrow my brow and shoot a glance at Zara. "What is it, Judge?"

"You said you've been chasing down leads. Have you looked into the Toscani Family yet?"

I shake my head. "Should we be?"

He leans forward. "Three weeks ago I denied a case appeal for Mario Toscani, the head of the family. Needless to say, he wasn't happy. Up until last year, he was living in luxury, until he got snagged evading taxes, which opened the door to his racketeering operation. It all went downhill from there for him, but his family and the rest of the Toscani mob are still operating out there. Though from what I hear they've gotten a lot better at covering their tracks."

"And you think they might have taken Hannah in retaliation for your ruling?" I ask.

He pulls a stack of papers off his desk. "I've been going through all of my old cases for the past year. This is the only one where I feel like the defendant has the resources and the vindictiveness to actually do it."

"Okay," I say. "So then what's the point? Where's the ransom?"

He gives me a humorless laugh. "The point?" His eyes widen and he seems more frantic, more on edge. "These people don't need money. Didn't you hear me? No, they want to hurt me. And because they can't get to me, they've decided to go after my family."

"Do you have any proof it was them?" Zara asks. "Any communication, any indication they were the ones that did it?"

He shakes his head. "I wish I did. But let me tell you, that Mario Toscani is one savage son of a bitch; excuse my language. I wouldn't put this past him. Not in the slightest."

"Okay," I say. "Well add them to the list and take a look."

I move to get up but a pleading look from him stops me. "Have you had any other luck? Anything to indicate where she might be?"

I'm hesitant to tell him what little we know, for fear of him going rogue on us. It can happen, especially distraught parents. If we tell him we think she was abducted by a ride-share driver, he could try to use his connections to retaliate, which would only further complicate the situation and make finding Hannah impossible.

"Nothing solid so far. But we're working some strong leads. As soon as we have a firm one, I will let you know, I promise."

He gives me a quick nod. I know that look in his eyes. It's the wild desperation I've seen in my own on more than one occasion. The one that says: "I know time is running out, and I'm willing to do anything to get the person I love back." That's a dangerous state of mind to be in.

We give him our regards, then head back out into the hallway, passing the guard again. "You know," Zara says, leaning in conspiratorially, "Betcha he'd sign off on a warrant in a heartbeat."

I chuckle. "I'm sure he would. But then anything we found would be completely inadmissible as having been obtained through a warrant that presents a conflict of interest. The Attorney General would have our heads."

"Yeah, but at least we'd know who picked up Hannah."

I have to admit it's tempting. But we can't break protocol like that. If it starts there, where does it end? What else will we justify in order to catch our criminal? I hate that I keep hearing Aruz in my head, telling me we need to go through the proper procedure to get access to his data. I know the second he saw the warrant signed by Judge Stewart and learned we'd be looking for Hannah Stewart, he'd call the priciest lawyer he could and look to hit the Bureau with a five-million-dollar lawsuit. And he'd be well within his rights to do so. We have to avoid any potential illusion of impropriety here, especially if we want to catch this guy for good.

"As much as I wish we could—"

"—yeah, yeah, I know," she says. "It's fun to think about though. A lot more fun than heading down into gang territory."

"Tell me about it," I reply. D.C. has never had the Mafia problem that a lot of other major American cities have had, but that doesn't mean we're immune from it. Often, smaller families will move into certain neighborhoods and run things until they're pushed out by someone else, or the community finally has enough. The constant shuffle has the benefit of keeping large-scale organized crime out of D.C. for the most part. But little pockets linger, and from what I remember, the Toscani's operate out of Brentwood. I'll need to talk to someone up in Organized Crime before we head over there, though. That's like walking into a viper's nest if you're not prepared.

"You think we should vest up?" Zara asks.

I shake my head. "No way. These places operate on respect. And we're not going to get any respect by going in there all suited up like we expect them to shoot us."

"So...what? We just go in there like this?" she asks.

I nod. "And let's hope the Judge is wrong about this one. Because if they really did take Hannah, our jobs just got a lot harder."

Chapter Fourteen

"EM?" ZARA ASKS. HER TONE STOPS ME COLD BECAUSE IT'S the first time I've ever detected a hint of uncertainty in her voice. At least, in this context. And I already know what it's about.

"Yeah?" I reply. After a quick visit with Organized Crime, I learned that the guy in charge of what's left of the Toscani family is a man named Santino, who is apparently Marco's nephew. Gilbert, who was part of the task force that brought down Marco, told me the Toscani's operate out of a warehouse block in Brentwood, right off the train tracks. It's already a sketchy part of the city, but down there near the rail yards, it's a lot easier to lose track of a body. I'm sure that's part of the reason Marco set up shop down there a few years ago. But according to Gilbert, the family has "gone straight" after what happened to Marco. I don't believe it, and I know he didn't either, but at the moment, they don't have anything on them. His last words to me were: "be careful."

"Look, I know I can seem cocky," Zara continues. "But I haven't really been in a situation like this before. Going up against a loudmouth like Aruz is one thing. But this…" She trails off.

"It's different," I reply.

"Yeah." She takes a deep breath.

"You remember that time you got up on stage over at L.J.'s for karaoke night?"

Zara grins. "Yeah."

"You were fearless that night. Go in here with the same confidence. These people can smell fear, and if you show even the slightest amount, they'll pounce. But I know you're not a fearful person. So don't let them intimidate you. They're just a bunch of thugs."

She nods to herself a few times. "Just like karaoke, got it."

I have to admit I'm feeling apprehensive myself. I'm used to putting myself in dangerous situations, but this really is asking for trouble. Were it not for Judge Stewart's insistence that the Toscani's could be involved, we wouldn't be here at all. But we have to investigate all leads and eliminate them when possible. I just hope we can cross this one off the list quickly.

A few minutes later I pull off the street onto a dirt gravel lot, kicking up some dust as I approach a warehouse marked with a giant "C-7" painted on the side. It's surrounded by a high chain-link fence that's open to a rudimentary parking lot. Along the side of the building are a series of trailers without the cabs, all backed up to the building for loading. In the very front is a small part of the building that sticks out, which must be where the offices are.

I pull up to the side, careful not to block the opening in the fence. I want to make sure we've got a clear exit point here if we need it. A couple other trucks and beat-up cars sit in the lot itself.

"Karaoke, karaoke," Zara whispers to herself a few more times. She's got a steely-eyed look now, psyching herself up for this. Finally she reaches for the door handle, and I do the same, stepping out into the sunlight.

I close my door, looking around at the lot. It's a generic

warehouse, not a speck of green or plant life anywhere. But we're not more than two steps from the car before the main door to the warehouse opens and two large men step out.

"Don't stop," I whisper to Zara. We keep walking with purpose toward the building. Around the side, another two men appear, watching us the entire way.

When we're about ten steps from the door to the main office one of the men who came through the door steps forward. "I think you two are lost."

I was prepared for this. I've already got my badge in my hand, and I show it to him, which gives me the advantage of not needing to reach into my coat like I'm going for a weapon. "Agents Slate and Foley. FBI. We're here to speak with Santino."

The man glances at his cohort. The sound of a rumbling engine echoes through the yard and moments later a truck attached to one of the trailers rumbles past, heading out the gate and on to the main road. In the distance I catch the sound of a train whistle, on its way to the yard. It's like a modern-day standoff, each side wondering which one will flinch first.

"What do you want with Santino?" the man asks.

"Just need to ask him a couple questions," I reply.

"Maybe he's not in an answerin' mood," the man growls.

"You really don't want to try and stop a federal investigation, do you?" I ask him. "The two of us being here? This is us doing you a favor. I could have brought my entire department with me. But I didn't think that was necessary. Are you telling me different?"

The man exchanges a glance with the guy beside him. "You armed?" he asks.

I pull my coat to the side to show my service weapon. Zara does the same.

"You'll leave those out here."

I shake my head. "No dice."

"Then you're not getting inside."

I glare at him. The tension in the air is practically crack-ling and all of a sudden I find myself calculating the odds of us walking away from this. I flick my eyes to the men standing off to the side, both of whom are tense, their eyes focused and intense. And who knows if Santino has anyone up high, lining us up in their sights.

"Fine," I say. "That's the way you want it, we'll be back. Get ready for some visitors." I motion to Zara that we should return to the car. I just hope she keeps it slow and purposeful. If she runs, they might panic and shoot us anyway.

"What the hell is this?" a different voice yells, coming out of the main door. The voice belongs to a man who looks to be just under six feet, with jet-black hair and a goatee, wearing gold chains around his neck that catch the sun's reflection. Otherwise he's dressed in all black, his shirt partially open. "Agents," he walks toward us, his arms open, "please excuse my men. They're jumpy. Bad experiences in the past."

"Santino Toscani," I say.

He nods, then turns to the two men standing off to the side. "You two, get back in there! You still got fifteen crates to load before the next shipment goes out. And you," He turns to the two men standing beside the door. "Go do your fuckin' jobs before I knock you upside the skull."

"But San, they're with the FBI," the bigger of the two men says.

"I know who they're goddamn with," he replies, glaring at his men. "You think if they were here to arrest me they'd send two agents? We'd have the whole of the FBI up our rectums by now. Get in there!" The men retreat into the office.

Toscani turns back to us, clasping his hands together. "Sorry for that unpleasantness. What can I do for you?"

I scan the yard, not willing to let my guard down. At least not until I know I'm out of the line of sight of anyone who might be perched up high, just waiting for an order from their boss. "We have a few questions," Zara says. "Do you have somewhere we can talk?"

"Sure, we can talk," he says, motioning for us to follow him. "You know, back when I first got in this game, the FBI agents were a lot uglier. You two are like a breath of fresh air."

I don't know if that's a compliment or he's being cheeky. I decide to leave it, continuing to scan the high areas of the yard until we follow him through the door.

Inside are a few desks, most with scattered papers. A young man sits at one, looking up as we enter. He can't be more than fifteen or sixteen. It looks like Santino is continuing the family tradition by passing things on to the next generation.

We pass all the desks and head out into the warehouse proper, where the sound of heavy machinery fills the air. People are shouting over the sounds of forklifts, manufacturing equipment and gigantic cooling units pumping air into the place. Santino motions that we continue following him, even as almost every eye in the place turns in our direction. The further in we follow him, the more I realize we're not going to be able to make a clean getaway if it becomes necessary. I'm beginning to question my decision to come down here without any backup.

Santino leads us into a finished part of the building, with drop ceilings and florescent lighting. He opens the first door on the left which leads to an office that seems to fit him. It's modest in size, but there are still a lot of flashy trinkets about, including on his desk. I can still hear the hum of the machinery from the floor, but it's dampened enough that speaking over it won't be a problem.

"Drink?" Santino asks, heading over to a makeshift bar he's set up behind his desk. I recognize more than one expensive label on that cart.

"No, thank you," I say. He pours himself one anyway as he indicates Zara and I take our seats.

"Surprised Gilbert himself didn't show up," Santino says. "He's normally the one to make these visits."

"We're not here to investigate your business," I say. His eyes flash a modicum of surprise. "We need to ask you about Judge Stewart."

Santino narrows his gaze. Clearly, that is not a welcome name in this place. "You're not here on Gilbert's behalf? And here I was hoping my fortune had changed."

I shake my head. "We're pursuing a kidnapping investigation."

His demeanor immediately changes, and it feels like the temperature of the room has dropped ten degrees. "Someone kidnapped the Judge?"

"His daughter, Hannah," Zara says.

Santino takes a sip of his drink, watching us closely. "And you're here…you think we had something to do with it."

"We're just asking questions," I say.

Santino shakes his head. It's like he's flipped a switch somewhere inside him. Apparently he was more than willing to cooperate when he thought this involved his uncle's arrest. "Don't know anything about it," he says. "Now, if you don't mind…" He makes a motion to get back up.

"Hold on," I say. "It's not too much of a stretch to think that someone in your organization might be feeling slighted after Judge Stewart's ruling. All we want to know is if you have seen or heard anything."

Santino shakes his head again. "Sorry, can't help you. Now if you ladies don't mind."

I bristle at the word *ladies*, but instead focus on the drilling down to Santino's soft spots. Had I known he was going in this direction, I *would* have brought Gilbert down here. "All that HVAC equipment out there," I make a motion with my head to the door. "Mind if we take a look?"

"A look?" Santino says, his face twisting. His glass is forgotten on the desk between us. "What for?"

"You never know," I say. "Just a routine search. Those HVAC units…lots of empty space in those. Might make good containers."

Santino's face goes a shade of red. "What are you…are you trying to manufacture some kind of operation here?"

I shake my head. "Nope. Just figured that while we were here, it might be worth a gander." He cuts his eyes to Zara, but I'm encouraged to see she's as steely-eyed as I am.

"You can't do that. Not without a warrant."

I lean forward. "Mr. Toscani. Your uncle was indicted four months ago for tax evasion and racketeering. He collected a lot of dirty money. I happen to know that he's remained silent on what has happened to that money, while your assistance in the matter helped seal your uncle's fate. Now, how do you think it's going to look if you refuse the FBI access to your facilities only a few days after your uncle's appeal was rejected? Might that rouse some suspicion?"

"Now wait just a goddamn minute," he says, holding up a finger. "I didn't have anything to do with my uncle's side operation. That was his business, not mine. I *cooperated.*"

I give him a pitying look. "But you see how it looks, don't you? Your organization is under extreme scrutiny right now. A second investigation could halt your operations entirely."

Santino shakes his head. "No, no, no. This is a *legitimate* business, Agent Slate. You think we'd be stupid enough to pull something right now? The whole reason I took over was so we didn't have any more…unfortunate encounters…with the law."

"Then you won't mind us taking a look."

His gaze shoots to the doors, then back to me again. Someone like Santino Toscani, no matter what he says, isn't just going to let stacks of cash go down the toilet. He's got a plan for cleaning it and redistributing it to further expand his little empire. Of that I have no doubt. In fact, I wouldn't be surprised if Santino was the one who ratted his uncle out, but

Gilbert said the details on it were sketchy. Regardless, Santino is the one left in power while his uncle rots in jail.

Santino drops the volume of his voice. "What do you want from me? I don't know anything about the Judge's daughter. Think about it, his ruling *helped* me. You think I want Marco back here?"

"Maybe not you," Zara says. "But one of your men. Someone still loyal to your uncle. Someone who thinks a grand gesture might be a good way to show that loyalty."

Santino glares at her. "None of my men are that stupid."

"You sure about that?" I ask. "None of them have aspirations of their own?"

He grits his teeth and sits back down, fuming. "So what? You want me to do your work for you?"

"I'm surprised you're throwing up this much of a fuss," I say. "If I had a mole in my organization, I'd want him found."

Santino doesn't respond. He just drains the rest of his drink, glaring at us. I take that as a good sign.

"She was abducted on Saturday night," I say. "Find out if any of your men was unaccounted for between say ten and midnight."

"Unaccounted for?" he asks, incredulous. "I don't have their fuckin' social calendars."

"Santino," I say, my voice serious. "You can either be cooperative with us on this or not. But if you decide not to, then I wouldn't be surprised to find the District Attorney come knocking."

He shakes his head. "You people are worse than my uncle."

I regard him and pull out my business card. "I'll take that as a yes. Let me know as soon as you have some information."

"I don't work for you," Santino says, not even acknowledging the card.

I give him a terse smile, then get up. Zara follows suit. Neither one of us take our eyes off him until we've reached the door. The entire time he stares right back. He knows it's in his best interest to find out if any one of his men is still running deeds for his uncle, he just doesn't want to admit it to us. Which is fine. Personally, I don't care about the inner politics of organized crime. I do care about finding Hannah Stewart before it's too late.

Before we leave, I give him one last look. "Soon, Santino. She doesn't have a lot of time."

Chapter Fifteen

"ARE THEY STILL WATCHING?" ZARA ASKS AS WE APPROACH THE car. I don't turn around to look. I don't want them to see me if I do. But when I reach my car door and turn the handle, out of the corner of my eye I see a man standing off by the warehouse, his arms crossed.

"Yep."

Zara doesn't say anything else, just gets into the car, staring straight ahead. For someone who has never done this before, she's got one hell of a poker face. We pull out of the lot without incident, and a few moments later, are back on the road. I look over to see Zara staring out the window.

"You okay?" I ask.

She turns back to me, her face a mask. Like she doesn't have a care in the world. "Sure."

I eye her for a moment, at least as much as I'm able while still keeping my attention on the road. "Yeah?"

"I mean, sure, it was a little rough in there. But nothing we couldn't handle. It was like you said, they're just thugs looking for a fight. I don't know about you, but bullies never scared me."

"Me neither," I say. Usually, I was the one who stepped in

front of whoever was getting picked on in school. And more often than not that earned me either a bloody nose or a trip to the principal's office. It's funny, when I was interviewing for the FBI, those records actually came up. "Still, for your first time out, that was pretty impressive."

"It was like you said, I just had to keep that confidence level up." She waits a beat before speaking again. "You think Santino will actually do it? Rat out one of his own guys?"

"Hard to say. It depends on how it looks for him. If he can twist it to make it look like he's getting rid of a rat in their organization, I think he will. But if for some reason Marco does still have a lot of support, he's going to have a hard time dragging one of Marco's men out without a lot of repercussions." I turn left, heading back for the city to the office.

"Do you really think they had anything to do with it?" she asks.

"Right now we can't rule anything out. These guys are good at staking out targets, they could have been watching Hannah for days, just waiting for her to be alone."

"But signing up with the ride-share company?" Zara asks.

I have to admit, it seems far-fetched. Not like something the Toscani's would do at all. They would just drive up in a black van and grab her, not entice her to get in one of their vehicles. But until I can prove that she was picked up by a driver for *Ryde 4 Lyfe*, this is what we're stuck with. I'd hate to find out later we were wrong and missed a potential suspect just because we assumed they wouldn't be smart enough to go through a ride-share. "It's probably nothing," I say. "But at least we'll be able to tell Judge Stewart we looked into it. Given how slowly the rest of this is progressing, I'd rather be able to give him that than nothing."

"Yeah, that's a good point. Even though I feel like I'm taking my life into my hands going down there."

"You're not far off," I tell her.

"They wouldn't really try to go after us, would they?" she

asks. "I mean, how would it look if two FBI agents suddenly disappeared?"

"Guys like that aren't always the smartest of the bunch," I say. "They're the kind who act first and deal with the consequences later. Or, at least, they can be that way if you piss them off enough. And yeah, they might go down for it, but we'd still be dead."

Zara chuckles. "Maybe I should head back down to analysis after all. Leave the dirty work to the professionals."

"Nah, you've got a knack for it. Even you have to admit it."

"Does kinda get the heart pounding, doesn't it?"

"It absolutely does," I reply. Now I know without a doubt she's hooked. Because that was just how I felt the very first time I went out on a job like that. I've been chasing that high ever since.

We head back to the office to keep working on the men we pulled from Arnie's security cameras. Zara keeps running them through the recognition software, but each time it comes up empty. All it makes me think about are those photographs hidden under my backseat. All I want to do is grab them and bring them in for analysis, but I can't do it with so many people here. I know that biding my time is the best chance I have for figuring out who this woman is and how I can catch up with her.

After a solid afternoon of coming up empty, finally Zara and I decide to head back out and start fresh tomorrow. I'm about to go back in and start uploading the pictures when I remember Timber is still at daycare and I need to pick him up. I make it over there just in time to grab him before closing. Fortunately, the happy smile on his face more than makes up for the fact that I didn't get to start my analysis.

Given the hours I work, most people would probably tell me to give Timber up for adoption, that I'm not giving him the time and companionship he needs. But at the same time, I can't. He's one of the last parts of Matt still in my life. I remember when I brought him home Matt glommed on to him immediately and they were like two best friends, the only difference between them being that one of them walked on four legs. After Matt died, I would spend days in bed with Timber, both of us leaning on each other for support. They say that animals can feel when someone in the house has died, and I absolutely believe it. For weeks Timber was a different dog. But after a while he began to get used to it and used to just having me around. The bond we managed to reforge after Matt was gone is completely different than the one we had when he was still alive. We depend on each other now, even if I'm not home a lot. The daycare seems like a good option in the short term. I'm not sure what I'll do when work begins to overwhelm me like it always does.

And given that my former dog sitter is now tailing me on my cases, I'll need to figure out something new.

After we get home and Timber is fed, I change out of my work clothes into some old sweats and grab a bottle of Pinot Noir from the pantry. I don't drink a lot of wine, but when I do I have to go for something a little drier. I used to like the sweet wines, but lately my taste buds have been shifting and I can't really stand them anymore. Plus, the advantage of drinking wine over straight liquor allows me to sink into it rather than just be knocked out for the night.

I take my glass over to my couch, along with the folder of pictures Parrish provided me. Timber is already asleep on his little rug by the time I pull my feet under me and start flipping through the images again.

It's not that I'm looking for anything new; I just want to see if I can get a sense of who this woman is using just the pictures alone. Up until now I've only had my memory to rely on. But with photographic proof I can go back over the scene as I remember it, second by second. See if maybe I can't pull some kind of profile on this woman.

I close my eyes. The doors to the elevator open and she's standing in front of me. She gives me a smile. I return it and we pass each other. She's on the elevator, leaving the scene of the crime. I have yet to realize a crime has even taken place. I'm still using a cane. As I make my way down the hall, I hear the code alarm sounding. Someone is in the process of dying.

I rub my eyes and open them again, thinking back to that moment. The way that woman looked at me, it was like she knew me. Like she knew what she had done to me by taking Gerald Wright off the board. I look up to the mantle over my small fireplace. On it sits a picture of me and Matt, on our honeymoon in St. John. She had known me because she'd seen my face. She'd seen it in our place together. This same picture had adorned the mantle in that home too.

How could I not have put this together before? It's obvious she knew who I was at the hospital. So then the question becomes, was she smiling at me because she recognized me and it was involuntary, or was it because she has some kind of twisted goal, and crossing Gerald Wright off was just the latest in a long string of events designed to…what? What's the point of all this?

I grumble, getting up off the couch return to the kitchen for a refill on my wine. On the way back I don't even sit down. I just pace around the couch. Timber looks up lazily, then lays his head back down, apparently not in the mood for my bullshit. I don't blame him.

Whatever this woman did, she did it in plain sight of the nurse station. She couldn't have been in with Wright more than a few minutes. And she clearly wasn't worried about someone seeing her face, or seeing her in the hospital. Otherwise why not wait until nightfall when she could have snuck in, taken him out then and no one would have ever been the wiser?

Because she's arrogant, the voice in my head says. *She knew she'd get away with it.* Which means she's either very stupid, very lucky, or a true professional. And that scares me more than anything. If someone can walk into a hospital and kill a man without anyone realizing it, what could she do to me in my own home? *Would* she even do anything, or am I just being paranoid?

I pick up the last picture Parrish showed me, the one from the long-distance lens. It's particularly clear, enough that I can see wisps of long blonde hair framing her face. She has on dark sunglasses, but otherwise is doing nothing to hide her face, which matches what I remember. I notice she's in heels, and her coat looks particularly expensive. So she has money, or at least likes to look like she does. But as far as I can tell there isn't anything about her that particularly stands out. Other than the fact that she looks like a woman on a mission.

I set the picture back down. As best I can tell from the photo, she looks to be in her late twenties, early thirties. Fit. Walking with purpose and without fear. Stylish, yet understated. Not someone you'd immediately notice, but once you do, you'd have a hard time taking your eyes off her.

And one other thing: she's a cold-blooded killer.

"Tomorrow," I say aloud. "Tomorrow I finally find out who you are."

Chapter Sixteen

I HEAD BACK INTO THE OFFICE EARLIER THAN NORMAL, FEELING slightly guilty for spending most of my evening obsessing over this mystery woman when I should really be concentrating on Hannah. That's one of the problems with this job: you're never really off the clock. Even when you're not at the office or on-site, you're still thinking about your cases. Turning them over in your mind, looking for things you might have missed, angles you haven't considered yet. And it's not like there's a reprieve when you solve one, because there are usually a dozen more where that came from.

Matt never said anything, but I could tell sometimes that the constant grind of this job was getting to him. I'd come home talking about a case and not shut up about it until we went to bed. Then, once I was asleep I'd even dream about it.

But unfortunately that's what the job requires. You have to keep playing these things over in your mind, looking for something you might have missed. Sometimes it can make all the difference.

When I stroll into the office, my folder in hand and ready to upload into the system, I'm surprised to see Zara already there, toiling away on her computer. Despite the fact she's wearing a suit, her shoes are off and her feet are up on the chair, her knees pulled to her chest as she types. This is the exact same posture I used to find her in back in her old job and it's how I can tell she's deep into something.

"Morning!" she calls out.

I slip the folder with the pictures under a couple other folders on my desk. They'll have to wait until later. "Morning. You're here early."

"I had a thought last night, couldn't sleep."

"About the case?"

She invites me over to her desk. The rest of the room is still dark, none of the other stations are on, meaning Zara is the only one here. Part of me thinks I might be able to get away with searching the database even with her right across from me. As long as she stays engrossed in her work.

"Okay, remember how you said we needed to find Aruz's pressure point if we were going to ever get him to show us his records? I think I may have found it."

"You're kidding," I say, looking over her shoulder.

"Remember Donaldson?" she asks. "Down in Finances?"

I wrack my brain looking for the name. "I think so? He's an FA, right?"

"Yep. Originally my idea was to get him to help me look into Toscani's business, see if he could find anything strange about their operations. But that would mean getting Gilbert involved and it would be this whole thing. Then I figured why not get his help with Aruz instead?"

I check my watch. It's barely seven a.m. "Donaldson works this early?"

"He does when I call him at four a.m. and ask him to come in early."

I smile, shaking my head. "Did you pull that with every case officer you worked with?" On more than one occasion Zara would often call and get me up early in the morning to begin working on a case.

"Only the ones I really like." She winks at me. "Anyway, he just sent over a bunch of financials he got from a friend at the IRS. Look at *Ryde 4 Lyfe's* tax returns. Look at his reported *income*."

"What the hell?" I say. "There's no way he's pulling in that much money from a ride-share alone. Especially not one that's only been operating what…two years?"

"Four," she replies. "Generally companies don't even see profit until the fifth year. Even with the rise in demand, based on what we do know about his company, he's pulling in at least three times the amount he should be."

"So where's it all coming from?" I ask.

She shakes her head. "I don't know. But I do think this looks like a case for an audit. The numbers in his most recent returns don't add up."

"You think he's evading taxes?"

"Maybe. But I think it's more likely he's got an illegal operation running on the side and he's trying to report it as legitimate income."

I shake my head. Math has never been my strong suit. It's why I became a Special Agent over a Forensic Accountant. "Is it enough to make him talk?"

"Unclear. He could just deny it all. But if we can get the IRS on his ass maybe he'll start singing. No one ever wants to be audited, especially not if they're hiding something." She looks up at me with that gleam in her eye. The one that tells me she knows she's on to something.

"This is good," I say. "But I don't want to take another run at him until we're absolutely sure we can nail him. I already bungled that once."

Zara relinquishes her feet and pulls her shoes back on. "You didn't bungle it. You just underestimated how much of an ass Aruz would be about it."

"I suppose."

"Then I guess we're still back at square one," she says.

"Until we can figure out where all that money is coming from, we really don't have any leverage."

I hate to admit it, but she's right. It might be enough to scare a normal person into helping us, but not Aruz. He won't accept anything other than a court order. And I'm not sure we could get one until the IRS performed a deep dive on his financials.

"You know what? Let's pull his bank records. Personal and business. Let's see what kind of deposits he's making."

"Are you thinking there might be a pattern?"

"Either that or a paper trail that leads back to the money," I reply. My phone vibrates in my pocket. I pull it out, not recognizing the number. "Slate."

"Hello and good morning, ma'am. Is this Emily Slate I'm speaking with?"

I screw up my face. "That's what I just said. Who is this?"

"Hi Ms. Slate, I'm with Dominion Loans. I was wondering if you'd be interested in a one-time offer of a six percent on your current credit—"

I click the call off, searching through my history until I find the number and block it. "Damn telemarketers. It is seven in the freaking morning. Speaking of which I need some coffee." I can't believe they get started so early. And I hate they've gotten hold of this number. Usually I can keep them off this phone as I only give it out to potential witnesses or anyone who can help with a case.

"Which one did you get?" Zara asks.

"I don't know. Some credit check crap," I say, pouring myself a cup of coffee from the maker in our small kitchen off to the side of the bullpen. "Someone must have tossed my business card and a shark snapped it up."

Zara is giving me the strangest look. Like she wants to ask me a question but also already knows the answer. "Is that the first telemarketer call you've received on that phone?"

"Yeah, wh—" It hits me a second later. It's no coincidence

that I receive this call not long after signing up for *Ryde 4 Lyfe*. No wonder he's got so much extra income. "That little weasel! He's selling his user's data!"

Zara runs back over to her computer, performing another search. "Current market prices for bundles of warm users could net him a hefty profit."

"I bet it could," I say. "Except he clearly states in his TOS that he doesn't sell his customer's data to anyone else. I bet you anything that's a big, fat lie."

Zara and I exchange looks. *Now* we have enough to nail him.

Chapter Seventeen

"I AM SICK OF SEEING THIS PLACE," I SAY AS WE GET OUT OF the car. We're back in front of the *Ryde 4 Lyfe* "corporate offices" and my patience has already hit rock bottom. I should have learned my lesson by now, but I'm nothing if not stubborn. And I know we're never going to get a warrant for the records, which means we have to get them using any other method at our disposal. And right now, that's Aruz's own ego.

I walk up to the door and attempt to tug on the handle, but it doesn't budge. I bang my fist on the plate glass, through the bars. It's barely after nine a.m., just long enough for Aruz and his assistant to get settled. We even watched them pull into the parking lot and unlock the building. Dana arrived first, about ten minutes before Aruz, who showed up at five-till.

I look inside and see Dana staring at us, her eyes wide. She grabs the phone and begins speaking into it, no doubt warning Aruz of our presence here. "Go around back," I tell Zara. "Don't let him slip away."

She nods and jogs around the building. I've locked eyes with Dana and I point at the door, reminding her of who she's dealing with by showing her my badge. I swear, if this wasn't such a tiny operation, I would have put in a request for a tactical team to join me. I'd have no qualms about breaking this man's door down, even though I know he'd raise hell twice over.

The longer I wait, the more frayed my nerves become. Dana is just sitting there, a terrified look on her face as she watches me. Aruz has obviously ordered her not to open the door for me. I just hope Zara made it around the back in time to nab him in case he decided to be stupid enough to run.

"May I help you, young lady?"

I turn, fury on my face to see a man in a brown tweed suit approach me. He's got white hair and a white mustache along with a jovial look on his face. As soon as I see him, all I can think of is Colonel Sanders.

"Sir, this is official FBI business, I need to ask you to keep your distance," I say, showing him my badge.

"My, that's shiny," he says with something of a southern accent. I can't tell if this guy is playacting or if Mr. Sanders here is the real deal. "You look a hair too young to be in the FBI, if you don't mind me sayin'."

"I do," I reply. "Now step back." Aruz's refusal to open his door is officially moving him into the obstruction category, which means I'm completely within the bounds of the law to break it down if I have to. I'd rather not, but given the circumstances, and the fact Hannah has been missing for three full days now, I'm out of patience.

I unholster my weapon.

"Ma'am, I wouldn't do that if I were you," the Colonel says.

"Sir, I said for you to stay back," I reply. I do not have time for this.

"You don't seem to understand. I'm Mr. Aruz's lawyer. He's advised me that the FBI has been harassing him. And given you're about to blow his door off its hinges, I'm inclined to agree."

I glare at the man a moment before holstering my weapon again.

He smiles. "Cornelius Cox the Third," he says, holding out one of his hands. "But you can call me Cornelius. Ever'-body else does. My offices are right down thataway." He points in the direction he came from, about four stalls down.

"Mr. Cox," I say, neglecting to take his hand. "Your client is willfully obstructing a kidnapping case in which the victim may have been picked up by one of his drivers. Now I have tried to be reasonable. But the fact of the matter is I am out of time and have given Mr. Aruz all the leeway I can afford. I need you to order your client to open this door so that we may begin looking at his files."

Cox smiles, though it's a difficult one. "I'm afraid that won't be possible m'dear. I've been instructed that all commu-nication meant for Mr. Aruz to come through me first and I can act as somethin' of a...buffer in this little matter. And I have to advise my client not to speak to you at this time. Unless you're willin' to charge him o'course."

I nod a couple of times, working my jaw. "Okay. Fine. Then I'm here to charge him. Open up."

Cox lets out a guffaw. "Young lady, you do know how the justice system works don't you? You can't just charge someone without evidence!"

"Call me young lady one more time and you're gonna find that mustache in the gutter," I growl. "I have all the evidence I need that shows Aruz is guilty of defrauding his customers, as well as illegally reporting his income. Something the IRS will be *very* interested in, don't you think?"

The man across from me clears his throat. "Perhaps we should go in, after all." He motions to Dana who comes running up and unlocks the door. I let Cox in first as I call Zara.

"Anything?" I ask.

"Nothing back here. He's staying put."

"Come back around. There's been a development." I hang up and put my phone away as I enter *Ryde 4 Lyfe* for the third time in two days. As soon as I'm in Aruz appears from around the open doorway in the back.

"What are you doing? What the hell did I hire you for?" He yells at Cox before turning on Dana. "And you, why did you let her in here again?" He gives neither of them a chance to answer before addressing me. "I'm not talking to you. Get out of here, I've already made myself clear."

I wait, it seems I have some patience reserves deep within after all. Zara appears at the door and follows us in.

"Cox! Are you just going to let them come in here? What kind of lawyer are you?"

"Mr. Aruz," Cox says, clearly uncomfortable. "These la— Agents are here to arrest you."

Aruz backs up, shaking his head. "On fake charges. Yeah, they already tried that once before."

I glare at him. "Robert Aruz," I say. "I'm placing you under arrest for fraud and tax evasion. As well as obstruction in the investigation of a crime."

He's still shaking his head, though I can see a glimmer of panic in his eyes. "No, what is this? Cox, stop them. They have no right."

"I can't tell the FBI how to do their jobs, Mr. Aruz," Cox says. I'm not sure if Cox knows exactly what he signed up for when he agreed to be Aruz's attorney, but I get the sense that he's beginning to regret it. He probably thought Aruz was just another young tech startup entrepreneur, unaware that he'd have to defend him against charges like this.

Cox turns to me anyway. "Agent, may I ask what evidence you have to support these charges?"

"For one thing, his balance sheets don't line up," I say. "Not with someone running a business like this."

"And he's selling his customer's data, despite the promises made in his terms of service," Zara adds.

"That's…you can't do anything. It's a fine or something. You can't arrest me for that." Cox tries to shush him, but Aruz pays the older man no attention.

"Then you admit it," I say, stepping closer to him. He takes a similar step back. "We've already flagged your financials for the IRS. And what we're seeing in your bank accounts doesn't match up with your reported income."

He keeps shaking his head, glancing behind him. "I've done nothing wrong here."

I pull out a zip tie from my jacket pocket. "We'll see about that. Federal tax evasion comes with serious time, Mr. Aruz. And just think, we wouldn't have found any of this had you just allowed us access to your records." I shake my head. "I guess it's a good thing you're as stubborn as you are. At least, it's good for us, not for you."

"Wait, no, you can't do this," he says as I close in on him. He's jumpy enough that I think he might try to run or fight me. Neither of which would be smart.

"Don't move, Mr. Aruz." I motion for Zara to walk around me to get behind him. I see a flash in his eyes and I'm sure he's about to bolt, but either he takes too long to make the decision, or he relents, as Zara is able to block off his other exit. I reach him and pull his hands behind his back, zipping them together.

"Cox! Can't you do anything?"

"Sorry, son," he says. "Gotta let the process work itself out. Just don't say anythin' until after they process you, hear? We'll get this worked out once the paperwork goes through."

"Okay, look, how about this?" Aruz says, panic rising in his voice. "I'll let you go through all the records you want. Okay? Just the driver ones. You can have the whole list. It's all right there, in my station." He nods toward the back.

"You don't seem to understand," I say, taking more pleasure in this than I should. "We're already going to look at the records. Now that you're in custody, you don't have any more hands to play."

"No, no," he says, some of that confidence returning. "Everything is encrypted. You'll need my personal login to access it."

I turn to Zara, motioning for her to get started. "We'll see about that."

"Give me a few minutes," she says, then disappears behind the back wall. I escort Aruz over to one of the few empty seats in the room and sit him down.

"She'll never get in," he says. "I use fractal encryption. Which means that unless she's a mind reader, she won't be able to keep up with the changing login algorithm."

I narrow my eyes, trying not to show any trepidation on my face. Zara is good—really good. But there's something I don't like about his attitude. Something that tells me he might not be bluffing about this.

I leave Aruz while Cox comes over to confer with him. Instead, I walk over to Dana's desk where she's returned, somewhat shell-shocked by the morning's events. "Does this mean I'm out of a job?" she asks.

"I don't know. Doesn't your company have a board of directors, or at least someone who can take over in the event of an emergency?"

She shakes her head. "Rob is big on automation. Most everything runs by itself with little need for support. I'm the only customer support representative the company has."

"Then he's done you a disservice," I say, drumming my fingers on her desk, waiting for Zara. I realize we've probably just made Dana's life more difficult, but that can't be helped. Aruz more or less just admitted to fraud. Which means we don't have a choice but to take him in now.

Growing impatient, I head back to find Zara sitting at Aruz's desk, surrounded by screens. It's cooler back here, industrial fans running to keep all the computer equipment from overheating. I feel like I've stepped into the matrix with the number of servers he has stacked on top of one another. "Anything?"

She glances back up at me. "It's not looking good. He wasn't kidding about this rotating algorithm. I think once I get into the system I shouldn't have any problems navigating it. But getting past this...whatever it is...is something I haven't run into before."

I grit my teeth. My hope had been that even if Aruz hadn't cooperated we'd be able to gain access to his systems anyway. I return to the main office.

"Can't get in, huh?" Aruz asks, a smile on his face. Cox tries to whisper in his ear, but it's lost to him.

"Give us access to the system," I say.

He stands. "Take these restraints off. And I want all charges dropped."

I laugh. "No chance. I don't think you understand just how much trouble you're in."

He shrugs. "Then I guess you don't get access."

I twist my face, doing my best not to walk over there and smack that little smile off his face. "Mr. Cox. Will you please tell your client what he can get for obstruction?"

He holds both his hands up. "I'm not here to do your job, Agent."

"Fine," I say. "Right now you're looking at five years max. I add an obstruction charge to that, and it could be twenty."

Aruz looks grief-stricken for half a second before his original swagger returns. He glances at Cox who nods. Aruz just shakes his head. "It'll never stick. This is all just a charade."

That's it. I've had it with his games. I get right in Aruz's face. "You think so? You so sure about that? Because right now I've got a missing woman. The daughter of a federal judge in fact. Young. Pretty. And what happens when the national media finds out that you, Mr. Aruz, you personally were responsible for keeping us from finding what we need to save her? How do you think that will look? Even if you don't get convicted, the court of public opinion will slaughter you. You will never be able to run another company in this country again."

His mask falters.

"Why put up such a fight now? You've already lost."

"Because of you and your kind," he spits. "So called officers of justice, when all you do is use the system to unfairly punish those who don't look like you."

I'm taken aback, though I shouldn't be surprised. It's true that some officers distort the law based on their own biases, but I've always worked hard to make sure I'm not one of them. "We're not all the same, Mr. Aruz. I'm not here because of the color of your skin, or your heritage. I'm here because you have committed a crime and the law demands you pay for that crime." I look him in the eyes. "But you're also in the unique position of being able to help someone else. Someone who can't help themselves right now. And I can tell you if you're cooperative, that will go a long way to favorability in your case."

Aruz looks back at Cox again and the older man scans my face, then nods. He knows I'm telling the truth. My only concern at the moment is Hannah.

"Fine," Aruz says, the fight going out of him. "You win."

Chapter Eighteen

ARUZ SITS AT HIS DESK, HIS HANDS NO LONGER BOUND BY THE zip ties, while Zara and I watch over his shoulder. Cox and Dana stand off to the side, neither of them saying anything. I have to admit this is not how I saw this encounter going. I was originally just going to use the information about Aruz's taxes to strongarm him into giving us access, but now it seems I have no choice but to actually charge him. The funny thing is if he hadn't been so defensive from the start, we might not have even found out about all his additional income.

Aruz's fingers fly over his keyboard as he logs into one system after another. They're a complete blur to me. "When did you start selling your user's data?" I ask.

He shrugs as he finishes the login. "I didn't have a choice. We were growing too quickly, and I needed an influx of cash. The bank wouldn't lend me any more, so I had to resort to other methods."

"Despite the fact your terms of service state the opposite," I say.

"It was never designed to be permanent. Just until the company was growing at a sustainable rate. Then I was going to shut it off again."

I hold up my phone. "I got a telemarketer call the morning after using your service for the first time."

He shrugs again, unconcerned. "What can I say?"

"Is that where all the extra income was coming from?" I ask. He nods. "I was hoping to keep it from the IRS so I wouldn't have to pay the taxes. They are killer on small businesses like mine. If I could, I would have moved to the Caribbean now, run it from there."

"Ah, the American dream," Zara says. "Shovel your money into tax havens and live by the beach."

Aruz rolls his eyes. "The system is up. Who are you looking for?"

"A customer named Hannah Stewart," I say. Half a second later her information pops up on one of Aruz's screens. It shows the date she registered with the company, how many rides she's taken, how often she takes them, the average length of the ride, the average tip she provides along with dozens of other statistics.

"Now, see if she scheduled a ride on Saturday evening," I say. "Around eleven p.m." I can already feel my heart beating in my chest. It honestly feels like we've run a marathon to get to this point, but I can almost feel Hannah is within our grasp.

"Nothing," Aruz says.

My heart drops into my stomach. "What?"

"She scheduled a ride at eight p.m., which dropped her off at 425 Arlington. That was her last scheduled ride in the system." He turns to me with a smug look on his face. "It's like I told you from the beginning, if there had been an error in the system, I would have seen it. And you still didn't believe me."

I shake my head; that can't be possible. We've eliminated every other avenue. I look at Zara who seems just as shocked as I am. "What are we missing here?" I ask.

She grabs Aruz's chair, rolling him out of the way as she

stares at the data. She backs up into the raw files, going through the lines of his proprietary system, one by one.

"What are you looking for?" Aruz asks. "There's nothing there. When will you ever stop harassing me?" He turns to Cox for support. "Is there anything we can do about this?"

"Agents," Cox says. "I'll have to ask you to—"

I spin on him. "Don't start. Not after the fight he put up. We're perfectly within the scope of our investigation to keep looking. You want to dispute it, bring it up in court."

He gives me a smile like he knows we're screwed, and he's going to try to use it to get his client a lighter sentence. It's as if I can see the whole thing falling apart in front of my face. All this work to get into these records, and she didn't take the ride that night? Then who could have picked her up? We cleared all the taxi services. All the private companies. The big ride-shares, all of whom were completely transparent with us. This was the only option remaining.

And yet she's not here.

I can feel this case slipping through my fingers by the second. I was so sure we were close. How could I have gotten this so wrong? Have I been spending too much time obsessing over finding the woman that killed my husband and not putting all my heart into this case? I'll have to update Janice on our progress when we leave here. And she's not going to be happy.

"Hey, Em," Zara says. "There's something strange in these records."

I look over her shoulder, but I can't make heads nor tails out of what I'm seeing. It all looks like gibberish to me. "What do you mean?"

"It looks like someone has been in here, messing with the code."

For a brief moment I consider what this means before turning on Aruz. "You. You erased her records."

He gives me a nervous chuckle. "What? I didn't even know

her name until two minutes ago. How could I erase the records?"

"Because you're in on it," I say. "You collaborated with the driver. Hell, you might even be the driver for all I know. And you deleted the transaction because you didn't want anyone finding out what you've done. You certainly had plenty of time."

"That's ridiculous!" he yells. "I worked for years on this system! You think I'd be so careless to go in there and screw it up? My algorithm is a masterpiece. I'm certainly not about to potentially corrupt it by trying to erase data. The entire unit depends on reliable information."

"Well, someone has been in here mucking around," Zara says. "I can see the artifacts from where they cleared out certain lines of code without properly reclosing the loops. It looks like a quick job. And look, there's one that points to the timestamp when Hannah was picked up."

"Let me see that," Aruz says, standing from his chair. I hold up a hand to keep him in place. "I just want to see if she's right."

I reluctantly withdraw my hand. Aruz squeezes in beside Zara, scanning the data. "This is impossible," he says as she points out the artifacts. I still can't see what she's talking about. I guess that's only something a data analyst would know to look for.

Aruz takes over the station from her and begins working on the system again. "What are you doing?" I ask.

"Trying to see where they came in. This system should be nearly impenetrable. I don't write bad code." He works for a few minutes. "Looks like you're right. Whoever did this, they were in a hurry. They left a trail half a mile wide."

"Do you know who could have done it?" I ask. "Who else has access to the raw code?"

He shakes his head. "No one. It would take a particularly skilled individual to do this, but it all leads back to the driver portal. I'd say whoever broke into the system, managed to brute force their way through there."

"Brute force?" I ask.

Zara turns to me. "Someone with a lot of computing power can momentarily overwhelm security systems if they know what they're doing and have enough computations per second to beat out a given system. We do that sometimes to terrorist organizations."

I look around the room at all the servers. "So someone would have to have more computing power than this to do it?"

"A lot more," Aruz says, still working. "Whoever they were, they didn't leave a trace of their identity. Sloppy enough to leave a trail, but smart enough to make sure the footprint wasn't identifiable."

"The driver portal, you said?" I ask, thinking. "The only reason I can think of for a driver to break in would be to erase a travel record, wouldn't you say?"

He turns slowly in his seat. "That makes sense."

"Then one of your drivers did pick up Hannah," Zara says.

"They're not *my* drivers," Aruz says. "They're independent contractors. And like I told you, we perform extensive background checks. I can't be held responsible for the actions of one rogue person."

"We'll see about that," I say. "I want a full list of all your drivers that were registered on the app last Saturday night."

"Em," Zara says. "Anyone smart enough to clear the record probably erased their entire employment contract with Ryde 4 Lyfe. Unless they were extremely stupid, they're not going to be in there."

"Right." She's correct, of course. I just wasn't thinking clearly. I have no doubt our kidnapper isn't stupid enough to leave their name in the system. I pull Aruz back away from the desk. He seems engrossed in trying to patch this hole that's been left in the system that his business is built on. "What about backups? Do you have any backups that wouldn't have been part of this system? Records this person wouldn't have been able to access?"

He huffs. "I want all of this to go into the official record," he says. "I feel like I'm being more than generous with my time and my expertise here."

I lean down so I'm in his face. "You act like all of this is a big inconvenience to you. Well trust me, you're going to have plenty of time to be inconvenienced when you're being held in a federal prison."

"Now, now, Agent Slate," Cox says. "I don't think we need to be throwin' threats around. Robert here would be more than happy to answer your question." He gives Aruz a pointed look, causing the man to grimace.

"We back the system up every month. Last one was seventeen days ago. I keep all the backup files stored offsite and off the mainframe in the event we have a catastrophic problem. That way the backup can be uploaded manually and reset the entire system."

"And these backups will have employee records?" I ask.

"Contractor records, yes," he replies.

"But how is that any better?" Zara asks. "It's still thousands of people to dig through. How do we know which one is the one who picked up Hannah?"

"Because," I say. "We'll compare the records today with the records seventeen days ago. Whoever isn't there now is our culprit."

"And if he didn't register until sixteen days ago?" she asks.

"Let's hope that isn't the case."

Chapter Nineteen

ZARA AND I ARE STANDING OUTSIDE A SMALL, RANCH-STYLE house in college park, just outside of the University of Maryland. The home, despite its small size, probably would go for a cool half a million even in its current state, which isn't good. But that just speaks to the insane home prices in this part of the state.

It's all brick with green shutters and a storm door with the letter "M" carved in wrought iron on the front door. It looks to me like the house was built in the fifties or sixties and hasn't seen much of an update since then.

"You think he was telling the truth?" Zara asks.

"I don't know," I reply. "He's been pretty combative this entire time." I glance over at her. "Did you see how red his face got when you started poking around in his system?"

"Part of me just wanted to do it to mess with him," she replies.

I chuckle. "Is it bad I really enjoyed arresting him?"

"For as much of a pain in our asses as he's been? Not at all," she replies.

After Aruz had helped Zara download a list of all their drivers, active and otherwise, we waited on the support unit to come pick up Aruz. We would have taken him in ourselves, but given the time-sensitive nature of this case, Janice was able to pull some strings for us. Still, since we arrested him without a warrant, he'll have to appear before a Magistrate Judge to determine culpability.

But honestly, I don't even care what happens to Aruz. Not until Hannah is back home, safe. Before they carted him away, he informed us all his backups are kept offsite at a second location. When he said that I hadn't expected the second location to be an unassuming single-family home ten miles away.

"Let's go see if we can add perjury to his list of charges," I joke, walking up the broken concrete walk leading to the front door from the small mailbox. If I had to guess, I would say this house belonged to a little old lady, given its condition. Though the plants out front need some care. It looks like they haven't been pruned in a while.

I knock on the door and step back, looking for any security measures and finding none. No video camera, no signs in the yard informing would-be thieves this house is protected by so-and-so. To house such secure data, Aruz sure isn't trying to protect it.

"Are we sure we have the right address?" I ask Zara. She only shrugs.

A few moments later the front door opens to reveal a young woman who can't be more than twenty-one. Her hair is a bright purple and she's wearing fishnets under torn black jeans, combat boots and a leather jacket, along with a large number of bracelets and even a choker.

"Yeah?" she asks.

I hold out my badge. "Agents Slate and Foley with the FBI. Are you Julie?"

"Jules," she says. "What do you want?" She doesn't seem perturbed in the slightest two FBI agents are on her porch. Either she puts on a good show or she really doesn't care.

"You work for Robert Aruz? With Ryde 4 Lyfe?"

She scans the street beyond us. "Yeah. So?"

"He's been arrested," I tell her. "On Fraud and tax evasion charges."

She crosses her arms. "Good for him. What's that have to do with me?"

"He told us you're in charge of all of Ryde 4 Lyfe's backups. That you keep them here?"

"That's classified."

I exchange a look with Zara. "Classified by who? Aruz was the one who told us."

"Mr. Aruz told me no one was to gain access. That's the last I heard."

I arch an eyebrow. "Yeah? You look pretty young to be a homeowner in a neighborhood like this."

"It was my grandma's house. She passed away six months ago. Left it to me."

"You a Terp?" I ask.

She shrugs.

"What's your major? Computer science?"

"And psychology," she replies.

"I like your hair," Zara tells her. "Mine used to be blue but I had to change it. Benefits of the job."

Jules softens a little. "Thanks," she says.

"Listen. We're just trying to get a copy of the driver records from the last backup. It would really help us out if you could let us access the system."

She nods to me. "You guys don't look old enough to be in the FBI."

"My specialty used to be infiltrating gangs," I say. "They never suspect the girl that looks like a teenager."

"Yeah?" she asks, opening up a little more. "Ever have any big busts?"

"Yep. Took down a huge human trafficking ring here in D.C. just a few months ago," I tell her. "Saved at least forty kids."

"No shit," she replies, a smile forming on her lips. "And you arrested my boss?"

"He was defrauding your customers. Selling their private data without their knowledge," Zara says.

"Man, I knew it," she replies. "Dickhead. Yeah, c'mon in." She unlocks the metal storm door and opens it for us. The first thing that hits me as soon as we're inside is the smell of pot. The front room, which would normally be a living room, is littered with beer cans, bottles, and there's a ping-pong table set up in the center.

Jules leads us through the house, which is in a similar state, until we reach the back bedrooms.

"You must be pretty popular," I say. "Since you have your own house close to campus."

"Most people suck," Jules replies. "I don't have massive ragers here if that's what you're thinking." She pulls out a set of keys that are attached to her belt and it's then I notice four bolts on one of the doors. She uses each of the keys in turn until the door finally opens to reveal what used to be the primary bedroom but has now been converted into a server storage room.

It's almost as many processing units as what Aruz had back at his office, except most of them are off. A few are running though, each with their own cooling units.

"Why would Aruz put all his stuff in here?" I ask, looking at the windows which are covered with blackout curtains. "This seems like a high-risk area. What if someone breaks in?"

"First, most of these things weigh fifty pounds or more," Jules says. "And second, Aruz is a cheap bastard. He pays me to store them here rather than paying the costs of a storage unit."

There's a terminal that looks like Aruz's unit back at his office. I motion for Zara to get to work. Thankfully this time she has all Aruz's information in order to log in. "Give me a few minutes," she says. "I'll need to find the most recent backup and locate the driver records."

I nod, noting how cool it is in here, just like back in the office. "So what's the future look like for you?" I ask Jules, looking around at all the servers. "Plan to keep working for Ryde?"

She shakes her head. "Nah. This is just temporary. I'll probably do coding work for startups that don't have enough money to pay me what I'm worth."

I nod, wishing I had a better understanding of stuff like this. But that's why I've got Zara.

"So what are you guys working on?" Jules asks.

"We're not really at liberty to talk about it," I say.

"But it has something to do with one of the drivers for the company? What'd they do? Kill someone?"

"Not exactly," I say.

Jules looks away and pretends to play with the keyring on her belt. "So, like if someone wanted to get info on what kind of jobs the FBI has, where would you say they should go?"

I sneak a glance at Zara. This is an unexpected development. "You thinking about applying to the Bureau?" I ask.

She shrugs. "Just curious what's available."

"A couple of different things," I tell her. "Zara and I are Special Agents, which are like the enforcement side. But there's other positions too, surveillance, linguistics, intelligence analysts. All kinds of stuff."

"Who are the people who, you know, track down the serial killers? Figure out what they're thinking and stuff?"

I guess I shouldn't be surprised she's asking me about this. It's probably the side of the Bureau that's glamorized the most on TV and in the movies. "I guess that would be us. But we really don't deal with serial killers that often."

"A-*hem*," Zara says.

"Wait, have you ever chased one before?" Jules asks, her interest clear now. "Did you catch him?"

"She did," Zara says. "Right before he was about to murder his own *children*."

"*Sick*," Jules says, but her eyes are wide with interest. "Any job openings for that?"

I glare at Zara. She's gonna get it for that one. "He was just a one-off," I say. "We run across them sometimes, but it's rare. Honestly, you're more likely to be arresting people like your boss than bloodthirsty serial killers."

"Still," Jules says. "I think I'd like to be the person who figures out what they're thinking. You know, before they know they're thinking it themselves? What's that called?"

"A profiler," I reply.

"Yeah. That'd be a cool job. I could handle that."

"I think I have it," Zara says. "I'm uploading the original file from Aruz and cross-referencing."

In my heart of hearts I know this is a long shot. But given the nature of this case, we don't have much else to go on. If it turns out one of Ryde's drivers really *didn't* pick Hannah up, I'll be at a loss. But given what we've managed to eliminate so far, I can't see how we could be wrong. I still don't have a lot of faith that one of Toscani's men was responsible, but I can't afford to leave any avenue unexplored.

Zara stares at the screen a little longer, then gives me the kind of look that means I'm not going to like what she has to say. "You're kidding me. Nothing?" I ask.

"Oh no, there's something. But the problem is it isn't just one name. It's three."

"Ugh," I drop my head. Of course. It couldn't have been simple. "Get a copy and let's head back to the office and get started. Combined with those two you found at the bar; we're going to be pulling a long night."

Zara gets up and we excuse ourselves from Jules's room. We're just about to the front door when she stops us. "Hey."

"Right, sorry," I say. "Thank you for your cooperation. It was a big help."

"You don't seem too happy about it," she says.

"It's just…time is of the essence in this case. We don't know how long we have."

Jules nods. "Is it worth it? The job?"

I don't think I would ever actively encourage someone to get into this line of work if they weren't suited for it. Or if they didn't have a unique skill that set them apart. It can be a brutal, unforgiving job. And more often than not, we see the worst humanity has to offer. But at the end of the day, I feel like we're providing a valuable public service. One which protects the public trust and ensures the safety of our country. As often as we get it wrong, we get a lot right too.

"Absolutely," I say, giving her a wink.

Chapter Twenty

THIS IS ALREADY PROVING TO BE A LONG DAY. AND IT LOOKS like we're going to be working well into the evening. Which means if I hope to use the system to search for my mystery woman, I'm going to have to stay at work even later. But that's going to require a solution for Timber.

"Dammit," I say, pulling out my phone as we make our way back to the Bureau.

"Hey," Zara says. "At least we got some names. That's good news, right?"

She thinks I'm upset about the names, which I am. But I have a more immediate problem that I don't want to face. Though, at this point, I don't see I have a choice.

"I was just really hoping there would only be one. It would have made this a lot easier," I say, dialing the number I really don't want to dial. Maybe he'll be more amenable now that it's been a few months.

I put the phone to my ear as it rings, my hand trembling ever so slightly.

"Hello?" his gruff voice says.

"Chris?"

"Emily." His voice is cold, just like I suspected. There's a good reason I haven't talked to him since the funeral.

"I need your help."

"Sorry," he says. "Can't do it."

"It's not for me. It's for Timber," I say quickly, before he can hang up.

"What?"

"Would you pick him up from daycare? Until I get off work?"

I can hear him sigh on the other end of the line. "How late?"

"I don't know. This is a complicated case. I can swing by later tonight though."

"Are they going to let me pick him up?"

"I'll call and make sure they have you listed as authorized," I tell him. "I wouldn't ask if it wasn't an emergency."

"Fine," he says. "What time do they close?"

"Six-thirty I think. It's the one off of Williams."

"Text me when you're on the way," he says then hangs up.

I sigh, replacing my phone in my jacket.

"How's *that* going?" Zara asks.

"It's not. You heard. He barely wants anything to do with me. Not that I can really blame him." Chris and I used to get along really well, until…well, until everything fell apart.

"You said he and Matt were close."

"As close as brothers could be. But after Matt died, it was like someone flipped a switch in him. I feel bad for him, for Dani, for everyone involved. You can probably guess I'm not someone they want around."

Zara shakes her head. "See, I just don't get that. They used to be your family. And they know you don't have any siblings or anything, so why are they ostracizing you? It's not like it was your fault what happened."

"I think…" I'm really not sure what to think about my brother-in-law and his wife. The four of us used to get along famously. "I think when he died like he did, they wanted someone to blame. Maybe out of pure grief, I'm not sure. I can see where they're coming from though, I should have been there with him when it happened. I'm sure they think if I had been I would have been able to save his life."

"Don't you do that to yourself again, not after everything we've been through," Zara says, her voice stern. She's usually pretty light-hearted, but right now she's not messing around. "It was not your fault. You need to remember that."

A few weeks ago I might have agreed with her. I'd gone through all the guilt, of course, but slowly I'd begun to accept that there was nothing I could have done to save him. But now that I know this woman was involved, that she did to him what she did to Gerald Wright, I can't help but feel a new pang of guilt coursing through my system. It's all I can do not to burst out and tell Zara what I've discovered. But I have to protect her. I can't let her get caught up in all of this again.

Still, I know if I'd been there, Matt would still be alive today. I could have stopped her. Which is why I don't blame Chris for hating me, even though he doesn't know all the details. I'd hate me too if I were him.

"You're still doing it, I can see it in your eyes," Zara says.

I shake my head. "No, just…thinking about the case."

"God, you are a bad liar," she replies. "Good thing you don't play poker for a living."

I push all the feelings away. I need to keep my focus on Hannah. We're actually making some progress; I can't forget that. "When you were in Aruz's system, how secure did it look to you?"

She gestures uncertainly. "To random attacks, it's fool-proof. Even I couldn't get in without some kind of key. But once you have access…it's like he built thirty foot walls with barbed wire and guard towers, but as long as you speak the right password, you can get in. The internal security is a mess. There aren't enough separations between all the inner work-

ings of his programs. I assume that's why this driver was able
to get in and modify the system."

"But not anyone could do it, right?" I ask. "They'd need a
certain level of skill."

"Definitely. Whoever was able to alter his records, they
have experience, and a lot of it. In fact, they were so confident
in their abilities, they didn't even cover up the fact they'd been
in there. Which tells you something about them."

"Classic case of over-confidence. The driver probably
thinks that because they cleared out their records, we'll never
be able to find them," I say, pondering. "In fact, I'm betting
the driver never expected us to get this far with as many
precautions that they took picking her up."

Zara looks away for a moment as I pull up to a stoplight.
"There's something we haven't discussed yet," she says. "We
still don't have definitive proof it was one of Ryde's drivers
that took her."

"That's true," I say, thinking back to the Toscani organization. "We can't afford to get complacent now that we've made
some progress." I just hope my instincts about this one aren't
wrong. There's no telling how much time Hannah has left.

Twenty minutes later we're back in the office. Zara is running
the names down while I fill in Janice on our progress. Part of
me was afraid she might tell us to quit pursuing this ride-share
angle, but thankfully she's always given the agents working
under her a lot of autonomy. After I finish my brief report I
head back to my desk, passing Nick on the way.

"Found your abductor yet?" he asks.

"No," I reply, not pausing to talk. "But we're making
progress." He lifts his mug to me in a half-salute. I don't know
why he's being so cordial lately, usually we're at each other's
throats. Maybe it has something to do with me going on leave

and coming back and then all that business in Stillwater. He might have finally buried the hatchet.

"Okay," I say, pulling my chair up to Zara's desk. "What do we have?"

"I'm running them through the system now," she says. "Daryl Thorpe, Nasir Galvan, and Douglas Krauss. All three men aged thirty to forty-five, and all three locals."

"We need to do full workups on all of them, see if we can establish alibi's, look for anything that might indicate behavior like this in the past."

"I can already tell you none of them have a prior record," Zara says. "Otherwise, it would have flagged them when they applied to Ryde 4 Lyfe."

"Do any of them have backgrounds in computer science?" I ask.

She shrugs. "Here, take Galvan. I'll start with Thorpe. Then we can move on to Krauss."

I take the name and what little data was in the ride-share back to my station. I've got a birthdate on Galvan, along with a current address. But most of the rest of the data on him is related to his time at Ryde. Number of trips per day, average amount earned, that sort of thing. But given he's on this list means at some point in the past three weeks he's quit driving for Ryde. Whether that was because his entire plan was to abduct Hannah or for some other reason I don't know.

I flip through the records one more time. "Hey, Z? When did Thorpe and Krauss start driving for the company?"

Zara goes through the records she has. "Thorpe was eight months ago. Krauss was six."

As I'm looking at Galvan's file, I'm already pretty sure this isn't the guy. He doesn't fit the profile I have in my head. "Galvan has been with them from the beginning. Two years. There is no way he's had this plan in motion for that long."

"Unless it really was a crime of opportunity," she says.

I shake my head. "It's too clean. Whoever picked her up

planned this. Down to marking where all the traffic cameras were so they wouldn't get spotted."

I plop down at my desk and run his name and DOB through the NGI. Within seconds I have his entire history from where he's employed to what kind of car he drives. "Well, mine's definitely a bust."

"Why do you say that?"

"Because he's dead," I reply. Along with everything else came Galvan's obituary. "He died two weeks ago. Cancer." I toss the file in the trash.

"Damn." Zara holds out the third file. "Guess you get Krauss then."

"Let's just hope they're not all dead," I reply, taking the file from her. "Because then we're really screwed."

"Mine's definitely not. And he graduated from Stanford with a degree in Computer Science." I perk up. "What kind of car does he drive?"

She scans her screen. "Looks like a Subaru Legacy." I exchange glances with her. "You wanna go talk to him?"

I shake my head. "No way. If it is him, two agents showing up on his doorstep will spook him. He might do something to Hannah. We'll need to tail him first, keep him under surveillance. Whoever took Hannah is smart; we won't get a second chance at him." I turn back to my file. "Let's see if I can eliminate Krauss and then we'll focus in on Thorpe."

It takes me a few minutes to run Krauss's name through our software. But the more I find, the tighter my stomach gets.

Finally, Zara stops what she's doing and comes over, I'm sure because she's concerned about the looks she's seeing on my face. But when her eyes land on my monitor she curses and stomps back to her desk.

This just got a lot more complicated.

Chapter Twenty-One

IT FEELS LIKE SHE'S BEEN IN HERE FOR A WEEK. OR MAYBE longer. Without any natural daylight coming through and no clocks, Hannah has no idea how much time has passed. But she's ready to do anything to get out of this box. Despite all the "window dressing", it's nothing more than a gilded cage.

She's been trying to keep track of her meals, but they seem to come at different times of the day. So far she's received seven? Eight maybe? But sometimes they are breakfast foods and sometimes they're not. Her entire body clock is off and she's not sure if she's staying up half the night or sleeping the afternoon away.

All she knows is she's scared, and she wants out of here. But it doesn't look like that's going to happen, not any time soon.

What's even worse is whoever this person who took her is, they don't seem to have anything to do with Alonzo. Which doesn't even make sense! She was sure this was some kind of retaliation of his for not doing as she promised. She can't help but feel a small sense of relief at the possibility, though. The only upside of this situation is she's safe from him in here. But being safe from Alonzo doesn't mean she isn't in trouble.

Given the choice, she'd rather take her chances out there with him.

There's a small click and Hannah looks up. A portal opens along the floor of the locked door, revealing a tray full of warm food. Whoever is keeping her here, they make a good cook. The first few meals she refused to eat, until the sensation of overwhelming hunger became too much and the smells wafting off the dishes was too much to bear.

This is...meal nine, Hannah thinks. Today it's a chopped salad with shredded chicken and apple slices, along with a bowl of tomato soup and some focaccia bread for dipping. She's also been provided a plastic cup full of iced tea.

Once the portal closes, Hannah walks over to the tray and picks it up, taking it to the small table along the blank wall. The funny thing about this place is how much trouble someone is going to in order to keep her comfortable. She's provided fresh clothing every day, warm food, and can take hot showers whenever she wishes. There are even books in the nightstand beside the bed, though she hasn't brought herself to touch them yet, other than to flip through them to make sure there was nothing she could use that might help her escape.

Someone is expending a lot of time and energy on her, and she can't figure out why. Especially since the only contact she's had with her kidnapper has been through a voice-modulated speaker embedded somewhere in the wall and the small cameras that sit in the corners of the room, always watching her.

Hannah sets her tray down on the table and prepares to eat. It smells better than it has any right to and a small amount of steam wafts off the soup.

"I thought we'd try something different today," the voice says suddenly, startling her. She puts her spoon down, looking up to the camera.

"What do you mean?"

"You seem to have settled into your new surroundings nicely. I think it's time we took things to the next level."

The words send a shiver down her spine. Whatever they're talking about, she doesn't like it.

"Until now, the line of visual communication has been one-way," the voice adds. "I believe it's time to change that."

Hannah is still trying to figure out what they're talking about when the wall beside her seems to shimmer as if it is water. A moment later, she's looking through transparent glass into an open space which seems made of mostly concrete. Three steps down from her level lead into a sunken area, which appears to be accessed from a door on the far left side. She can't see much beyond the edges of what used to be her wall, other than to see that this outer chamber seems to extend beyond the walls of her own.

In the middle of the sunken room stands a man, his hands in his jean pockets, staring at her. He's trim, with orange-reddish hair and a very light beard. He wears a well-fitted plaid shirt, and his skin is pale, like it's been a while since he's been out in the sun. But she can also see he's covered in freckles. It's the same man who picked her up in the car; she recalls his picture from the ride-share app. But beyond that, there's something familiar about the man, she just can't put her finger on it.

"Who are you?" she asks.

He smiles. "I know it's been a while," he replies, his voice no longer modulated. "But I'd hoped you'd still recognize me."

She screws up her face, getting a good look at him. He's not trying to hide anything about who he is, but for the life of her, Hannah can't place his face. She shakes her head. "I don't. What do you want with me?"

He pinches his features, and she can tell he's angry. She's seen that look on a thousand guys before, the ones who always ask her out at the bars, the ones who think they know her and get mad when she rejects them. It's the exact same look. Except this time, she's in this man's total control. She has no way out.

"Want with you?" he asks, as if the question is ludicrous. "I want you to be happy." The irritation in his voice is unmistakable. If she doesn't do something to salvage this soon, she's never getting out of here.

"You're right, I'm sorry," she says, doing her best to sound submissive. She just needs him to let his guard down for a few minutes. To unlock that door. Right now, that's her only goal.

His face seems to relax. He steps to the side to reveal a small table behind him, complete with a tray of food of his own. "I thought we could have lunch together. Catch up. It's been so long."

What kind of sick game is this guy playing? She needs to stall; she needs time to figure this out. Hannah looks around at what used to be the wall which is now all glass. "What is this? Has this been a window this entire time?"

"It's called switchable glass," he replies, matter-of-factly. "With the introduction of a certain amount of current, the glass transforms from opaque to clear." His eyes flick down to the tray on her table. "So? Care to eat with me?"

Hannah doesn't see she has much choice. Plus, the more she can learn about this man, the better chance she has of getting out of here. At this point she doesn't even care why he abducted her; she just wants out. And this isn't the kind of guy who strikes her as one of those alpha-male types she's always running into. He seems quiet, reserved. Like a person no one would ever notice.

She takes a cautious seat, which produces a small smile on the man's face. He rounds the table and sits as well, staring directly at her. The first few moments are spent in silence, though he never takes his eyes off her as they eat. She finds it unnerving, but does her best not to show it. There's no telling what this man is capable of.

"So?" he asks.

She glances at him, a current of fear running through her. It was too much to hope they'd be able to eat in silence. But with the wall no longer there she feels exposed, like she's on display. Nothing about this feels right. She doesn't even taste the food she's eating.

"So?" she repeats.

"How is it? I know tomato soup is your favorite."

It actually isn't, but she's not about to argue with him. "It's good," she says, trying to keep her voice even. He's acting like they're old friends, and Hannah racks her brain trying to figure out if she *does* know him. She's pretty sure she wouldn't forget a face like that, though. Maybe they used to go to college together? He looks to be about her age, maybe a few years older.

"D-did you go to UMD?"

Immediately she knows she's made a mistake. His face, which had been neutral before, twists into something ugly. He slams his fork down. "Why are you acting like this?" he says. It's more of an accusation than a question.

Something inside her snaps. Maybe it's the accusatory tone, or the fact he's locked her in this box with no way out. And even though some part of her brain knows it isn't smart, she can't help herself. She throws her fork down and shoots out of the chair. "What do you want with me?" she screams. "Just let me out of here!"

He shakes his head, standing from his seat. "I'd really hoped we were past this. I was hoping you'd started to remember."

"Remember *what?*" she yells. "I've never met you! I don't know anything about you, why should I?"

He lets out a long breath and approaches the pane separating them. Hannah instinctively backs up. "I see the amnesia has taken hold. I was really hoping you'd come through this time."

"What are you talking about, you sick *fuck*!" Hannah yells. "Just let me out of here!" She puts her hands to her skull and turns in the room. This can't be happening to her. She doesn't deserve this.

"You know I can't do that, Lisa. Not until you're better."

She's taken aback. "Who the hell is Lisa?"

"Don't you remember?" he asks. "You are."

Chapter Twenty-Two

"SO WE HAVE TWO POTENTIAL SUSPECTS," ZARA SAYS, "BOTH of them with computer science degrees and both who drive sedans. What are the odds?"

I shake my head. As I'd begun looking into Douglas Krauss I felt like we'd done nothing but hit another roadblock, given he and Daryl Thorpe are so similar. They're almost too similar. White males, approximately the same age, height, slightly different hair color, same general build. Both with similar backgrounds; both with enough skills to crack into *Ryde 4 Lyfe's* files and erase their records.

In fact, they're so similar it's enough to make me suspicious. Like someone engineered it that way.

"They both fit the profile," I say. "Almost to a fault. Which means we need to figure out a way to differentiate them from each other. Either one could be our man."

"And here I thought I'd actually be able to go home tonight," she replies.

"In your dreams," I say, looking deeper into Douglas Krauss. Pretty quickly I'm able to find out that both his parents are deceased, though he has an aunt and an uncle who live in Florida. He also has a sister, but I can't find much on her. But what's even more interesting is the fact that he's built himself a small fortune off his skills as a programmer.

"Listen to this," I say. "Douglas Krauss is one of the brightest stars in the field today, pioneering three different proprietary technologies that have propelled him to become a millionaire before turning thirty."

"I definitely went into the wrong profession," Zara quips.

"It says here the technologies he's developed are used by the aviation industry, local police departments and even...the federal government." I look up. "Have you ever heard of this guy?"

Zara pushes her lips out. "Wait a second...Krauss, right?" She works on her terminal a few minutes. "Yeah, I think he's the guy who helped develop the framework behind the Facial Analysis, Comparison, and Evaluation software. Jeez, no wonder he's a millionaire."

I glare at the information Aruz provided from *Ryde 4 Lyfe*. "So what's a millionaire doing driving for a ride-share company?"

"I dunno, maybe he gets lonely. He's not married, right?"

I double check my data. "No. And I don't see anything about a girlfriend. Which also fits the profile. But still...given the kind of work he does, you wouldn't think he'd spend his nights picking up strangers and dropping them off. Not unless..." I turn to her. "...he was looking for somebody." I motion to her. "What do Thorpe's financials look like?"

She pulls up his information. "Not good. Despite having a master's in computer science, he hasn't been able to hold down a steady job since he graduated three years ago. He's been jumping from gig to gig. Ryde 4 Lyfe just happens to be his most recent."

"It has to be Krauss," I say. "Thorpe needs the money, but this guy doesn't. He's out there patrolling the streets, like a predator." A chill runs up my back. "Zara? Check and see how many other missing person's cases are out there for this area."

"Um…" she says, squinting at her screen. "Sixteen for DMV. You want Baltimore too?"

I shake my head. "No. This guy is going to stay local. How many of those missing persons are women?"

"Nine," she replies.

"And how many under the age of…let's say thirty."

"Six."

"How old is the oldest case?"

"Hang on a second," she says. "I see where you're going with this." She works on her terminal a minute longer. "Okay. Three of those six have gone missing within the time Krauss has worked for Ryde 4 Lyfe. Beginning about five and a half months ago."

"He's taking them," I say. "He's just out there, taking women off the streets."

"But wait a second," Zara says. "They can't have all been through Ryde 4 Lyfe. It's like Aruz said. If someone were abducting their fares, it would show up in his system."

"Not if he broke into the system before he even began working there." I stare at Krauss's face on the screen in front of me. There's a coldness about him. A lifelessness in his eyes, and in my gut I know this is the guy. "Given his level of skill, who's to say he hasn't been manipulating the system from the start? What better way to get an unsuspecting woman into your car?"

"So then why stop now?" she asks. "If I'm out there, using a system that's proven to work for me, why stop now? What changed so that I erase my entire profile?"

I shake my head. "I'm not sure. But I'm willing to bet Krauss didn't know Aruz backed everything up offsite on a server that isn't connected to anything. Otherwise he would have erased the entire record of him working there. But as it is, he can only access the active system. Something must have changed. Either he grew tired of doing it, or he finally found the fare he'd been looking for all along."

"Hannah," Zara says.

I shoot her a finger gun. "Yep. For whatever reason she was his white whale. Once he had her, he no longer had a need for the ride-share." I sit back up. "We need to figure out what connects them. Why she was the target."

"So I'm assuming you want to put Thorpe to the side for now?" Zara asks.

"We won't eliminate him yet," I reply. "But given what we know so far, I think Krauss is our guy. Check and see if his contract with us is still open regarding all this equipment. It might give us a natural in to him without tipping him off."

A moment later Zara shakes her head. "No dice. The contract expired last year."

"Damn," I say. "I guess that would have been too easy."

"So what do we do? You said if we tip our hand, it could endanger Hannah."

"It still could. We have no idea what he's capable of. And now we might have these other missing women to contend with." I sit back in my chair. "We'll need to tail him. Keep an eye on him, see what he's doing during the day."

"That might not be as easy as it sounds," she says. "These rich guys often go to places the general public isn't allowed. Exclusive golf clubs, private events. Places where you and I would stand out like red grass."

I rub my face. The past few days have been exhausting. It seems like every lead we have only throws up more obstacles. Zara's right. People with money protect themselves, especially if they're out kidnapping people. The key is finding what Hannah means to him. If we can find that, we'll be in a much better position. Otherwise, why would he go to all the trouble?

Krauss is a man who can say and buy anything he wants. Why risk it for this one woman?

"Let's get to work on taking Douglas Krauss's life apart," I say. "We need as much information on him as we can get. Once we figure him out, then we'll worry about how to tail him without being spotted."

"You're the boss," she says.

As we get back to work, I'm reminded were it not for Chris, I'd have to go get Timber. But thankfully, even though he hates my guts, he loves my dog. Small blessings.

It's close to ten-thirty when I finally see Zara nod off at her desk. Her head pitches back, causing her mouth to open and a series of soft snores to begin. I go over and gently shake her, snapping her back awake.

"Wha—?" she looks up at me through sleepy eyes. "Helloooo."

"Go home," I tell her. "Get some sleep."

She shakes her head. "No way, if you're staying, I'm staying."

"No, you're not. You're no good to me or anyone else if you're exhausted. Go home, get a few hours, then come back."

"What about you?" she asks, standing up.

"I'm not far behind you. Just going to run a few more searches. I need to go pick up your boyfriend. My former brother-in-law has been more than patient."

She yawns, causing me to yawn in response. I hate that. "Kay," she says, then grabs her coat. "See you in a couple hours."

"A good night's rest!" I call after her, unsure if she'll actually listen or not. She waves me off as she passes through the double doors. I look around the rest of the office. The main lights are off and most of the stations are empty. Usually there are at least a few people working late, but it seems like I have the place to myself tonight. I double-check by dipping my head into Janice's office, then quickly stroll down through the bullpen. The place is deserted as far as I can tell.

I make my way back to my desk, my heart pounding as I pull out the folder Parrish gave me. It only takes me a moment to load up the pictures of the woman into the system. I set the parameters and begin the search, trying not to get my hopes up.

It isn't as if FACE has the picture of everyone on earth. And even if they did, these pictures would have to be clear enough to confirm a positive match. As it is, we only have the images of people of interest, or those with criminal backgrounds. And it's not comprehensive by any means. Agencies all over the country are notorious for not keeping their files updated. Which means if someone has committed a crime in the past month there's a possibility they aren't even in the system yet. It's horribly outdated, and I find it ironic that Krauss's technology helps run it. Maybe that's why he's in D.C. He could have moved here for the contract and just never left, especially since it seems like the only family he has lives in Florida.

As the search is running, I see the system beginning to create a small tally of names; possible matches, with the percentage of accuracy beside them. So far none of them are above forty percent. I need it to be at least seventy before I can act on anything.

A noise from somewhere behind me causes me to immediately spin in my chair, my hand reaching for a service weapon that isn't there. It's locked in my desk. But I'm in the middle of the J. Edgar Hoover Building, I'm not in any danger here. It's just a reflex. But it means someone else is here. Someone I've missed.

I switch off my monitor while the search continues to run.

"Hello?" I call out, but there's no response. I'm up and out of my chair, slowly making my way to where I heard the sound. I shouldn't be this jumpy, but performing an unauthorized search like this could get me into a lot of trouble, and I just found my way back into the Bureau's good graces.

When I reach the back of the room where the small kitchen is located, the lights are off. Though I was sure the sound came from here. I switch them on, bathing the open room in florescent lighting. On the ground, next to the sink is a metal spoon. I reach down and pick it up, replacing it in the sink. Someone must have left it too close to the edge of the counter.

I scan the room one last time, making sure there's no one else there before I turn the lights back off and return to my station. When I flip my monitor back on, it's completed the search. In total it came back with eighty-six possible matches. Of those eighty-six, only four are above fifty percent. And none are above seventy.

I print off the list of the four anyway, then make sure to go back into the system and remove the log of the search, along with the images of the woman from the system. Finally, I clear out the print request as well. I may need to ask Zara for her help covering my tracks in the morning. I'll have to come up with some reason as to why I need her help with it, without telling her the real reason.

As I put my coat on, I can't help but feel a stab of shame at what I'm doing. This may be exactly what the abductor did before he took Hannah. But I'm not trying to hurt anyone. I'm trying to prevent people from getting hurt. Still…I can't help but feel *off* about this decision. I tuck the folder with the original pictures and the names under my arm and head out.

But as I'm preparing to leave, I feel the hairs on the back of my neck stand up. I spin in place, scanning the room behind me for someone in the darkness, someone watching me. But there's no one there. It's because I'm so off-book here;

it's making me more anxious than normal. Once I find out who this woman is and confront her, everything will be back to normal. I'll finally be able to know peace again. I might not have Matt back, but at least I'll have answers. And that will be good enough.

Chapter Twenty-Three

"WOW, IT'S REALLY WARMING UP QUICK," ZARA SAYS AS WE step out of my car in front of a small apartment block on the west side of the city. The morning started out cool but has already warmed considerably, enough so that I pull off my overcoat and toss it in the back seat. Above us, fluffy clouds make a slow march across the clear blue sky.

"Are we seriously talking about the weather?" I ask, shooting her a glance.

"Okay, random fun fact time then," she replies, grinning. "Did you know polar bears have black skin under their fur?"

I arch my eyebrow at her. "No?"

"Yeah. If you ever get a chance, Google it. Shaved polar bears look like wolverines or something. Super scary. All that white fluff, it's just a ruse to draw us in. To make them look all cuddly and fluffy and soft."

"Why do you know so much about polar bears?" I ask.

"I fell asleep to it last night. Don't you ever fall asleep with the TV on?" she asks.

"No, I fall asleep to white noise and an eye mask to block out the light. And since when did you get cable?"

"Oh, it wasn't cable. It was on YouTube. Sometimes I'll

just pull up something random, just to have the noise on as I go to sleep. But then if I wake up, it's playing something totally different. Like last night. I woke up at about three and the polar bear thing was on."

Zara is one of those people who gets interested in everything. No matter what the subject matter is, she finds a way to peel it apart and find the thing inside that interests her. I wish I was like that, sometimes. But the fact is, some things just don't hold my attention. I nod to the building. "Want to do this?"

"If you're sure," she says.

We both came back in this morning, going over Krauss and Thorpe with fresh eyes. I also had the unfortunate job of informing Janice that our perp may have kidnapped more than just Hannah. We don't have physical evidence yet, but given the circumstances, I think caution is warranted. She told me she'd be happy to assign more people to the case if I need the extra manpower, which is encouraging. Two months ago, I wouldn't have dreamed she'd offer something like that. It means all the work I've been doing since returning from Stillwater has paid off in spades. But her confidence only reminds me I'm going behind her back searching for my mystery woman. That it could all come crashing back down in an instant.

As we stroll up to the building, I'm confident now the man we're looking for is Krauss. But Janice was adamant we eliminate Thorpe as a suspect. Which means we'll need to interview him. And since I don't believe he's our man, I'm not as worried about spooking him.

The building in front of us is a standard five-over-one apartment block, with retail and restaurants on the ground floor and four floors of apartments above it. Fortunately, because it's so early in the day we managed to find a spot on the street. Our records show Thorpe as unemployed, which gives me hope he's still home this early. Given what I know about his work history, I don't see him as the type who's up at five a.m. at the gym and in the office by eight. He strikes me more of a "roll out of bed around ten" sort of guy. Another reason why I don't think he's our man. The abductor is smart, methodical, and absolutely committed. And given where Thorpe lives, I don't see how he could abduct anyone and hide them in a place like this. According to his financials, he doesn't have any money tucked away or a second home of any kind. So unless he took her and killed her immediately, he would have run into a problem of logistics.

The probabilities that Krauss is our man just keep increasing.

The apartment block is security controlled from the street, but all we have to do is wait until someone leaves so we can gain access. The woman looks at us funny, but I show her my badge as we pass which seems to placate her. Even if Thorpe isn't our man, I don't want to give him a heads up we're coming. In situations like these it's often best to catch people off guard. It usually makes evaluating them easier as they haven't had time to practice how they're going to act.

When we reach Thorpe's door I rap on it a few times.

It swings open to reveal a woman probably no more than two or three years younger than me, with nothing but a sweatshirt on, which goes halfway down her thighs. She's got long, black hair which is as straight as an arrow. "Yes?" she asks.

I shoot Zara a glance. "Is this the home of Daryl Thorpe?"

"Hey, D!" she calls out, standing to the side.

Down the hall a bare-chested man appears, wearing the sweatpants that match the woman's sweatshirt. Though, perhaps "man" is too generous a word. Daryl Thorpe still looks like a kid, which is something I know a little about. But while it's just my face that looks young, Daryl really does look no more than eighteen. He just doesn't seem to have filled out yet. The term "skinny white kid" comes to mind. His dirty blonde hair sticks out from under a black cap emblazoned with the Yankees' logo and he walks with more swagger than someone of his position should have.

"Yeah?" he asks, coming up to us. I almost gag on the body spray as he enters our periphery.

"You're Daryl Thorpe?" I ask.

"So?" he says, with an air of nonchalance. I feel like he's putting on a show for his lady friend, who's still looking at us curiously.

I show him my badge, while Zara does the same. His eyes widen, but he quickly recovers. "Where were you Saturday night, around eleven?"

"Why? What's it matter to you?" It's like he's tempting us.

"We're investigating a case." Zara's voice already belies the impatience she's feeling. I'm right there with her. Thorpe strikes me as a man who doesn't seem to care much about anything, much less meticulously planning to abduct someone. But we have to do our due diligence.

Thorpe shoots the other woman a look. "I was here all night. Gettin' high and counting my bills."

"Alone?" I ask. His friend is giving Thorpe a strange look.

"Nah, I was with Tasmin here."

I turn to her. "Is that true? Keep in mind, lying to a federal officer is a felony. Punishable by up to five years in prison."

She swallows, hard. "Um…not exactly."

"Tas!" Daryl says, trying to shush her. I put my hand out to stop him from getting any closer.

"Tell us."

Thorpe looks positively mortified, glancing all around the place. I get the feeling he might try to run. Maybe I've called this whole thing wrong. Thorpe might actually be our abductor. He could even be a thrill killer.

"We were at the fifth street station until about midnight," she says. "Then we came home."

"Fifth street station?" I ask.

"It's a soup kitchen," she replies. "For the homeless."

"Tas! C'mon, these are Feds," Thorpe whines. "I've got a reputation!"

"Wait a second," I say. "You mean to tell me you were both working at a soup kitchen on a Saturday night?"

She shrugs. "Yeah. We do it 'cause my family didn't come from the best place. Try to give back, you know? D has been really supportive ever since we started goin' together." Thorpe has his hands on his head, walking back and forth like he can't believe she's spilling his secret. Any illusions we might have had about him have just been shattered.

"Who's your contact down there?" I ask.

"Marcia. She's always been good to us. Give her a call, she'll confirm we were there."

Wow. I knew Thorpe wasn't our guy, but this has gone in a completely different direction. "You mind if I take a quick look around?"

She shakes her head and steps aside while Thorpe looks at her with pleading eyes. Though I think it's more out of embarrassment than anything else.

The apartment is well-kept. Though there is some trash and dirty dishes in the kitchen. And there's a massive bong on the table in front of the couch. I can smell it from here. I give the other rooms a quick once-over while Zara stays with Thorpe and Tasmin. It's only a two-bedroom, so there's not a lot of space. But I don't see anything that would lead me to believe Thorpe is our man. He just doesn't have the means to carry something like this out.

I head back through the door. "You used to drive for Ryde 4 Lyfe, right?"

"Yeah," Thorpe says, though he looks miserable now.

"What made you quit?"

"Got tired of only running midnight shifts. I think that algorithm's screwed up. It only ever gave me ghetto jobs. Like it thought I belonged there. I just got tired of driving out where I might get shot, so I quit."

"Thank you both for your time," I say and motion that we head back to the car.

"Hey, you won't tell the other Feds about this, right?" Thorpe calls after us. "Right?" I don't even bother answering.

"That was kinda pathetic," Zara says as we get back outside. "What's he doing? Trying to be a baller?"

"Looks that way," I say. "Cosplaying as something he has no idea about. I'm surprised Tasmin puts up with it."

"Maybe he's great in all other respects," Zara laughs as she gets in.

"He'd damn well have to be to make me put up with that," I say. "I think we can cross Thorpe off our list."

"Do you want me to verify the alibi?" she asks.

I nod. "Go ahead, so we can document it in the file." Zara makes the call as I pull away from the curb, and based on what I can hear of the conversation I can already tell it checks out.

"Well, Marcia is just a treat." Zara laughs. "Can't say enough good things about 'D' and Tasmin. Apparently they're there all the time."

I have to admit I feel a little bad for stereotyping Thorpe when we arrived. To me he looked like someone without a direction, and given his employment history, I'd assumed that was actually the case. But now I have a new respect for him. Maybe he got the wrong degree at school and has been jumping from one job to the next because he's trying to find what he really wants to do. But I've regained my confidence from earlier. I know now that Krauss is our guy; he's the only one left.

Zara reaches back to grab the case file so she can make the notes while we're on the way. I don't realize what she's doing until it's too late and her hand is already back there. "Wait!" I yell, pulling the car to the side of the road and throwing it in park.

"Em, what the hell?" Zara says from being jostled by the sudden stop.

I look down at her hand; I'm too late. She's holding the folder with the pictures from Parrish in it. I forgot to take it back in last night after I did the search.

"Here, that's the wrong file," I say, which, of course, has the opposite effect. As she's glancing down at it all I can see is her promising career going up in smoke because of what I've done. Because of my mistakes. Everyone close to me ends up hurt in some way. It happened with Matt, with Nick, with my parents, and now it's going to happen with her. I'm like a human wrecking ball.

I reach for the folder, but before I can grab it, she pulls it away, inspecting the contents closely.

"Em," she says. "What have you been doing?"

Chapter Twenty-Four

I PUT THE CAR INTO PARK AND LEAN MY HEAD BACK AGAINST the headrest. Dammit. I never wanted her to have to deal with this—to have to make a choice because of me. I need to find a way to cover it up...to lie. She can't know anything about it.

"Emily Rachel Slate," she says, more forcefully this time. "What's going on?"

"I don't know how to answer that," I reply. I don't *want* to lie. Not to the only person left in my life who matters.

"Who's this woman in these pictures?"

I can tell from the tone of her voice she already knows. It was foolish of me to think I could pretend otherwise. Zara has never been stupid. But I'm grasping at straws here. If she pulls on this thread, she may very well be out of a job because of me.

"It's her. The one from the hospital," she answers for me.

I snatch the folder away from her, tucking it back into the backseat. I can't believe how careless I was, leaving it back there last night. I was just so tired when I got home, and I thought I might need them again, even though the initial search wasn't productive.

"Where did you get those pictures? I thought you said no one saw her."

I turn to her. "Zara, please. Just drop it."

"Drop it?" she asks, her face incredulous. I don't see Zara angry often, but it's very clear right now. "How am I supposed to drop it? You've been lying to me this entire time."

"Because if Janice finds out about this, I don't want you going down too!" I yell. I take a deep breath. "I'm sorry. But the truth is, I shouldn't even be looking into this. And I knew if I told you about it, you'd want to help, and I can't have you risking your job like that."

"Did you ever think of *asking me?*" I look her in the eyes, and I don't see anger in there. I see hurt and pain. "You don't get to make decisions for me," she says. "Just like I don't get to make decisions for you."

"Zara," I say. "I just couldn't risk it. She's already killed at least two people. Not to mention it would be career suicide if anyone ever found out you were helping me. I used the system last night. Without permission, to try and find this woman."

She holds out her hand for the folder. "Let me see."

I hand it back to her and she flips through the pictures. "Where did you get them?"

"Zara—"

Impatience surrounds her. "Where?"

It's clear she's not going to drop it. Maybe if I tell her everything, she'll be smart enough to turn me in. That would be the appropriate thing to do. But I know that's about as likely as me winning the lottery. "I hired a private investigator once I got back to D.C. He spent a few weeks up there gathering information and was able to piece these together. It's the only evidence I have."

"Did your search turn up anything? Were you able to find out who she is?"

I shake my head. "Only four names came back that were above a fifty percent accuracy. But it's obvious none of them are her. I checked all the records on the names; and even the pictures don't really match. One's a soccer mom in Idaho who got stopped for a traffic ticket. Another is almost a grand-mother by now, she was convicted back in the seventies for some drug charge. The other two are prostitutes, one in Cali-fornia and the other in Texas. It was a zero for zero in the end."

Zara looks through the pictures again then hands the folder back to me. "I wish you'd told me. I'm supposed to be your friend."

"You *are* my friend," I say, her words stinging at my heart. "But I can't afford to lose anyone else. You're all I've got left. If something happened to you…I don't know what I'd do." I sigh. "No, I know exactly what I'd do. I'd throw myself into my work and never come up for air. I'd become an extension of the FBI itself. That is, if they didn't fire me for misappro-priating resources."

Zara flashes an upturned lip. "This? This isn't misappro-priating resources. You're looking into the death of Gerald Wright, that's all."

"Despite the fact his death was ruled an accidental heart attack."

"Yeah. Exactly. You suspect foul play. Maybe you're not the most unbiased person to take the case, but I don't think it's the career-ender you think it is."

"Then should we go tell Janice?" I ask. "Right now? We can grab a box of doughnuts on the way."

She gives me a mirthless chuckle. "Maybe don't go that far. I'd wait until you actually have a suspect you can point to. Who knows where this woman is right now?" She glances back at the file as I stuff it in the backseat under all the rest. "But I'm willing to help you look."

"You don't need to do that," I say. "It's like I said, I don't want you getting too wrapped up in this."

"And it's like *I* said," she replies. "It's not up to you. That would be like me deciding to keep Timber without even asking you. Which I still might do."

I scoff. "Are you kidding? You work longer hours than I do now." I look away, momentarily overwhelmed. "But thank you. I don't expect you to put your job in jeopardy for me."

"What, you mean when that red guy told me to sign away my soul for your personal wellbeing I should have refused? I think we need to put out an ABP on him. Note, he had black horns and a forked tail."

"Very funny," I reply.

"Listen, I need to know that you trust me to know what's best for me. And I'll trust you know what's best for *you*, okay? If something is too heavy for me to handle, I'll tell you."

"Okay," I reply, feeling like a fool.

"Though, there hasn't been anything yet I haven't been able to lift," she adds. "You should see me in the gym."

"When did you start going to the gym?" I ask.

"When I got approved for field work. You were the one who told me, remember? You said all those martial arts classes were practically mandatory. I know being in the gym isn't quite the same, but I gave the heavy bag a good thrashing. Agent Phillips was impressed, at least."

I chuckle. Zara has a petite frame. I can't imagine her doing much to those heavy bags. "I'll have to come see that next time you're down there."

"You can't tell because of my suit jackets, but I've been growing some major guns under here." She flexes her arm for emphasis. Even though I lied to her, she isn't dismissing me. She isn't turning away from me.

"What would I do without you?" I ask.

"Your life would be a lot more boring," she replies. "But you'd figure it out. I don't guess you have any additional information from your P.I., do you?"

I shake my head. "He talked to everyone. Most of these

pictures were a coincidence that he got them at all. One was from a survey crew a quarter mile away."

"Jeez," she replies. "I guess even an assassin can't escape all the cameras these days. It's a good thing we live when we do."

"That word," I say. "Assassin. Is that what you think she is?" I'd briefly considered the possibility, but I hadn't wanted to admit it to myself. Because a trained killer going after my husband and Gerald Wright opens a host of questions I don't want to face. It means someone had a grudge or was hired for a job. I don't like the implications of either scenario.

Zara shrugs. "What else would you call someone who killed at least two people and covered it up to look like an accident both times?"

"Dangerous," I reply.

"I second that." We sit in silence for a moment. "So what are you going to do about it?"

"Do about it? What do you mean?"

"If she's not in FACE, what's your next step?"

I shake my head. "Honestly, I'm out of ideas. She could be anyone, and she could be anywhere by now. All I know is I need to find her. Face her and get the truth about what she did." I ball my hand into a fist. "I don't care what it takes."

"It's not going to be like you can just haul her in. This is obviously a very smart and cautious person you're dealing with here. What happens if she figures out you're trying to come after her?"

That's another factor of this equation I don't like. A woman like this can obviously kill with impunity. Which means if she knows I'm looking for her, I'll be looking over my shoulder until we either have her in custody or she's dead.

I rub my temples. Despite the sleep I clocked in last night, I'm still tired. I think the week is beginning to wear on me. The longer we go without finding a solid clue to Hannah, the more exhausted I become. No wonder the agents who make it to retirement all look like they've lived at least two lifetimes. "I guess I'll have to deal with that when it happens. The truth is, I don't know."

She reaches over and pats my forearm. "Just know you're not alone. You've got me. And I'm willing to bet you still have Liam too."

I chuckle. "I don't think I ever *had* Liam."

"You said he heard what Wright said that night, right? Have you talked to him since coming back to D.C.?"

I shake my head. I hadn't wanted to make an already sticky situation worse. Liam and I might have worked on Victoria Wright's case together, but there was something brewing under the surface between us. Something that I can't act on, not while Matt's death is so fresh in my mind. I don't know if I can even have another romantic relationship after what he and I had, but I know that right now is not the time. I figured contacting Liam would only making things harder. "As far as I know, he's still in training."

"But he heard it, right?"

I shake my head. "I'm sure he thought Wright was just saying anything he could to keep from going to prison. People have said crazier."

"You guys didn't talk about it after it happened?" she asks.

"Not really. I kind of…lost a lot of blood right after. And then we had the whole deal with apprehending Chief Burke… it never really came up again. And honestly, I didn't want to bring it up. Not until I had a chance to speak to Wright in earnest."

She pulls out her cell. "Let's call him."

I grab her hand. "Don't you dare."

She tugs on it, both of us grappling for the phone like fools in the front seats of the car. Before long we're both laughing our asses off before she finally relents. "Okay, okay!" she says. "You win. We won't call him…today."

I toss the phone back at her, but there's a wide grin on my face. "Or ever. I will literally kill you."

She waves me off. "Whatever. I'll just wait until I see him in person. When he gets done with training you know they're gonna assign him to the head office. At least for the first six months."

My smile falters. I hadn't really considered that. It means we could run into each other in the building. Which wouldn't be the worst thing. I like Liam, and he really had my back in Stillwater. He's a good person. It's just...there are a lot of complicated feelings that come along with him.

"Anyway, my point is, if you need extra backup, I bet he'd be there. Especially if you told him what happened with Wright."

"I think I'm already putting enough people in jeopardy, don't you?" I ask.

She gives me one of her signature noncommittal shrugs. "I guess it depends on how lethal this assassin is. If she's like a ninja, then yeah, you're definitely on your own. I cannot deal with katanas and throwing stars. But if she's just really good with a gun, then I think I can show up for that fight."

I shake my head. "We better get back on it. We've still got another suspect to run down."

As I reach for the steering wheel, Zara snatches my hand, holding on to it tight. "I'm serious, Em. I'm not going anywhere. Okay?"

I nod, thankful that I have her. But I know in my heart of hearts that no one can really promise that. We don't know what will happen today or tomorrow. And Zara may think she's all in, but there's a difference between saying and doing. When the time comes, I won't blame her if she decides to abandon me.

"Okay." I say. "Let's go find Krauss."

Chapter Twenty-Five

"Is this the place?" Zara asks. I look up through the windshield of the car at the twenty-story building looming above us.

"I guess. Integrated Technology Solutions. Krauss's business enterprise." I pull up the picture of him on my phone. He's not what I'd call conventional-looking, but he's not ugly. I can see how he might be appealing to young women. Why someone like this would go out of his way to abduct people is beyond me. He has everything he needs in the world, money, looks, power. What do these women provide for him that he can't buy or coerce out of someone?

"So what do we do?" Zara asks.

"Wait," I reply. "I want to get a good look at him. And see where he goes when he leaves." Unlike Daryl Thorpe, Krauss *does* strike me as the kind of man who is up at five a.m. every day. I see him as one of those people who thinks sleep is for the dead and time is money. Given what we know about him, he's been working all of his adult life on his ventures, though he stays out of the public eye as best he can. No interviews with magazines, despite numerous requests by WIRED and FORBES, no in-person interviews with even local TV, not to mention national stations. There were a few early videos online, but those are mostly of just him coding. Apparently people like to watch that kind of thing. To me, it seems about as exciting as watching paint dry. But even in those videos he's very withdrawn.

"It says here, he's not even the CEO of his own company," Zara says, reading off her phone. "He handed over management of the company when they grew to over a million dollars in business back in 2018."

"So then…what? Does he still work here at all?" I ask.

She nods. "Looks like he's in charge of special projects, but as far as I can tell that's a dead area. The company hasn't produced anything out of that division, or if they have, they've kept it quiet."

"How many employees?" I ask.

"Sixty total."

I look up at the building again. "I wonder how many of them interact with him on a daily basis?"

"Are you thinking you want to try and get to know him through his coworkers?" she asks.

"I don't know. If he's who we think he is, he may have crafted a carefully-curated persona that he only displays when he's around other people. Something that obscures the real man underneath."

"Yeah, but how long can he keep something like that up?" she asks.

"Oh, trust me. People can do it for decades. It becomes second nature. They just change who they are based on who they're around. It's a trick sociopaths use to blend in better. The more they mirror the people around them, the more likely they are to be accepted into the group dynamics and the more those people like them. People like it when their own behavior is mimicked, even if they don't realize it."

"Seems like a lot of extra work," she says.

"Maybe. But for someone who doesn't naturally fit into

society, it can be like a coping mechanism. Or even a coat of armor that gives their true 'inner-self' protection from the world. In the case of men like Krauss, it can obscure who they really are to those that feel like they're close to them. Think about it: anytime anyone goes on a killing spree they always interview the neighbors. And what do the neighbors always say?"

She grins. "He was the nicest, quietest boy. I never would have thought he was capable of something like this."

"Exactly," I say. "It's how they blend into our world and walk among us."

"You make them sound like alien reptiles or something," she laughs.

"That's not far off. They are alien, in a sense. Especially some of the people we hunt. Some of these crime scenes…I don't know how another human can do something like that."

"So we're just going to wait," Zara says.

"I don't see that we have much choice," I reply. "We need to get a sense of him, figure out a way into his world. Because if he's done kidnapping women, that means we can't bust him for it again. And who knows how much time those women have left, if they're still alive at all. But given none of the bodies have been found yet, I'm cautiously optimistic."

"Okay," Zara says, settling in. "Let's watch."

Almost four hours later, I'm barely keeping my eyes open when I see a Passat pull out of the parking deck for Krauss's building. I nudge Zara, who is lost in her phone on something. "Doesn't Krauss drive a Volkswagen Passat?"

"A gray one, I think." She perks up, looking out the windshield. "Like that."

"Thought so," I reply, turning over the engine and putting the car in gear. I'm careful to stay at least three cars back from

Krauss; I have no idea how paranoid he might be. He could be looking over his shoulder every second, waiting for someone to pounce on him.

"Where is he going?" Zara asks. "It's two-thirty."

"Late lunch?" I suggest, keeping the tail long. We stop at a light while he continues on, but I've still got him in my sights.

"I dunno," she replies. "There are plenty of places to eat around his office that he could walk to. Why drive somewhere?"

I don't have a good answer for her. All we can do is wait and find out. The light turns green, and we're back on him, still keeping our distance. We end up weaving through D.C. traffic for a while until he starts heading out on New York Avenue. He stays on it until it turns into Hanson Highway and before I know it, we're leaving the confines of the city. "He's headed home," I say.

"Kind of odd to leave at this time of day," Zara says.

"But it also means we can't follow him." Krauss's house is out near the shore, right off the South River. There are some huge homes out there, but not a lot of traffic, and his has a private gate anyway. He'll definitely pick up on our tail long before we reach his home, and then he'll *know* someone is looking at him. "I'm going to have to turn back," I say.

"That's it? What are we supposed to do, just let him go?" Zara asks.

"We don't have any evidence it was him," I say. "Other than the circumstantial fact that he quit the ride-share we *suspect* Hannah Stewart took the night of her disappearance. We've got nothing linking her to him."

"But..." Zara says as I pull away and leave Krauss to head home on his own. I know exactly what she's feeling. The frustration of not being able to pursue the suspect, the anger that he could have those women doing God-knows-what and there's nothing we can do about it. The helplessness of it all. I've been there.

"Look, we'll head back to the office and go over all of it again. Deep dive. School records, childhood friends, teachers. Distant relatives, anything. If anyone has so much breathed on Douglas Krauss, I want to know about it." I'm thinking about calling in that favor from Janice. I could use a few more people on this. My only concern is what if I'm wrong? What if we're still chasing the wrong man?

"So we just did all of that for nothing?" she asks.

"It's like that sometimes. This job is a lot of feeling around in the dark, working a problem from the inside out."

She slumps back down in her seat. "I guess I never real-ized how many roadblocks you run into out here. I'm used to having someone hand me a problem and I hand them back the solution."

"It's a completely different animal out here," I say, turning back for headquarters. "We don't always get the answer we want."

"Should we keep surveillance on Krauss?" she asks.

"Not until we can connect him to Hannah or one of the other missing women," I say. "But we should look into their cases as well." I huff. Which means coordinating with the Metropolitan Police Department. I'm sure they're going to be super helpful when we call and ask about the disappearances.

"You've got that look in your eye," Zara says.

"What look?"

"The one that says you're gearing up for a fight." She's not wrong. Most of the time I'm able to work with local P.D. without a problem. Sometimes I'll run into a few assholes that make my job harder, but not impossible. But coming off the case in Stillwater, and after going up against Chief Burke, I think he's changed my threshold for patience in this regard. The man was an absolute wretch, and he deserves everything that's coming to him, including the corruption and obstruc-tion of justice charges brought against him not only by the State of Virginia, but the federal government as well. I'll be happy once he's sentenced and behind bars, but I realize now that he's really tainted how I view local P.D. I take a breath, allowing the stress of the moment to leave my body.

"There, that's better," she says, patting my hand. "Let all the stressies out. Everything is fine. You can go back home and have a nice drink and collapse into your bed."

I glance at the clock on my car. "That *sounds* nice, but it's barely three p.m."

When I glance over, she's got that gleam in her eye. "I'll cover for you."

She's right. I need to take a minute to breathe. I've been holding on to this case with an iron grip. I'm never going to get anywhere because I'm wound so tight. Once I take a minute to relax and reset myself, I'll be clear-headed and ready to pounce on Krauss. Maybe I'll even figure out a way to connect him to Hannah. "You know, you're not such a bad friend after all," I say.

She gives me a wink. "Told 'ya so."

We're just about to pull onto Pennsylvania Avenue when my phone rings. "Slate," I say.

"Agent," a smooth voice says on the other end. "I've got something for you."

"Santino?" I'd nearly forgotten about the Toscani's given everything else going on with the case. "What's going on?"

"Why don't you come on over to the warehouse. I've found your kidnapper."

Chapter Twenty-Six

"I DON'T LIKE IT," ZARA SAYS AS WE PULL UP TO TOSCANI'S warehouse in Brentwood.

"What's to like?" I ask. "We just got a call from a mob boss to meet him in his den. And this time, he knows we're coming."

As soon as Santino hung up, I dialed Janice to let her know what was going on. She's authorized backup on the Toscani warehouse in the event we run into trouble. I don't want to go in there guns blazing, but at the same time, we need to be cautious. This could all be a trap, especially considering what he told me.

Though from what I could hear in his voice, he was being sincere. Either that, or Santino is one hell of a liar.

I pull up to one of the parking spaces and turn off the engine. This time there's no one outside, waiting for us. The place is quiet. No trucks rumbling by today.

"I've just confirmed with Phillips," Zara says. "They have a tac team set up on the other side of the tracks, ready to go in if we get in trouble."

That should make me feel better, but it doesn't. If Santino has decided to double-cross me, I'll be long dead before the tac team can breach. I guess my only consolation would be that Santino and the rest of the organization would go down for good if they murdered two federal agents. I flip the clasp on my service weapon before I even open the door.

"You ready?" I ask.

"No. How do you get ready for something like this?" she asks.

"I guess you don't." Just as I grab the handle to open the door, my phone trills again. It makes my heart jump and I fumble for it, angry with myself for being so on edge. "Slate."

"Have you found her?" My heart drops when I hear the voice. I turn to Zara and mouth *Judge Stewart*. Her expression matches my own. We don't have time for this, not right now.

"Judge," I say. "I'm sorry, but I can't talk right now. I'm in the middle of something."

"You promised me you'd keep me apprised, Agent Slate," he chides. "I understand you've had a development regarding the Toscani's."

What the hell? How could he know that already? We just found out less than an hour ago. "There are some things in motion. But I can't talk about them, not right now over an open line."

"Very well," he says. "But I expect to hear from you this evening. It's been four days and I haven't heard a word."

"Trust me, Judge. This case is all I've been thinking about." I shoot a guilty glance at the files on my backseat. "We think we're closing in on finding Hannah. But please, I have to go. This is delicate."

"Understood," he says. "I look forward to hearing from you later." Finally he hangs up.

"What the hell," I say, putting my phone away.

"What?" Zara asks.

"He knew about the Toscani's. Someone talked. We've got a leak somewhere."

"Is it a leak if it's a federal judge?"

"It's a leak if anyone outside the operation knows what's going on. Right now it's you, me, Janice and the tac team. And that should be it."

"Then it's someone on the team," she says. "Someone with a big mouth."

"We'll have to deal with that later," I say. "C'mon, we need to get in there. I don't want to keep Santino waiting. He's already probably watching us, wondering what's taking us so long."

We step out into the warm afternoon air, though it's beginning to cool as the sun moves toward the horizon. I don't have my hand on my weapon as we approach the main warehouse office door, but it's close enough to grab it in an instant. Zara already has hers in hand, though it's still pointed at the ground. She had prior training with a weapon when she first started with the FBI, but hasn't used one in years. A refresher course was all she needed to qualify for field duty. I just hope it was enough if it comes to it.

"I still don't get it," she whispers. "How can he have the abductor if it's Krauss? We saw him heading home."

"I don't know," I reply. "As far as I'm aware, Santino and Krauss's orbits don't intersect, anywhere in this city. They shouldn't even be aware of each other."

She shakes her head. "Something is off about this."

We reach the door and I rap on it, four times, hard. We wait a moment before a latch is thrown on the other side and the door swings open to reveal one of the large guards we saw earlier. He glances at Zara's weapon, but it doesn't seem to bother him this time. He's the kind of man who looks like he wouldn't be stopped by anything other than an elephant gun.

"Come on. Boss is waiting." He turns and leads us through the office, which causes Zara and I to throw nervous looks at each other. We're taken the exact same way we came before, when we first met Santino. But now, the warehouse is dark and none of the machines are running. All the HVAC equipment sits on the factory floor, unopened and unloaded into any trucks.

"Shut down production?" I ask.

"Temporarily," the man replies, which makes me wonder what could be so big to shut down one of their primary sources of income. You'd think, especially if they were going to shoot us, they would want a lot of noise to drown out the sound.

The man finally leads us to the office section of the building, where he takes us straight to Santino Toscani's office, near the back. A familiar coppery tang hits my nose and the back of my throat as soon as the guard opens the door to let us in. A half a second later, I see him.

Bound to a chair halfway between the door and Santino's desk, is a man with dark hair and a Mediterranean complexion. He hangs limp, by bound hands and feet, his face bloody and swollen. His shirt is ripped, showing off a hairy chest. And his face is so puffy, I can't tell if his eyes are open or not.

"Ah, Agents!" Santino says, standing from his desk. I hadn't even noticed him there. "Thank you for coming."

"What the hell is this, Santino?" I ask, indicating the man. "Some kind of intimidation tactic?"

"What?" he says, looking at me through feigned hurt. "I would never, Agent Slate. I got you what you asked for, the man who kidnapped your victim. Here he is for you, all wrapped up." He gestures to the man. "Turns out you were right after all. One of my men was still working for my uncle. Thought it would be a good idea to take the girl in exchange for his release."

I exchange a skeptical look with Zara. "He's admitted this?"

"Oh yes," Santino says. "Quite vociferously." He kicks the foot of the poor man tied to the chair, producing a low moan. "Didn't you, Federico?"

The man moans again.

"What did you do to him?" I ask.

"This?" Santino says as if it's nothing. "This was all self-defense." I shoot him a look. "I swear. Once I realized he couldn't account for his actions on Saturday night, we confronted him, and he became belligerent. It took three of my men to restrain him, but we finally calmed him down. We wanted to make sure he was in good shape when you arrived."

"You call this good shape?" I ask. "You've beaten him to a pulp!"

"No, no, look, he's fine," Santino says. "He'll have a fat lip and some bruised ribs come tomorrow, but there's been no permanent damage done."

I put my hands on my hips, unsure what to do with this situation. This can't be the man who took Hannah. "Did he say anything else? Like what he did with her?"

Santino shakes his head. "Unfortunately, he's been tight-lipped about that part. But I figure I'd let the professionals handle it. You can interrogate him yourselves."

"How did you find out he was unaccounted for on Saturday?" Zara asks. "You said yourself you didn't have their social calendars."

Santino perches on the edge of his desk, nodding. "I did say that. But I started asking around. Most of my boys stick together on the weekends. But no one could account for ol' Federico here. Seems he was missing at the normal gatherings."

"That's not enough," I say. "Just because he wasn't where he normally was doesn't mean he took Hannah."

"Of course not," he says, mocking hurt again. "Do you think I'd really waste your time with something so trivial?" He kicks at Federico's boot again. "Tell her, *stronzino*."

"I did it," he says, his voice muffled and sounding like it's coming through a wad of cotton.

"Did what?" I ask.

"I took the Judge's daughter."

I crouch down, trying to get a good look at his face. The problem is it's so screwed up there's no way I can tell if he's telling the truth or if he's just been coerced. For what reason, I don't know. "Where is she, Federico? What did you do with her?"

He shakes his head once, which clearly causes him pain. I look up at Santino. His face seems like a mixture between pleasure and loathing. I don't think I've ever seen anything quite like it before. And I can't tell if it's directed at me, or at Federico.

"You better tell her, Federico. Marco's not gonna protect you in prison. You know that, right?"

Federico looks up for the first time, his swollen eyes meeting mine. They're full of pain, like he just wants to die. A few bruised ribs my ass. This man has been beaten within an inch of his life. We need to get him to a hospital before he flat-lines on us.

"Zara, call in the paramedics. We need to get him trans-ported out of here," I say. I stand back up, facing Santino. "You know this is unacceptable. When I asked you to find out if any of your men had anything to do with this, I didn't mean for you to bring your own version of vigilante justice down on them."

Santino stares at me, a gleam in his eye. "What can I say? It was self-defense, Agent Slate."

"That's bullshit and we both know it," I reply.

Santino gestures to the other men in the room. "You can ask anyone here. We have plenty of witnesses."

"I'm sure you do," I reply.

"Paramedics are two minutes away," Zara says.

I motion for the door. "Show them how to get back here." She heads back to the front, while the man who escorted us in follows her. I'm no longer concerned Santino is going to do something as stupid as trying to jump us. He obviously has a different objective here.

"What are you playing at, Santino?" I ask.

He shoots me a noncommittal look then rounds his desk and takes a seat. Federico moans again. "I have no idea what you mean, Agent Slate."

I know I can't trust the man. But I also can't ignore this bombshell he's dropped in my lap. That's the problem with this job, there's always a certain level of uncertainty. We never had any solid evidence on Krauss, only my hunch and the information from *Ryde 4 Lyfe* that just happened to line up with a theory. This is something completely different. This man has confessed to the crime, to my face. I have to face the possibility I've been chasing the wrong person this entire time and Judge Stewart had been correct all along.

Moments later Zara comes rushing back in the room with two paramedics who are wheeling a gurney. All of us work to free Federico from the chair and get him on the ground before they hoist him up on the gurney, strapping him in and giving him oxygen and fluids. They have him back out of the office in less than three minutes.

I stare down at the chair he was tied to, blood stains on the carpet underneath.

"Ambulance was close," Santino says. "I certainly hope that wasn't because you thought I might hurt you or your partner."

I shoot him a look. "I guess it was just one of those lucky coincidences." Nothing about this whole situation feels right to me. It's like someone has thrown a stick in the spokes of my bike and launched me off into the underbrush. Where I was cool, collected and sure of myself before, now I don't know what to think.

"Keep me up to date on the rest of your investigation," Santino says. "I'd love to know how it turns out."

"Sorry," I say. "We don't talk about active cases with the public." I turn and head for the door, Zara right in front of me.

"Oh, and Agent Slate," Santino calls, just as I reach the door. I turn back to him. "I hope this little favor isn't forgotten in the future. We always like to help out our friends at the FBI, whenever we can."

So that's his game. The fact that I walked right into it makes me want to throw up. Instead, I do everything in my power to not let him see he's gotten under my skin. Instead, I leave him there, a wicked smile plastered across his face.

Chapter Twenty-Seven

"IT'S A CONUNDRUM, I AGREE," JANICE SAYS.

Zara and I are sitting in her office, having just come from the hospital where we watched as Federico went into emergency surgery to survive all the damage Santino's men inflicted on him. From what I understand, he's going to need his jaw wired shut. Which means answering questions about Hannah is going to prove difficult, for at least a few days. Time we don't have.

"They literally broke his jaw. This is all just a ruse from Santino. He's betting Hannah is already dead and gone, and if he can put up one of his men as a patsy, then he'll have given the FBI a golden egg that we just can't ignore."

She taps the end of her pen on her desk, glaring, not at me or Zara, but at the wall behind us. Deep in thought. "But you heard the man admit to taking her," Janice says.

"He was barely conscious and in no condition to answer questions," I reply. "He would have told you he was from Mars if you'd asked him." I stand up, pacing the room. "Plus, Santino probably primed him, telling him only to give us nuggets of information. Just enough that we couldn't use any of it. And all the while, Hannah is still out there somewhere.

Not to mention these other women who he conveniently didn't mention."

"Of which you still have no evidence that connects any of them," Janice says. "We can't ignore the implications of this. We'll need to interview this Federico as soon as he's out of surgery." She holds up a hand before I can argue. "I get it. And I agree with you. But if the Director hears that we have a confessed abductor in custody and we're still chasing down other leads, he'll pitch a fit. Especially considering this has to do with the Judge's daughter."

I shake my head. "It stinks, Jan. The Toscani's are trying to play us."

"You think it's this Krauss character," Janice says. "Despite the fact he has no motive."

"He has a motive, we just haven't found it yet," I say.

Janice purses her lips and turns to Zara. "Hell of a first week in the field, huh?"

"It certainly isn't what I expected," she replies.

"You two have been putting a lot of time in on this. Let me get another agent to interview Federico. I don't want you burning out."

"I'm not—" I stop myself before I get going. I don't want her to bench us, we need to keep going after Krauss. "Can we at least keep an eye on Krauss? Until we've confirmed Federico is the true kidnapper?"

I don't like the look on Janice's face. It's one made of politics and making concessions, even though she knows it isn't right. "Krauss isn't a nobody. Because of what he's done for some of the biggest businesses in the city, and for us as well, he's made some powerful friends. You run the risk of making an enemy out of someone who may have nothing to do with this."

I blow a frustrated breath out and rub my temples.

"I'll assign Hogan to speak with Federico. When is he supposed to be out of surgery?"

"Four hours," I say, checking my watch. It's already eight p.m. Chris is going to throw a fit after having to take care of Timber again.

"Both of you, go home. Get some rest. Come back in the morning refreshed and we'll decide how to proceed. We should at least have a preliminary statement from Federico by then." She pauses. "I'm not usually an optimistic person, so I'm not going to blow a lot of smoke up your asses. The fact is, it's been almost a week since she went missing. Odds are she's already dead. You both worked your hearts out on this one, I know you did. But sometimes we just come up short."

We both head out, back to the bullpen. I can't say meeting with her made me feel any better. I may not know Santino personally, but I know his type. And I wouldn't put it past him to try and pull a scheme like this. Whether he thinks it will help him gain respect, that he can say he has the FBI in his pocket; or if it's part of a larger power play, I don't know. What I do know is we can't trust a word that comes out of his mouth.

"You okay?" Zara asks as we reach our desks. I pull my coat back on.

"No. Are you?"

"Not really. But I don't know what else we can do about it now." She stares at her desk for a moment. "It seems too convenient, doesn't it?"

"Yeah, it does. I've never had someone drop something like that in my lap before. We just don't get that lucky."

"Are you thinking what I'm thinking?" she asks with a mischievous grin.

"Absolutely," I say. "Let's go stake out the son of a bitch. See what he does in that big house all by himself at night."

"Oh, wait. I meant we should go get blackout drunk and gossip about people we hate. What were you thinking?"

I stall for a second. "I—"

"God, you are so easy sometimes," she says, cracking a

grin. "Let me go get the equipment. What do you think? Thermals? Night vision? Long-range lenses?"

"I hate you sometimes," I say, though I'm smiling as I say it.

"Yeah, you do. Anything else you can think of?"

"Are you sure you can get all of that?" I ask.

"Absolutely. You know Gary down in tech services? He owes me like, twenty favors. He won't bat an eye."

"Okay, I'll meet you down at the car." My heart is pumping like crazy. This is more like it. Janice doesn't have to know we're putting Krauss under surveillance if we do the surveillance ourselves. Plus, it just *feels* right. I want to nail him so bad I can taste it. Even if he already has disposed of Hannah, I'm not going to stop.

Zara winks, then heads off down to tech services. I pull my coat all the way on and make sure my desk is clear of anything else. This is going to be a long stakeout, and I want to make sure I'm not missing anything important.

"Still working on the case?"

I turn to see Agent Nick Hogan, still holding what looks like the same mug of coffee I saw him with last time.

"You ever give that stuff a rest?" I ask.

"Nah. Keeps me awake. I just got the call from Janice. She wants me to interview your 'suspect'."

"Yeah, good luck with that," I tell him. "Considering the guy can't even talk."

Nick shrugs, and all of a sudden, I realize there's something different about him. He's got that swagger about him again; the one I'm used to. I've never liked that swagger. It was the first thing I noticed about him when we started working together and it's the same attitude he carried all those years he was trying to one-up me. Recently I thought things had improved, that he'd moved past this childish competition that only exists in his mind. But apparently, I was wrong.

"He may not be able to talk, but I bet he can still write."

"Good luck verifying anything he tells you," I say. "It's not like he's the most reliable source of information."

"No, you're probably right," he replies. "Still. We have to do our due diligence, right?"

"We do," I say.

"Nice that you got the evening off. Have anything fun planned?"

"Why, are you looking for a date?"

He takes a long sip of coffee, eyeing me and suddenly, I feel exposed. Like he knows what Zara and I are up to. But how could he?

"I saw you last night," he says. "Using the system to search for that woman."

My heart jumps to my throat and I feel like I'm about to be sick. *What?* How could he have seen me? The entire place was empty. Then I remember the spoon in the kitchen area. I look down at the mug in his hand. He doesn't like his coffee black. Instead, it's more of a light beige. It would take a lot of creamer to get it that color.

"What are you doing, *spying* on me?" I growl, allowing my anger at having been seen to take over.

He holds up his hands in mock surrender. "Just ensuring the integrity of the Bureau," he says. "Though I do wonder what you were searching for. And why I can't find a record of the search in the system anymore."

"What do you want?" I say under my breath. I'm *this* close to decking him.

"I just want to make the world a safer place," he says.

"Cut the shit, Nick. I don't have the patience to play these games."

He licks his lips, then looks around, making sure no one else is within earshot. "Okay, Slate. Here's the deal. Both you and I know this Federico guy is a big nothing-burger. He's either a patsy for the Toscani's or he's a complete moron.

Either way, he didn't do it. That Uber driver you've been zeroing in on did."

"Have you been looking at my *case notes*?" I say, furious.

"Hey, don't blame me," he says. "Janice gave me access. This is your first big case since your trial period was up. She was just covering her bases in case something went wrong."

"Does Zara know?" I ask. "Does anyone else?"

He scoffs. "Please. Foley is too close with you to be objective. Janice knows that and so does everyone else. No, this is a strictly low-key operation."

"And so, what, you're my chaperone?" I can't believe Janice did this to me. I thought I'd finally earned back the Bureau's trust. That I could work with full autonomy again.

"Let's just say I've been keeping an eye on the investigation, making sure it stays on track. You've always had good instincts, Slate, I'll give you that. And this bombshell by the Toscani's has really thrown a wrench in things. But it doesn't mean you're wrong."

"Get to the part where you forget about the search last night," I say.

"Fine. Here's the deal. You bring me evidence Krauss is the real deal, that he kidnapped those women, and you're off the hook. I'll forget all about it."

"You can't be serious," I say. "You're *extorting* me? There's a woman's life at stake here."

"You and I both know she's already dead," he says with an air of nonchalance that makes my skin crawl. I never knew Nick could be so cold.

"You want the collar, is that it? So you can take the credit?"

He glares at me, then rubs his side. It's the exact same spot he got shot four months ago. "I think you owe me, don't you?"

"Look, I already told you I was sorry about that. I can't go back—"

"You never should have been on the case that day. I told

you, Janice told you. Everyone tried to get you to go home, to mourn your loss. But no. Emily Slate won't be stopped, it doesn't matter how much bad shit happens in her life. Even if it means getting her partner shot."

I turn away, tears stinging my eyes. I hate him for doing this to me, for making it seem like it's my fault when I had no control over that situation. Maybe I shouldn't have come in for the operation, but if I hadn't, all those kids would still be under someone else's thumb. Instead, they're back at home, right now, because of what we did.

"I'm sorry you got shot," I say, slowly and evenly. "But I won't apologize for doing what I did. We dealt a major blow to that kidnapping ring."

"Yeah, we did," he says. "Except you walked away, scot-free, while I was intensive care for five days. I had to watch my wife go through more pain than I've ever seen her go through before, all because you were careless in the moment and blanked."

Wife? I didn't know he was married. Though, given I've never asked, that's not surprising. Like a lot of us, he doesn't wear a wedding ring. It tends to make us higher-value targets.

"And what if I can't find any evidence he's done anything wrong? I might be wrong about him." Zara must have most of the equipment by now. She's probably already down at the car.

Nick shakes his head. "Slate, you are one of the most ruthless investigators I've ever seen. The way you broke down that poor ride-share owner just to get a look at his files? Brutal. The point is, if the evidence is there, you'll find it. I know you will. And I trust in your theories because they usually turn out to be right, even if your actions surrounding them aren't."

Wow, talk about a backhanded compliment.

"You think I don't already know what you and Foley are planning? I used to see that look in your eye when we worked together. You're going to stake him out. What I'm saying is as soon as you have the evidence you need for a warrant, a search, anything, you call and relay it to me and get out of there."

"And you'll call in the cavalry while taking all the credit," I say.

"Those are the terms." I make a disgusted face. "Oh, come on, like you've ever cared about who gets credit for what before anyway. You're all 'Ms. High and Mighty', defender of truth and the public trust."

"It's not the credit I care about," I reply. "I couldn't give two shits whose name goes on the board. It's the underhanded way in which you're going about it that bothers me."

"Well," he says, taking another sip from his mug. "I guess life just isn't going to be fair to either of us today. Either get me what I want, or I go straight to Janice in the morning."

He turns, walking away and whistling at the same time. I just want to put my fist through the back of his skull. Or give him a good roundhouse kick, right to the kidney where he got shot. That would take him down for a week.

My phone buzzes in my pocket. *You coming?* Zara asks.

Shit. Now what do I do? There's a good chance I might not find any evidence on Krauss. It's still possible, however unlikely, that Federico is the culprit. But my gut tells me different.

Still...I'm not sure I can ask Zara to take that risk. Knowing about the pictures is one thing, but if I can't find anything, and Nick goes to Janice, we're both on the hook. She won't differentiate between us. And despite what Zara told me, I can't flush her life down the toilet because of my bad choices. I have to do better by her.

I sigh, heading down to the parking garage. This isn't going to be a fun conversation.

Chapter Twenty-Eight

HANNAH HAS LEARNED TO BE A GOOD GIRL.

Those are the words he uses: *good girl*. Like she's a dog. Though, given the treatment she's received, that's not far off.

The days have continued to run together, and she has no idea how long she's been here. It feels like a month, but she knows that's not possible because she hasn't had her period yet. She was due in two and a half weeks. Given the fact it hasn't happened means only a week or two has passed since she's been in this room, even though it feels like much longer. Without any daylight to regulate her body, she's taken to sleeping in fits, only getting a few hours at a time, despite the bed being more than comfortable.

Though she has to admit, she's looked at those sheets differently these past few days. Instead of using them for their intended purpose, she now sees them as a possible way out. A last resort, if she needs it.

She hates how fearful she's become; how withdrawn. She recalls thinking this place was better than dealing with Alonzo; that she was safe from him here. She now sees how naïve and foolish that was. She would face ten Alonzo's if it meant she could get out of this place.

But she's trapped here. With no way out. She's fought back, refused everything and none of it has worked. If she acts up too much he just shuts the lights off and lets her sit in darkness for a while. It's strange what total darkness will do to a person. The complete absence of sensory inputs. In here she can't hear anything, smell anything...so when the lights are out, she's left with little more than touch. Moving around the rooms to touch everything is all that keeps her from losing it.

She's had the lights cut out on her twice now, and she's learned how to avoid it. First, she must act in a pleasant and submissive manner, at all times. Because even when the wall is solid, he's still watching. She can't act unappreciative, even though all she wants to do is bash this man's face in. She does it over and over in her mind, many times a day.

Second, she must engage in active conversation during their shared meal times. She must be animated, nonchalant, like she doesn't have a care in the world. And she must act interested in his life, asking questions about his days and providing him comfort when he needs it.

Third, she must completely—and this is important—embody the persona of *Lisa*. She must respond to the name as if it's her own, and she must act as if she and her tormentor have known each other a long time. She still has no idea who Lisa is, as it would be counterintuitive to ask about her "self", however she's figured out she is someone important to this man. Whoever he is, he cares for this Lisa very much. As long as she inhabits this role, she is relatively safe.

Thank God she took some theater in college. She should have seen it earlier, the need for her to be someone she wasn't. But the strange thing is he hasn't tried to come into her room or bring her out to his. He likes the separation between them, at least for now. Or perhaps he suspects she's not fully committed to the role yet. Maybe once she managed to convince him, he'll take things to the next level.

That will be her chance.

But what if it never comes? What if he decides to keep her in this box forever? Theoretically, she has everything she needs to survive long-term in here, given the food continues to arrive on schedule. But she also wonders what would happen if she just refused to play along. Other than the sensory deprivation, what other steps would he take? Would he feed her an IV if she stopped eating? Would he restrain her if she attempted to harm herself?

What lengths would he go to in order to keep her alive?

She still doesn't know why he chose her, or what significance she plays in his life. After mulling it over for what feels like a week, she can't come up with any instance in which she's met this man before. He's a freak, a total stranger, who stole her off the street to have her perform in this little game.

Hannah can't stay here forever. Eventually she's going to crack, and she knows it. She can already feel the trembling of her hands when they eat together.

In fact, they're doing it right now.

"You're quiet this evening," he says, taking a bite of his steak.

Hannah looks down at the half-eaten plate of food in front of her. She hasn't had an appetite since she arrived here, other than after her self-imposed fast failed rather quickly. Somehow she manages to produce a rueful smile for him. "I'm just not feeling that well, sorry."

He snaps to attention. "Are you sick?"

She waves him off. "No, nothing like that. I just haven't felt well all day. I think I may just need some rest."

"Lis, if it's something serious, I have plenty of medicines. Just tell me what you need."

About five hundred milligrams of cyanide would do the trick, she thinks. But instead she grins at him again. "No, really, I'm fine. I don't want you to worry. I'm sure I'll feel better tomorrow." This is a "dinner" meal, which means it must be evening. She is only served food like this for dinner. Her next meal will be pancakes and eggs. A morning meal.

"Okay," he says, sounding disappointed. She hates when he does that. He makes it seem like she's the one hurting *his* feelings. She's the one locked up in a room! If she could, she would reach through this glass and strangle him where he sat. "Just put your tray back at the receptacle when you're done."

"Sorry," I say again. "Sometimes I just can't control it."

He huffs, like he'd hoped this evening would have gone better. Instead, he pushes his own plate away. "It's fine. I'll see you tomorrow. Feel better."

She's just able to watch him stand just before the wall shimmers back to opaque again and the small light comes on the camera in the corner. Hannah picks up the tray of food and deposits it at the receptacle beside the door which will take it and spin it back to the outside. She's wondered about that receptacle, thinking it might be the means of her escape, but it's much too thin for her to fit under. A cat might be able to make it, but a human? No way.

She's barely halfway back to the bed when the lights shut off and she's plunged into darkness.

Son of a bitch is throwing a tantrum, she thinks. Even though she can feel the anxiety creeping up her spine, she forces herself to remain cool. This is what she's been waiting for.

Reaching through her collar, she manages to unclasp her bra and slip her arms out without taking her dress off. Once she gets the bra free, it takes her a moment to fumble with it, though she lays down on the bed anyway with it still in her hand. Her back is to the camera, which she's sure has night vision, even though she can't prove it. But thankfully, she doesn't need to see to do what she's about to do.

She only needs to feel.

It takes her a few minutes of working the bra, but eventually she manages to wear a small hole beside the cup, exposing the underwire. It's delicate, but she manages to pull the underwire out, without snapping it. Then she goes to work on the other side, extracting the other one in exactly the same way.

Once they're in hand, she allows the bra to fall to the ground, feeling for the flat edge of the first wire. It's thick enough for her purposes, she thinks. Though she's never tried anything like this before.

Using the other end as a fulcrum, she manages to bend and fashion one end of the second wire in a jagged pattern. It's not perfect, but it will have to do.

It takes her about fifteen minutes, but once she's finished, she slips back over to the door, reaching down and pretending to take items off the tray. If he's watching, he'll think she decided she was hungry again after all. But really, she feels around for the protrusion of the deadbolt. She slips the first wire with the long, flat piece along the bottom, while inserting the jagged edge along the top, against the tumblers.

She has no clue if this will work, but she has to give it a try. It's all she's been thinking about for what seems like a week. She just needed the opportunity to make it happen.

Taking another piece of food from the tray, Hannah begins working the pieces of metal in the lock itself, listening for anything in the mechanism that might indicate she's succeeded. After a moment, she hears a click. Followed by another, then another. Three tumblers, all in place. Gently, she begins rotating both pieces of metal in the housing, feeling the bolt turn as she does.

She's doing everything she can to keep her clammy palms from dropping the wires, while her heart hammers in her chest. Finally, the bolt turns all the way, and clicks a final time.

She'll have to be fast. If he's watching, there's no telling how long it will take him to reach her. She needs to find the exit, and find it quick.

Hannah gently removes both of the wires, then turns the main knob of the door itself. It clicks, and turns all the way.

In an instant Hannah flings the door open and is met by

light brighter than the sun. She shields her eyes as she moves forward, her hand waving in front of her as her pupils adjust to all the extra input. Within moments she can see she's in what looks to be a concrete hallway. Down to her left are four more doors, all like hers. But to her right is an open corridor, that leads somewhere else. She dashes down the corridor, feeling the exhilaration of being able to move freely again. There are no alarms, no guards anywhere. But this feels like an underground bunker of some kind. Each opening she passes connects with another, all of them with sunken centers and a utilitarian feel.

Hannah spots a set of metal stairs, and races up them, only to encounter a second door. She tries the handle, but it's locked as well.

If she did it once, she can do it again.

Using the same technique as before, Hannah goes to work on the door, but her movements aren't as coordinated as last time. Her whole body shakes at the possibility of getting out of here. The first tumbler clicks and Hannah flinches, working on the second. She knows she doesn't have much time.

When the second tumbler falls, Hannah is yanked back by her leg, causing her to hit her face on the metal stairs. Immediately she knows she's either cracked or lost a tooth. Her mouth fills with the coppery taste of blood as she's dragged down the rest of the stairs, flailing to keep her face from hitting any more of them.

"I can't *believe* you'd do this to me!" the man roars. "After all I've done for you!" Hannah hits the concrete floor. She's so stunned, and her mouth is so sore she can barely open it, much less speak. To ask him to stop. She tries kicking at him, but he swats her leg away, pulling her back in the direction she came.

"No!" she yells, her voice muffled.

"I've tried to do everything I could for you, Lisa," the man says. "I've tired to make you comfortable while you get better.

And this is how you repay me. Were you just pretending this entire time?"

Hannah reaches up and stabs the man's hand with the end of one of her wires. He yells and drops her leg, which gives her just enough time to scramble up and start running.

"You ungrateful *whore!*" he yells, hot on her heels.

She can practically *feel* his breath on the back of her neck as she zigs and zags through the concrete supports. She cuts back just as she feels his hand slice through the air past her head. He's forced her back in the opposite direction, away from the stairs, but all that matters right now is getting away. She runs until she recognizes her surroundings; she's on the other side of the wall, in the chamber where he normally sits. Her "window" is to the right. But as she looks, she realizes there are more windows, beyond hers. Four more, in fact. She dashes forward, even though this room ends in a dead-end. There's someone else in one of the other windows, looking back at her. Someone who looks...like her.

He slams into her from behind, knocking her to the ground.

She hits the floor with an *oof*, the wires flying from her hand.

"I give you the *perfect* life here, a chance to start over, fresh. And what do you do? You try to escape?" He grabs a fist full of her hair and yanks her head up. It tears from her scalp as she cries out. "You're *never* getting away from me, do you understand? Such a disappointment. And here I thought you weren't going to give me any trouble."

He throws her back down to the ground, then gets off her, standing up. As she tries to get back up as well, he plows his foot right into her midsection, pushing all the air out of her lungs, leaving her gasping. He grabs on to her leg again, dragging her back out of the chamber. Hannah barely has time to look up and see the other woman, her hands on the glass, watching as Hannah is dragged away.

Chapter Twenty-Nine

"What happened?" Zara asks. "I thought we were all set to go show them how wrong they all are."

"We were," I reply. "But maybe we should give them a chance to interview Federico. I thought about it. Janice is right. We don't want to go antagonizing Krauss just because of my hunch. If I'm wrong, it could be disastrous for the Bureau."

Zara shakes her head. "Nope. Something's wrong with you. You never let something go once you've got your teeth in it. What's going on?"

We've been going back and forth like this ever since I came down to the garage. The problem with Zara is she knows me too well. And while I am great at pretending I'm someone I'm not, ironically I'm not that good of a liar. I really have to inhabit a role in order for it to become convincing. The "method acting" of FBI work, I suppose. But if I'm going to pull this off the way I plan, Zara can't be there, not even to watch my back. Because it's illegal. She has to have complete plausible deniability, otherwise it's like Nick said, everyone will know she helped me. Everyone will assume that already anyway, but if she's got a rock-solid alibi, they won't be able to deny it. The story will be that I went rogue all on my own.

And potentially made an enemy of a very powerful man in this town.

"I just think Janice is right, is all," I say, opening my side door and tossing my bag inside. "We can still do it tomorrow night. Just sign the stuff out for one more day. But let's give them a chance with Toscani before we go blowing it all up."

"What about all that talk, about Toscani being nothing more than a patsy for Santino's operation?" she asks. "If that's true, then Krauss is free to roam for another twenty-four hours. He could be kidnapping someone right now."

I sigh. This is more difficult than I thought. "We can't second-guess ourselves to death. That's why we have a set of procedures we follow. And right now, I agree with Janice. We should hold and see what pans out on Toscani's man. Then, if it looks like he's still lying, we start going after Krauss."

I can tell she doesn't believe a word of it from the skeptical look on her face. She's right. I never would let something this big get away from me. If there is even a small chance Krauss took Hannah, I'd much rather eliminate him as a suspect than wait another day for him to do god-knows-what to someone else. Without a ransom, we have to assume Hannah is dead. But that doesn't mean I'm about to give up on the person who took her. And thanks to Nick's ultimatum, I'm going to need to take a few risks I normally wouldn't to make sure we get the right guy.

Zara folds her arms on top of my car, looking over the roof. It's comical because she's probably on her tiptoes to do it. "So then, what? Go home? Take a bath? Open a bottle of wine?"

"Sounds nice, actually. After I pick up Timber, of course."

"Can't forget Timber," she says, staring directly into my eyes. I know what she's doing. She's looking for the unconscious tells we broadcast when we're lying. It's the same thing I look for in a suspect, or a witness to determine how much we can trust what's coming out of their mouths. It's hard to train yourself to overcome what most people would ascribe to involuntary tics, but if you know what you're doing, it can be mastered.

"Remember what I asked you?" she says, her voice serious. "About trusting me?"

"That street goes both ways," I say, watching her reaction closely. "You have to be willing to trust me too."

She bites her lower lip, pushing off from the roof of the car. "If you say so," she says. "Guess I'll go home and try to get some sleep. You want me to take all that back to tech services?" She indicates the bag she left on the ground; no doubt full of surveillance equipment.

"I'll take care of it," I say. "Enjoy your night off."

"You too," she says without an ounce of enthusiasm. She's going to be pissed at me tomorrow. Hell, she's already pissed at me right now. But I can't help that. Not when I know there's so much at stake for her. For everyone involved.

Finally Zara gets in her car and drives off, without a final wave or even a glance. I toss the bag of equipment in my backseat. Damn Nick for putting me in this position. It seems like no matter what I do, people don't seem to be able to let go of their grudges around me. I have half a mind to report him myself, for extortion. But I know he'll just bring up the illegal search and then I'm done, no matter what. An agent can't have that many strikes on their record in such a short amount of time, they just can't. No department head would look at their record and want them on their teams. Even if I were to be transferred to another field office, they'd still be able to see what I had done, and what it cost me. No one would trust me with their secrets again.

I press the ignition on my car and pull out of the spot, heading up the ramp and out into the evening. Unfortunately, because she's not an idiot, I expect Zara to be waiting out here for me, somewhere. Sure enough, after the second stoplight I spot her, five cars back. She's tailing me, determined to find out if I'm going to Krauss's place or not.

Instead, I take the exit that will take me out to Chris's house.

Fifteen minutes later, I pull into the driveway of their craftsman home. Chris and Dani renovated it themselves a few years ago when they first bought the place. Matt and I were over here almost every weekend I had free helping them with the place. It was a complete gut, start to finish, but the house is beautiful now. I check my rearview to see if Zara is still back there, but there's no sign of her. She's really getting the hang of this tailing thing. She must have pulled in somewhere back further in the neighborhood, waiting for me to come back out.

I tread up the steps to the house and knock on the door. All the lights on inside remind me of a warm embrace, almost like the house itself is alive, waiting to welcome me in.

But when the door opens I see anything but a friendly face.

"You're late," my brother-in-law says, his face drawn down. Chris is a well-built man, someone who obviously works with his hands. His hair is darker than Matt's and he has a full beard and mustache, but he keeps them short and clean.

"Can I come in a second?" I ask.

For a second I think he's going to say no, but he steps aside, allowing me inside. Timber is laying in the hallway. When he sees me, his eyes light up and he jumps up, bounding down the hallway. I crouch down and take him into my arms as his little tail about wags itself off.

"Hi buddy," I say. "I'm sorry I'm so late. It's been a hard day."

I look up to see Dani approaching with his leash in her hand. Her long, dark, curly hair frames her face well, falling down to her chest. She's not that much older than I am, but I hope to God I still look that good when I reach her age.

"Emily," she says, handing me the leash.

"Hi. Thanks." I clip it on his collar. "Did he do okay?"

"Perfect, as always." Her tone is cold, though she's not as shut off as her husband. Since Matt was his brother, I expect him to be angrier with me. But ever since it's happened, Dani has maintained a level of neutrality regarding me.

"I don't know what you have going on lately, but we're not your babysitting service," Chris says.

"I'm sorry," I say. "It's a big case. But I wanted to talk to you about something."

Chris huffs and walks past me into the kitchen, grabbing a beer from their fridge. Dani takes up one of the stools along the perfectly clean countertops. I take that as an invitation to speak.

"I know I'm not exactly welcome here," I begin, trying to maintain my composure. "But I hope that doesn't extend to Timber."

"He didn't have anything to do with it, did he?" Chris asks sarcastically, then takes a long drag from the bottle.

I shake my head. "I was just wondering…with everything going on at work lately…if you guys would agree to take Timber…in the event something happened to me."

Dani leans forward, though I can't read her expression. I want to think it's supportive, but I can't tell. She's one of those people who I believe could pass a lie-detector test without any preparation.

Chris scoffs. "What have you gotten yourself involved in now?"

"It's not about any one case in particular. But this case I've been working on, it's taking more and more of my time. And I realize I might not always be there for Timber, that it hasn't been fair to him these past few months."

"Because Matt was always there with him when you weren't," Dani says.

I nod. Chris looks like he's about to say something to his wife, but he keeps his mouth shut. Instead, he turns to me. "So...what? You want us to take him?"

"Not permanently," I say. I pull my keys out of my pocket and unlatch the spare key to my apartment. "Just...if you don't hear from me, will you come check on him? Make sure he's okay?"

"Emily, what's going on?" Dani asks. "Are you in some kind of trouble?"

I shake my head. "It's just me being cautious."

Chris eyes the key, then takes another sip. "Sure. Whatever." He pulls it across the counter and hooks it to the ring of keys hanging off the side of the refrigerator.

By my side, Timber whines. I give his head a little scratch. "I know, bud. We're going home." I turn back to my in-laws. "Thank you. Really. It means a lot knowing he'll be taken care of."

"Well, he was my brother's dog too," Chris says.

I nod, knowing they're not doing it for me. But as long as Timber is covered, that's all that matters. If something happens to me at Krauss's place tonight, or I'm hauled in and arrested by my own Bureau tomorrow, it's a small relief to know my dog will be okay.

I take him by the leash and lead him to the door. But before I reach it, I hear footsteps behind me. I turn to find Dani, holding herself across the chest.

"We could take him, you know," she says. "On a permanent basis."

I pull my features into a frown. "Thank you, but I don't think that's necessary."

"Think about it," Dani says before I can grab the door handle. "You said yourself you work strange hours. He needs consistency, a routine. He needs to know you're coming home every night. He's already lost Matt."

I shake my head. I wanted to make sure he was taken care of, not have him taken away from me. "Thanks, but we'll be okay, at least for a little while."

"I know why you don't want to let him go," Dani says, stepping forward and speaking a little louder. Her features soften again. "He's your last connection to your husband. I get it. But you have to think about what's best for him. Not for you."

I thought I was already doing that by asking them to take care of him when I couldn't. Maybe she's right. My job isn't the kind that has a lot of routine. Sometimes I have to go to work in the middle of the night. Often I'm gone all day. It's not like that for every agent, but it is for me. Probably because if I had to sit around my house any more than I already do I think I'd go crazy.

"Thanks, Dani," I say. "I'll see you later."

I leave her standing there in her doorway as I make my way down to my car with Timber by my side. I think I see the flash of movement somewhere down the street, but I can't be sure.

Once he's in the passenger seat, I head for home, keeping an eye out for Zara's tail but seeing nothing. I try not to think too much about Dani's offer. I can't give this dog up, not now. If I had to come home to an empty apartment every day…I would lose my mind. Truly.

Another fifteen minutes later and I pull into my complex, parking beside my building. I can't tell if Zara is still out there or not, but I'm going to assume she is. Between her and my encounter with my in-laws just now, my stress is at about its max.

We get inside and I quickly change into something darker and more utilitarian. If I'm going to find the evidence I need, which means I need to find Hannah, I'll need to move swiftly and quietly. And thanks to Zara's studiousness, I have an entire bag full of goodies at my disposal.

I make sure Timber is settled in his bed with a bully stick to chew on. He should be good for the night with that thing. I give him a kiss on the top of his flat little head before flipping off the main lights, leaving just my lamps illuminated.

I head back down to my car, checking the time. It's close to ten-thirty. If Zara is still out here, she's been waiting almost two hours. I could wait longer, but I've already got a forty-minute drive ahead of me and there's no telling how long it's going to take to get into Krauss's place.

Keeping to the shadows, I make it to my car and turn it on without turning on the lights. I pull the car around the side of the building, next to the service entrance, which is off the cross street, not the main entrance on Davidson. There's never any traffic on this street, not even parked cars. Which is good news, because it doesn't give Zara anywhere to hide. More than likely she's staked out the main entrance, waiting for me to leave.

"Going somewhere?"

I nearly yell out, spinning and going for my weapon at the same time. She's standing off in the shadow, right in the spot where I can't see her, arms crossed and leaning up against part of the fence that surrounds my place.

I take a few deep breaths, willing my heart rate to come back down. "You are too smart for your own good," I say.

"I have to admit, it was a pretty good ruse. Picking up Timber, driving home, turning off the lights like you were really done for the night. Had I not known you better, I would have been convinced."

"Zara—" I begin.

"Don't even start," she says, stepping out of the shadows. "We had a deal. You weren't going to lie to me anymore."

"You're right, we did have a deal," I reply. "But that was

before Nick threatened my job if I didn't get the evidence on Krauss for him so he can look like the hero."

"Wait," she says. "He did *what?*"

I give her the brief overview of our discussion from earlier that evening, all the while watching her grow angrier and angrier.

"That little prick," she says, once I'm done. "I'm going straight to Janice in the morning. He's extorting you."

"For good reason," I say. "Misappropriation of federal resources is a big deal. Especially when it's coming internally."

"Not with this it's not. He can't get away with that," she says.

"I don't see I have much choice. And at the moment, it aligns with my goals. We find out if Krauss is really our man or not. I just have to deal with a little backstabbing in the process."

Zara shakes her head. "Okay. Well, I get why you didn't tell me *now*. But still. I'm not letting you go out there by yourself. What are you planning to do to obtain this evidence?"

I sigh. I guess I don't have much of a choice but to tell her. "Break into Krauss's house. See if I can find any evidence of Hannah."

Zara breaks out laughing, almost doubling over.

"What's so funny?"

"Break into someone's house? You? You're not a cat burglar, you know. You're more like…a raging bull. Not to mention Krauss probably has a pretty intense security system. You're going to need some equipment if you want to pull that off. How were you planning on getting in?"

I shrug. "I was just going to wing it."

"In true Emily Slate style," she says, grinning. "First, I can't let you commit an illegal entry because Nick Hogan says so." She pulls out her phone, showing me what look like blueprints. "See this? I had to do some serious digging to find it. It's the construction documents from when Krauss built his home. I don't know about you, but this looks like some kind of holding facility." She zooms in and shows me some additional details, though I have to admit I have a pretty hard time reading blueprints. "Could be nothing more than an elaborate sex room, but—"

"—but it could also give us probable cause," I finish.

She nods. "Yep. Second, you're gonna need something a little more off-book to get into a place like that. Fortunately for you, I know a guy who can help us out with some additional equipment. An old contact back from my analyst days."

"Contact?" I ask.

"One of the people I'd often call when agents in the field needed some less-than-legal equipment. We get requests for it more often than you think." She walks over to the car's passenger door. "Unless I'm still not welcome."

I shake my head. "What would I do without you?"

"Dead or in jail," she says, not missing a beat. "Probably jail."

Chapter Thirty

"OKAY," I SAY, LOOKING THROUGH THE NIGHT VISION GOGGLES at Krauss's house. "You weren't kidding about this guy. He's got a concrete fence about eight feet high that surrounds the grounds. Bordered by trees on both sides."

"That's not a problem," Zara replies. "I'm more worried about what we'll find on the other side of that fence." She turns to me.

We're perched on a small hill about twenty meters away from Krauss's house, which sits close to the edge of the water. He's got a massive amount of land out here, almost an entire peninsula to himself. There's a lot of open ground between us and where we need to be. Thankfully there's only a crescent moon tonight, and a bit of cloud cover so we won't be totally exposed.

"Did you ever think you'd be sneaking around like this in the FBI?" Zara whispers as she gathers up her backpack. "I mean, normally, we just go up and knock."

"Not an option in this case," I say. "If there's even a possibility that he's got Hannah and those other women in there and they aren't dead yet, I don't want him to take them out in some last-ditch effort. We need to find evidence that they are there, then we take him into custody."

"Yeah, and fuck Nick Hogan and his ultimatums." She gives me a reassuring nod. I'm not sure what's going to happen with Nick, but I know capturing Krauss is more important than what happens to me or anyone else at the Bureau. We'll call in backup as soon as we confirm Krauss is our man.

"Okay, let's head down there," Zara whispers.

I deactivate the goggles and slip them up off my head. My pack is full of equipment we may need to get into Krauss's house. Since we don't know exactly what we're dealing with, Zara got a little bit of everything. I obtained the satellite photo of his home, but that's about all the information we had beforehand, other than what Zara dug up. We're going way off-book here, though I'm not worried about the local P.D. showing up. I'm more worried about what Krauss might do when he figures out we're snooping around his house.

We both keep low and run through the tall grass from the edge of the clearing to the base of the trees that make up the outer section of one of Krauss's walls. Zara turns me around and opens my pack, pulling out a long, metal contraption. Above us, the wall is about eight feet high, with no handholds anywhere.

As I'm standing there, Zara begins extending the device she pulled from my pack. It starts as an extendable pole, but then I see little ledges flip down from the body of the pole itself. When it reaches its full height, it's about six and a half feet tall. She leans it up against the wall. "After you."

"A portable ladder?" I ask. "How do you know about all this stuff?"

"When you're stuck at a desk all day, dreaming about doing *anything* else, you find yourself looking at a lot of different things online," she says. "Now get up there."

I climb the rungs with ease, which allow me to push myself up on top of the concrete wall. Zara is right behind me, and I take her hand to hoist her all the way up. She brings the ladder with her and collapses it back down. "For getting back up if we have to get out of here unnoticed," she says, putting it back in my pack.

The only reason we'd need to leave unnoticed is if we don't find anything. That'll be the worst-case scenario, given what could happen if Krauss finds two FBI agents sneaking around like a couple of cat burglars in his house. But come hell or high water, we're doing it together.

I hang down off the edge of the wall, then drop the additional three feet to the ground. Zara does the same and we crouch down, staring at our target. "Here," I say, pulling a pair of nitrite gloves out of my pocket and handing them to her. I put on a second pair. The last thing I want to do is leave fingerprints.

The house is long and flat, and very modern by design. There's not a pitched roof in sight. Instead, clean lines, large windows and sharp angles make up Douglas Krauss's home. The number of windows is good on one hand, as they allow us to see a lot of the inside. But they'll be a problem once we get in there and want to remain unseen. Lights are on all over the place, though I don't see Krauss anywhere.

"This guy isn't social and he should live alone, so we probably won't encounter anyone else," I tell Zara. "Do you see anything concerning?"

She's looking at the house using a small scope. "I only see two…wait, three motion sensors. No cameras though, which is strange. I think if we stay close to the wall and move around to the back, we'll be out of their range." I nod and follow her so that we stay between the trees on this side and the concrete wall.

Around back, Krauss has a large swimming pool, and a small maintenance building off to the side. The pool deck is lit up with accent lighting, though there's no one outside. "Hang on," I whisper to Zara. I make my way over to the maintenance building, finding it unlocked. Inside are just a bunch of pipes and pumps. All to control the pool.

"Nothing," I say when I get back to her. "Let's keep moving."

She nods and we make our way across the backyard, staying in the shadows as much as possible. Zara is checking all the angles for any motion sensors, but I assume she doesn't see any as we don't stop anywhere. We reach one of the back doors, which happens to be all glass. There's a small lock built into the metal frame.

From this angle, if anyone were to walk into the living room, which is what is on the other side of the back ceiling-to-floor windows, they'd see us immediately. I peer into the room, spotting a small box with a flashing light near the ceiling. "Is that what I think it is?"

Zara is pulling a small case out of her pack when she looks up. "Yep. Monitoring station." She digs in the pack some more. "Here, get ready to use this." She hands me a small, black device with an orange button on it while she uses a keyset on the lock itself. In less than ten seconds, she has it unlocked. "Get ready to push and hold that button," she says.

I nod. She motions and I push and hold. Zara slides the back door open and crouch-walks in. I follow and she closes the door behind us. She motions that I can take my finger off the button. "What is this?" I whisper.

"A radio frequency jammer," she says. "Uses the same frequency as those." She points to the still-blinking station over the door.

"Let's get started," I say. "The quicker, the better." More than likely Krauss is asleep in his bedroom. I pray the proof we need isn't in there. We're both on the lookout for any cameras Krauss might be using inside the house, but I don't immediately see any. It doesn't really surprise me, considering those cameras can be easily hacked. Krauss doesn't want anyone else looking in on what he's doing, which makes me even more certain he is our guy.

The house is spotless and minimalist in nature. He doesn't seem to have anything that's out of place, and no clutter anywhere. Instead, every surface is clean and what little he does have is organized. I don't see a personal or family photo anywhere. The only things up on the walls are art pieces.

As I make my way into the kitchen, it's as immaculate as the rest of the house. The cabinets are all modern, without any handles or hardware, and the counter is a smooth, solid piece of marble that goes all the way to the floor. It seems Krauss has a flair for fancy décor. But walking through this house, it comes across more like a museum than a home.

I meet back up with Zara near the back door where we came in. "Anything?"

She shakes her head. "The place is clean as far as I can tell. But I have three closed doors down on that side of the house. I wanted to meet back up with you before we decided to go in."

Smart. In the event Krauss is behind one of those doors, sleeping, it's better we're together. I can't help but think about just how crazy this is. But I know Federico isn't our guy. He never was. It's this man, who managed to break into *Ryde 4 Lyfe* and delete his own record.

"Wait," I whisper. "This guy is a computer whiz, so where's the computer?" I haven't even seen so much as a cell phone charging cord in this place. "We're missing something big."

Zara motions for me to follow her to the doors. One is at the beginning of a long hall that heads down the east end of the house, while the other two are at the far end. I unclip my service weapon and motion for her to open the first door. She does and I make a quick peek around the corner only to see nothing but darkness. No windows in the room at all. I pull out the goggles again and put them on, only to find it's not a room, but a staircase leading to the basement.

I give her the signal to follow me, quietly. Thankfully, this house doesn't seem that old so it doesn't have all the creaks and sounds a settled house would have. The stairs make a ninety-degree turn halfway down, which leads us into the room below. I search for a switch, finding it and turning off the goggles before I flick it.

"Huh," Zara says, her voice still hushed. "I was expecting something…more scandalous than just a game room."

A pool table dominates the front part of the basement, while a large television and a leather couch sit off to the side. Compared to the museum upstairs, this is the coziest part about this house. There's even a makeshift bar over beside one wall, complete with a couple of stools.

I look around, my hands on my hips. "So where's the sex dungeon?" I ask.

"Yeah…I'm not sure." She pulls her phone out and begins examining the blueprints again.

"This doesn't look anything like the house upstairs. It looks like two different people designed these places. Doesn't this basement strike you as small for the size of the house upstairs?" The room itself is barely as large as the whole kitchen.

"Yeah," she says. "You're right. None of this matches the original documents, there has to be more somewhere."

"And they wouldn't have poured a concrete slab, just to dig this part out," I say. "For someone who has a ton of money at his disposal, this is downright pitiful for a game space."

We take our time going over every inch of the room, looking for anything Krauss might have hidden. I'm wary, given the fact I still haven't seen any evidence of his equipment. I also feel like this is taking too long. I don't know how light a sleeper Krauss might be or if he's even up there at all.

"Hey, Em," Zara says. She motions over by the bar. She's

pulled back the rug that covered the space between the bar itself and the back wall. Underneath is what looks like a hatch of some kind. "Secret entrance?" She grins.

I can't see that it's anything else. And whatever is down there, Krauss definitely doesn't want people to find. My pulse is racing.

"Open it," I say.

Chapter Thirty-One

ZARA LIFTS UP ON THE SMALL RING SET INTO THE HATCH ITSELF and it swings up, revealing another staircase, descending even further.

"Whoa," she says. "Cool."

"How deep does this house go?" I ask. "We have to be at the water table by now, right?"

"Doesn't look wet down there to me," she says. This stairwell is different than the other one. It's completely poured out of concrete, with small lights inset into the walls as the stairs descend. "Whatever is down there, it's not looking too good for Krauss."

"No, it's not," I say, taking the lead. The stairs take us down another level, into what I can only describe as an antechamber. Here, a large, metal door with a keypad sits in the middle of a concrete wall. The only other thing in the room is an old wooden chair off to the side. For some reason the chair creeps me out more than the door does.

"You were right, Em. This guy definitely has something going on. No one good keeps an underground bunker like this."

I survey the room and spot a camera in the upper right-hand corner. But I don't see a light or anything to indicate it's active. "We need to hurry. We might be visible. Can you get inside that thing?"

"Give me just a minute," she says, pulling out a small electronic box. She sets it on top of the keypad and toggles the switch on the side. "I kinda feel like Batman right now."

"If I'd known you had access to so much illegal technology I would have quit years ago. We could have just robbed a bank or something. Set ourselves up for life."

The machine on top of the keypad beeps, showing a sequence of numbers. Zara enters the sequence and the bolt on the door slides, allowing us to open it. I pull out my weapon, ready for anything.

On the other side of the door is a metal staircase, leading even further down. But this space is much larger, with higher ceilings. And the entire place is made out of concrete. Pillars form the basis of the large room, sectioning it off into smaller rooms. The entire place is lit with florescent lighting.

"Definitely not a sex dungeon," Zara says behind me.

When we reach the bottom of the short stairs, I look down, noting a crimson stain on the ground. "Look at this." I crouch, looking at the stain, and realize there is something small under the stairs. I reach in and pull it out. "Shit."

"That's a tooth," Zara says.

"Get an evidence bag," I say. It's not conclusive, but it's a step in the right direction. There's nothing to say this isn't Krauss's tooth, but a quick check with his dentist would reveal if he'd ever come in with any missing teeth. Unfortunately, that will have to wait until tomorrow.

I slip the tooth into the evidence bag and seal it, tucking it in my pack. A couple more crimson stains lead off in one direction. We follow them, only for them to abruptly end.

"Something bad happened here," I say.

"Hey, Em," Zara says. She's over on the far left side of the room, beside another metal door. Except this one doesn't have a lock. She tries it, and it opens to reveal what looks like a command center of sorts.

There's a desk in the middle of the room, with a dozen different monitors, all showing different parts of the house. "He *does* have cameras," I say. But either he wasn't watching, or us being in the home didn't set off any additional systems. But five of the screens show rooms we haven't seen yet. Each one identical, and all look like they have the lights off as we're seeing the rooms in the green of night vision.

In each room is a woman, all of varying ages as far as I can tell. Three are on their respective beds, one is on the floor and the other is standing, up against the side of the room, her ear pressed to the wall.

"Holy shit," I say. "We found them."

"Can you tell which one is Hannah?" Zara asks.

I can't. All the women look eerily similar. A couple of the other monitors show programs running, but I don't recognize any of them. "Does any of this make sense to you?"

Zara sits in the chair, inspecting the monitors. "I've never seen anything like this before. These must be programs he's developed for himself. Maybe to control what goes on in those rooms? I'm seeing temperature controls, light levels, humidity, and a few other things I don't recognize."

"He's got them caged up, like his own personal zoo," I say. That's when my eyes land on the only personal photograph I've seen since entering this house. It's a portrait of a young woman, long blonde hair, blue eyes. If I didn't know better, I'd say she was Hannah Stewart's sister. "Who is this?"

"Em, we need to call for backup," Zara says. "We've got him. Cold."

I nod, pulling out my phone. But unsurprisingly, there's no service. "I think we're too far underground. We need to get back up to the top level."

"And we need to get them out of there," she says. "Look at this one, on the ground. She doesn't look too good." It's hard to tell, but I think she's right. The woman isn't moving, and it seems like she's laying at a strange angle.

"Where are these rooms?" I ask.

"Probably somewhere down here, in this little maze he's built. But good luck getting into them."

"Can you do it?" I ask. "Can you find a way to unlock the cells so we can get them out of here?"

She shakes her head. "Maybe. But this is Aruz all over again. Without a key, I may not be able to do anything."

"Get working on it," I say. "I'll head back up to call for backup. Get those doors open. And keep your safety off. If anyone comes in here but me, you know what to do."

Zara gives me a strange look, but pulls out her weapon and sets it on the desk beside her, then turns back to the terminals. I head back out to the main chamber, looking around for what might be the rooms, but the place is such a maze that it would take me ten minutes just not to get turned around. I head back to the metal staircase and exit through the door to the antechamber. Unfortunately, my phone still doesn't have any bars. I head back up to the "basement" level through the trap door. Thankfully, when I make it into the room, one bar appears on my phone. I keep an eye on the staircase, just in case Krauss decides to come down.

"I actually didn't think you'd call," Nick says on the other end.

"Not now, Hogan," I say. "We've got—"

I feel him before I see him.

The hair on the back of my neck stands up and I instinctively turn, only for a syringe to plunge into the side of my neck. "Ack—" is all I'm able to get out as I try to knock it away, though I know it's too late. It's one of those fast-delivery syringes, shooting the entire dosage into me all at once. I catch sight of Krauss's face and raise my weapon, only for him to knock it out of my hand. It seems like I'm moving in slow motion, and I find I'm much too concerned with where he came from than the fact I'm rapidly losing consciousness. I don't even know where my phone is anymore, but I can feel the darkness pressing in on my vision and I do everything I can to keep myself up. But each time I blink, I feel my world growing smaller. I fall to one knee, then collapse back, looking up at the ceiling tiles of this shitty basement he's got set up. Krauss's face comes right into my view just as I close my eyes.

Chapter Thirty-Two

THE PAIN IS WHAT WAKES ME. IT BEGINS AS A DULL ACHE, pulling me from an unconscious state. But as my body slowly begins to work again, I find I can lift my head, only to realize my legs and arms are strapped down to a chair. Strangely, the image of Federico goes through my mind.

I open my eyes and blink a few times, realizing I'm back down in the sub-basement. Nothing but concrete floors, pillars and walls. Though I'm in a different part than I was before. To my right are a series of "walls", though they're not actually walls. Instead, they're windows, each looking into a different room. And in four of those rooms, women stand beyond the glass, staring back at me. These are the kidnapped women. And strangely, they all look very similar, though some are younger than others.

"Impressive, isn't it?" a voice asks.

I turn my head, something that causes a headache to erupt in my brain and I'm forced to close my eyes again until it begins to subside.

"That's the edetate disodium," he says. He has a smooth voice. Unassuming. Not overly cocky or elitist. A voice of someone you wouldn't think twice about. "It will wear off in a few minutes." I look to my left to see Zara, bound to another chair. The chair we passed out in the antechamber. She isn't moving. But I can see the subtle rise and fall of her chest. At least she's not dead. He probably hit her with the same cocktail he used on me. How long have I been out?

"Krauss," I say, my throat sore and my voice sounding like it's been through a wood chipper. "Give up. It's over."

"That'd be convenient for you, wouldn't it, Agent Slate?" he asks.

"How do you know my name?"

"I know more than your name," he replies, crouching down in front of me. "I know your address, your phone number, the names of everyone in your family. I know your mother died when you were twelve, and your father passed just a few years ago. I know you've been with the FBI for four years, and that you were suspended four months ago for improper conduct on the job. I know you have a pit bull you rescued from a dog fighting ring. And I know up until three months ago, you had a husband."

"How—" I begin, but before I can finish, he shows me his phone. On it, is a picture of me, from earlier in the evening, when Zara and I had just entered the house. It's a clear shot of my face, when I was sure he wasn't watching. Below my picture continues to scroll strings and strings of biographical information. There's more information on his phone than is collected anywhere else, including my own computer at home. "You broke into the FBI's system," I say. "It's a back door."

He barks out a laugh. "You wish. The system I sold the FBI is a toned-down version of the one I built for myself. Using a complex algorithm which scours the internet for any and all information on a person, I am able to build a complete biographical profile off of nothing but a picture. Here." He walks over to Zara and lifts her head, snapping a picture of her face. He turns the phone toward me and a second later, information begins to populate, showing Zara's address, her contact information and all her background biographical information.

"You built that? Why?" I ask.

"You already have the answer," he says, then points to the rooms on my right. I look at each of the four women, they're all watching me, intently. On the floor of the fifth room, I can see the woman's immobile body.

"That's how you located them," I say. "You saw them, didn't you? And then you took their picture, used it to find out their habits, and abducted them. But what did you do to them? They don't look like they used to."

"All I've done is restore them to their original looks," he replies. Each of the women now have blonde hair, though they all had blue eyes before. Something I should have picked up on. If I recall their case files we suspected could be connected, only one was a blonde originally.

"What the hell is this, Krauss?" I ask. "What are you doing with these women?"

"You know," he says, standing back up and slipping his phone in his pocket. "I've never had anyone else down here before. Not anyone who was ever on this side, with me, I mean. And now I've got two of you, and nowhere to put you."

"You're going to let us go," I say. "We're federal agents. And I've already notified my team. They're on their way."

He shakes his head. "Do you really think they're coming? I managed to scramble the GPS signal in your phone before it was too late. They'll have a fifty square mile area they'll have to search before they find this place. And even when they do, they'll never find you down here."

"We found our way down here," I say. "It honestly wasn't that hard."

I see his face falter for a moment, the illusion that he's untouchable gone for a brief instant before it's back again, with a vengeance. "And I watched you the entire way," he replies. "Imagine my surprise when I find what I think are two cat burglars attempting to break into my house. Except they've got some heavy-duty equipment to get past my systems. That was when I knew you were special. I looked you up, and here we are."

I want to bite back, to argue with him. Nick already knows we were headed here. Even if the call didn't fully go through, he heard my voice. He'll be sending everything the FBI has. I just need to hold out until they get here.

The only problem is, I still haven't sent him any proof. Janice could still shut this whole thing down, on the account of not wanting to piss off Krauss. If she only knew what we know now. "What's the point of all this, Krauss?" I say, trying to keep him talking. My arms and legs ache like crazy, but if we're going to get out of this, I have to keep him talking.

"This?" he asks. "This is me dealing with two home intruders on my property. The State of Maryland allows for Castle Doctrine, which means I can shoot anyone who comes into my home and threatens my wellbeing."

"I *know* what it means," I say. "But you can't just kill two federal agents and think everything is going to be okay."

"I didn't know you were federal agents," he says, innocently. "You never identified yourselves to me, broke into my home, raided my things. I'm afraid I was forced to shoot to protect myself."

"Then what's the point of all this?" I ask. "Why not just shoot us as soon as you saw us?"

He seems to consider the question. "I admit I was curious. When I learned you were FBI, I knew I needed some answers from you first. So here goes. How?"

"How what?" I ask, trying to play dumb. I need to string this out as long as possible.

"How did you manage to trace everything back to me? I erased all the records, made sure I wasn't on any surveillance cameras."

"Ryde 4 Lyfe backs up their driver data at an offsite location," I say. "Their boss is a little paranoid."

He snaps his fingers, standing back up and pacing the room. "Damn. I knew I had been in that system too long. But it was necessary to establish some credibility."

"Why Hannah?" I ask. "And why these other women? What are you doing down here?"

"Don't you understand?" he asks. "They are my collection. Perfectly curated. Though, I'll admit, one of my pieces was recently damaged. Unfortunately for me, it's the most valuable piece. If I can't repair her, I'll have to find a replacement." He gives me a curious look, like he's sizing me up. And as he gets closer, I can smell his aftershave. I try to pull away from him, but being bound to the chair limits my options.

"You'd never work," he says. "Face structure is all wrong. The hair we can fix, but everything else is off." He turns to Zara. "Too small. Neither of you are of high enough quality. Which means I don't have a place for you in the collection."

He turns and begins walking away. I don't like how ominous those words sounded. He doesn't even see us as people. Instead, he sees us as some kind of specimens for his display and amusement. "Wait," I call out. He stops. "Tell me about your...collection. When will you ever have another chance?"

He considers it, then turns back. "I'm not stupid, Agent Slate. Your attempts to stall me are futile at best."

"But it's like you said," I say, silently willing Zara to wake up. "You'll never have anyone down here again. What is a collection if you can't show it off to someone?"

He gives me another one of those curious looks. This is a man who likes for other people to be impressed by his accomplishments, though he pretends to remain humble. He gets off on people talking about him and saying that he doesn't do interviews, that instead he works hard for the betterment of humanity, instead of basking in the spotlight. But there is one spotlight he can't resist, and that's the one he can't tell anyone about. "That's just the thing, though. This isn't for anyone else; this is specifically for me."

"Still," I say. "You must take some pride in having curated it to this level so far."

"It wasn't easy," he replies. "I had to create the software just to obtain the first piece."

"How long have you been...collecting?" I ask.

"Roughly two years," he replies.

I honestly can't believe what I'm seeing down here. Some of these women have been down here *two years*? I look back over at them. None seem to be in bad shape, in fact, they all look very healthy.

"You take good care of your...pieces," I say.

"I have to, if I want them to last," he replies. "It's important to keep them in optimal condition. If a piece begins to deteriorate, then it risks falling out of the collection."

I look at each of the faces of the women, all of them watching us, watching *me*. Some of these women probably haven't seen another person, other than Krauss for a long time. I recall the picture I saw in the control room. Finally, it falls into place. "They are all...they're your sister, Lisa." I hadn't seen a picture of her in Krauss's file, because we just hadn't gone that deep on him yet. But I knew he lost his sister a few years back.

"Very good, Agent Slate," he replies. "You have a keen observational mind."

"But..." I say, turning back to him. "Why five of them? If you were looking to replace Lisa, why not just one?"

"Lisa is the most fascinating, complex person I have ever known," he says. It doesn't escape my attention that he's using the present tense. "She's a multi-faceted jewel, someone who cannot be defined by just one characteristic. Or one season. Each piece in the collection represents Lisa in all the different ways I know her." He walks over to the first window, where the youngest of the women looks back out. She can't be older than seventeen, at best. "This is her inquisitive phase, where she has an insatiable lust for knowledge." He walks to the next. She seems to be about nineteen, maybe twenty. "This is her prim phase, where she becomes more concerned with how people see her than how she sees the world. This is a difficult time for her." He seems particularly proud of this one and hangs on a moment before moving to the third window. This woman is in her late twenties, early thirties. "This is her maturing phase, where she puts all she has learned to good use and builds a life." He walks to the final window. A woman who is almost forty looks back at us. "This is her ascension phase, or the last phase of her life. As I've most recently known her." Finally, he walks to the last window, where no one looks back. "This is supposed to be her rebellious phase, where she breaks free of the constraints of the world and goes out to meet new challenges. But I'm a bit embarrassed, as the piece is no longer fit for viewing at this time."

"Why?" I ask. "What happened?"

"Not your concern," he replies, walking past me back toward the control room. "Though you were right, Agent Slate. I did enjoy showcasing my collection for you. It's just too bad you won't be around very long to enjoy it as much as I have."

"That last phase," I call out. "That was how she was when she died, wasn't it?" He stops, and turns again, his eyes burning with anger.

"What is wrong with you?" he spits. "She is *right there!*" He points to the windows.

"Listen to me Krauss," I say. "I know what it's like to lose someone you love. You know I know what it's like. My husband has only been gone four months and to be honest I don't know how I get out of bed most days. To have lived with this pain for years…it's almost unimaginable to me. But you've done it."

"My sister isn't *dead*," he says, vitriol coloring his words. "She's *there*, preserved. A perfect specimen." He glances over at the windows, but I see the briefest hint of a falter in his eyes. Part of him knows it's all an illusion, a mind game he's playing with himself.

"You and I are the same," I say. "We are both trying to deal with this grief in the best way we know how. You are trying to keep your sister alive by surrounding yourself with different versions of her. But you know in your heart none of them are really her. You'd have to combine all five of those women into one person to equal your sister. Me, on the other hand, I'm risking my job, my friends, maybe even my freedom to find out who took my husband from me. We're both obsessed with this idea that we can't let our loved ones go. But we have to."

He looks at me, earnestness in his eyes. "I feel for your plight, Agent Slate. But you and I are not the same. Your husband is dead. My sister is very much alive, right there. Right where I can always see her. Where I'll always be able to see her."

He walks over to a table where he has all our equipment laid out. It seems he's removed everything from our packs, including our phones and our weapons. But he's far enough away that I can at least try to wake Zara.

I attempt to shift my chair, only to find it's in some kind of groove in the floor, which means I can't move it without getting up. I try to reach over with my hand or my leg, but the ropes around them are too tight. Zara is too far away.

"Zara, c'mon, wake up," I whisper. But she's not moving. I tug on my restraints, pulling against the wood boards of the chair as hard as I can. I think I start to feel one of the arms give when Krauss takes another syringe from the table and walks back over to me.

"As much as I'd like to shoot you here and be done with it, I have to get you back upstairs first," he says. "They need to find you right inside the door, where I'll confess to shooting two intruders out of self-defense." I know if he manages to stick me with that needle, I'm never waking up again. I can't let that happen. I flex every muscle I can at once and use all the strength in my body to pitch myself forward, pulling the chair up out of the groove in the floor just as Krauss goes to jab me with the needle.

The surprise move causes him to jump back out of the way as I crash to the floor, face down, hitting my face on the concrete. It sends a shockwave of pain through me, though I realize the force of the abrupt stop has loosened the arm on the old chair. I wrench the entire arm of the chair off just as I flop to the side, catching Krauss off-guard again. He's got a determined look in his eye as he attempts to jab me in the side, but I strike his hand with the wooden board that is still attached to my arm.

Krauss drops the syringe as he yelps in pain, cradling his hand. Using my free hand, I manage to loosen the restraints on my other arm enough to pull it out from under the ropes. With both hands free, I try to grapple my way across the floor with my legs still attached to the chair.

He sees I'm going for the syringe and Krauss runs over, trying to pick it up first. I swing my legs around and hit him with both them and the chair, knocking his legs out from under him and sending him down to the concrete. His head bounces off the ground and his eyes flutter, but they're still open. My legs are now pinned under Krauss and it's all I can do to continue clawing my way to the syringe. He moans and turns over, his legs flopping off the chair and I find I have some more freedom of movement, but not much. The syringe is too far away for me to grab, so I start working on my legs, trying to unbind the ropes holding them there.

"Zara!" I yell. "Zara, wake *up*!" Even in my manic state I still think about how she's only here because of me, and that we're both in mortal danger because of my foolish choices. I finally manage to get one leg free just as Krauss rolls over onto all fours, then rubs the back of his head where it hit the floor.

Our eyes meet and I can see the panic in his. He knows this is all about to come crashing down around him. The syringe is too far away for him to grab without having to go over me and he knows I can trip him up. Instead, he looks to the table where he laid out all our items. Where he laid out our weapons.

Working furiously on the last knot, I do everything I can to get my leg free while trying to inch toward the syringe at the same time. Finally, I pull my foot out from the loosened rope and scramble up, grabbing the syringe just as a bullet clips the ground at my feet.

I look up, and Krauss has my weapon in his hand. I dive behind one of the pillars, with the syringe just as another bullet hits the pillar between us.

"This isn't how I wanted this to go," he calls out. "I could have made it painless for you."

"Pretty sure that's off the table," I call back. "Krauss, the FBI already knew we were coming here. They're on their way. You need to give yourself up."

He laughs, though it's forced. "You really don't know me, Agent Slate. Do you think I got where I am today by *giving up*?"

I examine the syringe in my hand. If I can just get close enough, I can impale this into his bloodstream in less than a second. But I don't know how good of a shot Krauss is. So far, he's been too close to the mark for me to risk it. I glance to my left. The row of cells is just beyond the next pillar.

Taking a deep breath, I dive for the pillar as another shot rings out. I can almost feel the bullet whizz by. "Enough of this!" he yells out. I use the distraction to jump to the left again, and even though I'm in the open, he doesn't fire.

"What's wrong?" I ask, opening my arms like wings. I

know I'm taunting him, but I'm also standing right in front of the cells. "Are you afraid of damaging your specimens?"

He's looking down the barrel of the gun at me, hatred seared across his face. The weapon is shaking in his hand, but he's not shooting.

"You can't bring yourself to do it, can you?" I ask. "You're too afraid of hitting one of the cells. That glass is strong, but it's not bulletproof, is it? It'll shatter if you shoot it."

Krauss grits his teeth but doesn't move. I take a step closer. "It's over," I say. "The FBI is on their way. You can't sustain this any longer."

Rage forms across his face and in an instant, he turns the weapon on Zara. "No!" I rush him as fast as I can, slamming into him just as I hear the shot. I stab him in with the injector, then knock the gun from his hand. He tries to knock me off, but a few seconds later, I feel his body begin to go limp. I scramble off him, and go to my friend. The only friend I have left. The friend whose life I've put in danger.

And then I see the blood.

Chapter Thirty-Three

"LOOK AT ME," I SAY, FRANTIC. "LOOK AT ME." I'M SHAKING Zara, doing anything I can to get her to open her eyes. A small moan escapes her mouth. "Dammit, Zara!"

"Cheese fries," she says, her voice soft.

"What?" I ask, then tap her cheek with my palm, doing anything I can to get her to open her eyes.

"Want some cheese fries," she says, her eyes finally opening. She's smiling but it quickly fades when she sees my face. "What's wrong?" She looks down, realizing, I think, for the first time she's strapped to a chair. "Krauss, where is he?"

I step to the side, but I'm careful to keep my hand on Zara's neck.

"Why are you holding me like you're going to strangle me?" she asks.

"Because of this," I say, pulling my hand away for a moment. It's covered in dark crimson. "He almost killed you. The bullet grazed your neck, I'm trying to get it to stop bleeding for a second so I can untie you."

"He shot me and I didn't wake up?" she asks.

I've been trying to wake her for the past four minutes. I don't know how the bullet didn't cut deeper through her throat, I just know a millimeter to the right, and she'd be bleeding out right now. "He gave us both a heavy sedative. What happened in the control room? I thought I told you to shoot anyone who came through that door."

"I didn't have a choice," she says. "He had you with him, dragging you down the stairs. He said if I didn't inject myself, he'd kill you right there on the spot."

"You should have just shot him then and there," I say, keeping my one hand on her neck while I keep working on the rope around her arm.

"Couldn't risk it," she says. "I had no idea what kind of mental state he was in. How did he get the drop on you?"

I shake my head. "There must be another hidden compartment up there we didn't see. He got me from the back when I was trying to call for backup."

"Did you get through?" she asks.

"I don't know. I couldn't tell them anything before he stuck me with that needle." I finally loosen the rope enough that she's able to get her hand free.

"Here, I'll hold, you keep working on the ropes." She puts pressure on her wound, freeing up my hands. I run back over to the table with all our equipment and grab a tactical knife, which I then use to saw through all her bonds, as well as the remaining one on my arm.

"Stay there," I tell her. "I don't want you to rupture something by moving too fast, at least not until they check you out."

"Where are you going?" she asks.

"I need to check on that final room. I think it's Hannah, she looks hurt. Did you ever figure out how to get inside?"

"No," she says. "I don't think the rooms are connected to the system. I think they're individually locked, like with an actual key."

That doesn't make much sense, given all the rest of the equipment Krauss has around here. "Maybe in case of power failure? He didn't want the doors to open?"

I go back to the table and grab a zip tie, then roll Krauss over and bind his hands together. On the back of his belt, I notice a particular keyring, with five golden keys. I hold them up for Zara. "This guy."

"It's always the narcissists," she replies.

"Stay there," I say. "I'll be right back." I grab my phone and run around the pillars I was hiding behind, looking for a way around the "cells" to the sides with the doors. After a few minutes I manage to make my way around to a long hallway, with five doors set into the concrete walls. I can't even imagine what the general contractor who built this house must have thought Krauss was going to do down here. He probably assumed it was some sort of sex dungeon.

I try two keys before the third fits the first door, which is the "empty" one. The lock clicks and I open the door to reveal Hannah Stewart, splayed out on the floor, her face and mouth bloody. Her face is covered in so much blood she's barely recognizable and for a minute my heart drops because I'm not even sure she's breathing.

But then she gurgles out and I get under her, sitting her up to try and clear her airway. Blood flows freely from her mouth and she seems out of it, even though she's still breathing.

"Hannah, my name is Emily, I'm with the FBI," I say. "You're going to be all right, but I need you to sit up on your own, okay? Can you do that?"

"FBI?" she says weakly, and I can see enough of her mouth that I realize where the tooth I found came from.

"That's right. You're okay. We have him in custody. You're safe."

Tears begin to leak from her eyes, and she tries wrapping her arms around me. I gently pull her into a hug as she cries into my shoulder. I give her a few moments, then set her back up against the bed, and pull a few pillows down. "I'm going to leave the door open. Just sit tight and I'm going to get help," I say.

She shakes her head and tries to get up. I guess I can't blame her. If I'd been trapped in this room for a week, I wouldn't want to spend another second in it either.

I relent and help her to her feet, and get her to the door-way. Once we're in the hall, I try to help her back down again. She shakes her head. "No, I can help," she says, her voice muffled by her swollen mouth. I can see now she looks a lot worse than she actually is. Most of the blood seems to have come from the tooth in her mouth and possibly a broken nose.

"Okay," I say, handing her the set of keys. "Open the rest of these doors and help the women out, get them into the center. My friend is over there. She's been shot, but she's an FBI agent too. You'll be safe."

She takes the keys. "I got it."

I leave her to it and make my way back through the small maze until I'm back at the door to the antechamber. I open it back up, leaving it open and then ascend the stairs to the base-ment level. The hatch is still open and as I look carefully, I see a small inset beside the bar where a false wall leads to a small room. It looks like a makeshift panic room, though there's very little inside. He was right beside us while we were discovering the hatch and we never knew it. Who knows how many other secret chambers are in this house?

Climbing the stairs, I reach the top level to find red and blue flashing lights coming up the driveway. I take a deep breath and put my hands on my knees. They got my call. It went through.

I think we're going to be okay.

Chapter Thirty-Four

"OBVIOUSLY, WE DROPPED THE CHARGES AGAINST TOSCANI'S man," Janice says. Zara and I are back in her office, sitting across her large desk. Zara has a bandage on the right side of her neck that goes from her ear down to her collar. She's already complained about it a dozen times over.

"Bet he wasn't too happy about that," I say.

"Who, Santino or the guy?" Janice asks.

"Either," I reply. "Santino doesn't want him back because it makes him look bad, and Federico won't be able to sleep at night knowing he's been ousted as still supporting Santino's uncle. We'll probably find his body in less than a week. The victim of a 'tragic accident'."

"Unfortunately, you're probably right," she says. "But he's not being discharged from the hospital for a while. The funny thing is, he finally did break when Nick went in there to interview him. Said he dumped Hannah's body in the swamp."

I shake my head. "Santino really was counting on us never finding her, wasn't he?"

"He's trying to build his network, expand his influence," my boss says. "Fortunately for us, he's somewhat inept."

Both Zara and I share a chuckle. But Janice doesn't join us. She reaches down and pulls out a file folder. "But now the real purpose of this meeting." She taps on the folder. "There's been a serious accusation made against you. Misappropriation of resources."

I exchange a glance with Zara. I suppose it was too much to hope Nick wouldn't follow through with his threat. But I'm glad I didn't cave to his demands. "Okay," I say.

"Did you?" she asks.

I don't hesitate. "Yes."

"Why?"

I think back to Krauss, and how he had spent the past few years chasing after the death of his sister, to the point where it had literally driven him mad. He'd been so consumed by grief he'd built a fantasy world in which his sister still existed, in whatever form he chose. I don't want that to be me. I thought finding Matt's killer would give me a sense of peace. That it would close the book on that chapter of my life. But I realize now that's impossible. I will never find peace and it will never be done. I just have to learn to live with it.

"I allowed my feelings regarding my personal circum- stances to override my better judgement," I say. "I was so obsessed with finding answers, I put my own personal needs above those of the Bureau. It won't happen again."

Janice huffs, then opens the folder before closing it again. "Normally I'd overlook something like this. But given your recent history, I'm not sure I can. You see how this looks."

I nod. "I do."

"What she's not telling you is that Agent Hogan was extorting her to try and increase his standing here. He told Emily that if she made it so that he collared Krauss, he wouldn't release that information." I turn to her, my eyes wide. "What?" she says, shrugging. "You might be too big of a person to tattle, but I'm not. That's not the kind of person we want working here."

"Agent Slate, is that true?" Janice asks.

"Look, all I'm going to say is I made the wrong call by using federal resources without authorization and I'm going to leave it at that."

She looks at the folder again. "I'll take care of this internally. But that doesn't absolve you of what you did."

"No, ma'am," I reply.

Zara raises her hand. "I also have to admit I knew about it too. Though I found out after the fact. By accident."

"I assumed as much," Janice says. She regards us a minute, then looks down at the file. "Given your exemplary performance in apprehending Krauss and returning all five missing women to their families, I don't believe this warrants any action at this time." I look up. "It wasn't as if you were pulling resources from another case, or putting anyone in jeopardy. This was…personal curiosity. And I'm not going to make a fuss about one of my best agents over something so trivial." She tosses the file in her wastebasket. "Just try not to do it again."

"Yes, ma'am," I say, suppressing a smile.

Janice resets herself. "I got word this morning, Krauss is being remanded to the Maryland State Mental Ward. He won't be in genpop with everyone else, which I think is for the best."

"So do I," I say. "He's obviously suffering from some mental imbalance."

"The worst part of it is, the Bureau now has to do a systems review of the FACE program. We can't in good conscience keep using a program from an individual like that. I'd say give it a month before we find a new vendor, and get ready to learn a new system."

Both of us groan in unison.

"I know. Me too." She clears her throat. "I was also asked to pass along a message from ASAC Coleman, down at Quantico. He thanks you for recommending Liam Coll. He says he's an exemplary student and thinks he'll be a great addition to the Bureau."

"Glad to hear it," I say. "I happen to agree."

"Anything else?" she asks. We shake our heads. "Very well. Foley, you ready to take some on your own?"

"Absolutely," Zara says. "I think I've learned everything I can from this old bag anyway."

"Hey!" I give her a not-so-gentle push.

"Good. Last I saw, both your desks have stacks of new cases. Get on them."

We nod and head back out to the bullpen. "She wasn't kidding," Zara says, looking at her desk. "Is this what happens when you're in the hospital for two days?"

"In my experience?" I say, "Every time."

I pull up the driveway and step out of my car, hauling out a large bouquet of flowers along with me. Before I'm even halfway to the door, it swings open, revealing Amanda Stewart, running at me with her arms spread wide.

"Agent Slate!" she practically yells. "Thank you so much for coming!" She wraps me in a light hug. "Here, let me take those from you."

"I can't stay long, I just came to see how she's doing," I say as Mrs. Stewart leads me up the stairs. I tried to get Zara to come with me on this little visit, but she wasn't having any part of it. She was more interested in starting in on some of her own cases.

At the top of the stairs stands Judge Stewart, his hands in his pockets. "Agent Slate, wonderful to see you again," he says.

"This really isn't necessary," I say before Mrs. Stewart ushers me into the house.

"Nonsense," she says. "You brought our daughter back to

us. You're practically family now." I recall first coming to this house two weeks ago. It feels like a lifetime now. Back then it had seemed subdued, cold even. But today the house is bright, airy and seems like it is filled with life. I walk into the sitting room just off the main foyer to see Hannah sitting on the couch, a book in her hand. She still has a small brace over the bridge of her nose.

"Emily!" she says, getting up. "I didn't realize what time it was." She comes up and wraps me in a hug as well. "How are you?"

"Good, I suppose," I say. "How are you doing?"

She flashes me a brilliant white smile. "Whaddaya think? The dental surgeon said it was a pretty easy job, all things considered."

"I can't even tell," I reply. It's remarkable, like she never lost the tooth at all. "How's the therapy going?"

"Well. I'm sleeping a little better now. I can't even imagine what some of those other girls are going through. I was thinking about maybe setting up some kind of support group for the five of us. Do you think something like that might help?"

"In time," I say. "Some were there a very long time. And one of them is still a minor."

"I still can't believe it was only a week," she says. "It felt like months. I guess that's what happens when you don't have a clock and can't see the sun every day."

"Please," Judge Stewart says. "We've made you a cake and I had a friend send me a bottle of France's finest champagne."

"Oh, you really didn't have to do that," I say, wondering if it's too late to run for the door. I don't do well when all the attention is on me. It's one of the reasons I don't like birthday parties.

"Of course we did!" Mrs. Stewart says. "Come on now, it won't hurt."

"Actually, I need a moment with Hannah. It relates to the case," I say. This was the real reason I came here, knowing I'd still have to endure this little "party".

"Oh, of course," the Judge says. "We'll go pour you a glass."

As soon as they're out of earshot, I lean in close to Hannah. "I spoke to a friend at the DEA. They apprehended Alonzo this morning for possession."

"Oh, thank God," she says, putting her hand over her heart.

"And I spoke to my boss. Considering the ordeal you had to suffer, the AG isn't going to bring any charges against you for the drugs we found in your apartment."

She shakes her head. "It was so stupid. I never should have gotten involved with them."

"What were you trying to do, anyway?" I ask.

She makes a motion with her head toward the door her parents disappeared through. "All my life I've been reliant on them. And then I finally move out, get a good job. But in this city, it's still not enough to cover all my expenses. I thought with the promotion I could afford living on my own, but everything just piled up so quick and I panicked. Dealing for Alonzo was a means to an end; just a way to supplement my income until I could get a raise. I was just going to sell it to people I knew personally, people with extra cash. I didn't want to come crawling back to *them* for help. I've been doing that my entire life." She looks around. "Though, I guess I ended up back here after all."

"They're your parents," I say. "They may not be perfect, but try not to take them for granted while you still have them. Trust someone who knows."

"You're right," she says. "Poor little rich girl problems, amirite?"

I can't help but chuckle. At least she has enough self-awareness to make fun of herself. "I'm glad we got you out of there," I say.

"Me too. I'll do better in the future. Now, how about some cake?"

Chapter Thirty-Five

IT'S BEEN SIX WEEKS SINCE THE CONFRONTATION WITH KRAUSS at his home. In that time, Hannah has returned to her old life, though she gave up her apartment and moved back in with Margaret for the time being. And the other four women he'd held are doing well with therapy, though it's going to take them a long time to recover.

As for Krauss, from what I understand he's in something of a catatonic state. He's facing five counts of first-degree kidnapping, one count of aggravated assault against Hannah Stewart, and two counts of attempted murder of federal agents. To say it's not looking good for him is an understatement. But the good news is I heard from one of my contacts in the Attorney General's office yesterday telling me that his expensive lawyers came back with a no-contest plea. They know we have him dead to rights and there's no wiggling out of it. Thankfully that means Zara and I don't have to testify or sit through a lengthy trial. It saves everyone a lot of unnecessary time and trouble.

My phone vibrates in my pocket as I'm finishing up the details of my most recent case: a public corruption investigation involving some local prosecutors who I found were in Toscani's pocket.

"Slate," I say, answering the phone.

"Slate, this is Calhoun down in tech services. I've got that item you requisitioned."

My heart lurches to my throat. It had been so long I'd pushed it to the back of my mind. "I'll be right down." I hang up and glance over at Zara. "Psst," I say.

She glances up, narrowing her eyes at me. I make a motion toward the door with my head and immediately her eyes widen.

She takes her feet off her desk and replaces her keyboard, then joins me as I make my way toward the doors. We pass Nick's empty desk along the way. He hasn't been in for weeks now, though I don't think he's been fired. But Janice won't talk about it.

"What's going on?" she asks as we push through the double doors.

"Tech services just called," I say.

"Already? That was fast."

"No trial, no need to use the evidence," I reply.

"And no family to release it back to," she adds. "Which means it all just goes into storage."

I let out a small laugh. "Not like they'd let any of that back in the hands of the public anyway. It's too dangerous."

We make our way down to tech services and meet up with Calhoun, who is in the process of cataloging all the items that were confiscated from Krauss's home. The room is full of equipment, most of it from his "control room".

"Is this everything?" I ask him.

Calhoun is something of a squirrelly guy. He's thin, with dark hair and glasses, and he has the undeniable aura of being one of those people who keeps to himself most of the time. He's maybe a year or two older than me, but you'd never know it by looking at him. The premature lines on his face make him look older than he really is.

"Everything," he replies. "I understand you were particularly interested in this." He holds up Krauss's cell phone. The same one he showed me down in his little dungeon.

Before I take it from him, I stop. "You don't need any of this for the case, right? It's all just going into storage, to never be used again?"

He nods. "I got the call from the prosecutor yesterday. He said to box it all up, that we wouldn't be needing it for a trial."

I exhale. Maybe I'm still skirting a line here, but I wouldn't call this misappropriation of resources, because the items have all outlived their usefulness. No one will touch or see these things ever again, all things being equal. At least not until they clean out the evidence in sixty or seventy years after Krauss dies. And maybe not even then.

"Can you unlock it for me?" I ask, handing it back to him.

"Sure." He inputs the code and the phone comes to life. He hands it back to me and I scroll through the apps, looking for the one I need. "What did you want with it, anyway?"

"Just needed to check something," I say, then nod to Zara. She retrieves her own phone and brings up one of the images of the woman from the hospital. The paper copies are safe in my apartment. But we both have digital copies on our phones.

I find the app I'm looking for an open it. It's mostly source code, but this is definitely the same program Krauss showed me when he demonstrated his "genius". Using the camera on the phone, I take a picture of the image on Zara's phone, making sure the woman is as clearly visible as possible. Krauss's phone accepts the image, then I get the dreaded wheel of death as it processes.

"What is that?" Calhoun asks.

"A more sophisticated version of our own facial recognition programs," I say. "This man needed a way to find people who looked a certain way."

"And you need it for a case?"

I shoot a glance at Zara. "No. This is a personal matter. Which is why I waited until after everything with Krauss was wrapped up. I didn't want to use it while it was still technically evidence."

"Oh, yeah, that makes sense," he says. "Though I will need for you to sign that you had access to these items today."

"I can do that," I reply, looking at the phone again as it seems to mock me with its spinning. I might not be able to find peace by figuring out who killed my husband, but I'm damn sure not going to let her get away with it. I'm an officer of the law, and if for no other reason than this woman committed two murders, I need to find her and bring her in. But until I have absolute proof, I need to do it on my own time. Not the Bureau's.

I shake my head. "It shouldn't be taking this long. He did it on you and it pulled the results in half a second," I say.

"Maybe she's the kind of person who can't be found," Zara suggests. "We'll just have—"

Krauss's phone gives a little buzz at the same time the circle disappears. Below the woman's image, the fields start populating. "Wait. It has something." As I start reading the information, my eyes widen.

Zara must see my expression because she comes over. "What is it? What's wrong?" she asks. When she looks at the information coming up, she grimaces.

"This just made things a lot more complicated," I say. "You sure you're up for it?"

Zara seems to reset herself, then gives me a firm nod. "Always."

"Then pack your bags. We need to book a flight."

The End?

To Be Continued...

Want to read more about Emily?

When FBI Agent Emily Slate discovers a series of fires are being used to cover up the murder of fire-fighters, she'll need all her skills as an investigator to flush out the killer.

A string of arson cases brings Emily to the historic city of Charleston right as she's in the middle of trying to find the woman who killed her husband. Her personal investigation will have to wait, however, because the local community is on edge, having already lost two firefighters in these tragedies.

But before she can get very far, more blazes erupt throughout the city, causing a panic within the ranks. In each one, the victim is burned alive, from both the inside and out. And at each scene, a strange symbol remains in the rubble, leaving Emily to believe they're working with a sick and twisted individual who has their sights set on something even bigger.

With the number of fires increasing by the day, and a city in panic, Emily must race against the clock to uncover the killer before they burn the entire city down with their rage.

Find out what happens in *Smoke and Ashes*, available now on Amazon. Click HERE to get your copy now!

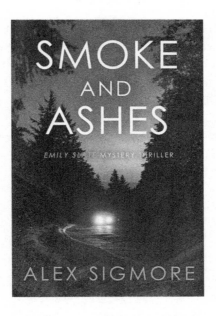

Click **HERE** or scan the code below with your phone to get your copy of **SMOKE AND ASHES**!

FREE book offer!
Where did it all go wrong for Emily?

I hope you enjoyed *The Collection Girls*. By now you're aware of the tragic circumstances surrounding her husband's death. If you'd like to learn about what happened to Emily in the days following, including what almost got her kicked out of the FBI, then you're in luck! *Her Last Shot* introduces Emily and tells the story of the case that almost ended her career. Interested? CLICK HERE to get your free copy now!

Not Available Anywhere Else!

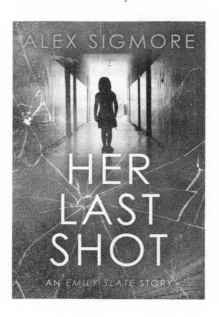

You'll also be the first to know when each book in the Emily Slate series is available!
Download for FREE HERE or scan the code below!

The Emily Slate FBI Mystery Series

Coming Soon!

A Note from Alex

I hope you enjoyed *The Collection Girls*, book 2 in the new Emily Slate FBI Mystery Series. My wish is to give you an immersive story that is also satisfying when you reach the end.

But being a new writer in this business can be hard. Your support makes all the difference. After all, you are the reason I write!

Because I don't have a large budget or a huge following, I ask that you please take the time to leave a review or recommend it to fellow book lover. This will ensure I'll be able to write many more books in the *Emily Slate Series* in the future.

Thank you for being a loyal reader,

Alex

Made in United States
Orlando, FL
25 May 2024